Acclaim for Bear Like Me

"In his fur-filled and fulfilling first novel, *Bear Like Me,* author Jonathan Cohen lays bare the bear subculture with incisive wit and seductive satire. Yet this comical cavort through the thick forest of hirsute gay/bi male animals entertains as it illuminates. *Bear Like Me* will have you alternately howling (with laughter), growling (with self-recognition), and of course, woofing."

—Ron Suresha,
Author, *Bears on Bears;*
Editor, *Bearotica*

"There is a madcap pleasure to *Bear Like Me,* a cheekily improbable comic read which is both an insider's appreciation for the contemporary bear community, and something of a caring send-up of it, as well. Jonathan Cohen writes about bear customs, mores, and quirks with charming archness, coordinating a sociologist's keen eye and a gossipmonger's sharp tongue with gleeful precision. That's the fun part; what delights is Cohen's old-fashioned way with romance, as his undercover bear unexpectedly falls away from the twink he thought he loved, and falls for the hefty hunk he meets up with as he finds himself rendezvousing with burly, hairy handfuls of men at every turn. Self-identified bear readers will find images of themselves lumbering lustily and lovingly through these cheery pages; nonbears, or curious cubs-in-waiting, will enjoy Cohen's saucy take on one of the queer world's proudest subcultures."

—Richard Labonte, Reviewer,
Book Marks and *Q Syndicate*

"Novelist Jonathan Cohen takes the reader on a trip to a new and mostly unknown world. By turns hilarious, melodramatic, thought-provoking, and utterly entertaining, Peter's discovery of his 'inner bear' is a classic coming-out (as a bear) story. Cohen weaves narrative with documentary (as a writer's diary) to bring to life the reality of West Coast bear culture, creates some lovingly memorable characters along the way, and leaves the reader wanting to see the movie version. *Bear Like Me* is highly reminiscent of the early novels of Paul Monette, and Cohen is a writer to keep your eye on."

—Les Wright, Director,
Nashoba Institute (Bear History Project);
Editor and Co-author,
The Bear Book and *The Bear Book II*

NOTES FOR PROFESSIONAL LIBRARIANS AND LIBRARY USERS

This is an original book title published by Southern Tier Editions, Harrington Park Press®, an imprint of The Haworth Press, Inc. Unless otherwise noted in specific chapters with attribution, materials in this book have not been previously published elsewhere in any format or language.

CONSERVATION AND PRESERVATION NOTES

All books published by The Haworth Press, Inc. and its imprints are printed on certified pH neutral, acid free book grade paper. This paper meets the minimum requirements of American National Standard for Information Sciences-Permanence of Paper for Printed Material, ANSI Z39.48-1984.

Bear Like Me

HARRINGTON PARK PRESS
Southern Tier Editions
Gay Men's Fiction
Jay Quinn, Executive Editor

Love, the Magician by Brian Bouldrey

Distortion by Stephen Beachy

The City Kid by Paul Reidinger

Rebel Yell: Stories by Contemporary Southern Gay Authors edited by Jay Quinn

Rebel Yell 2: More Stories of Contemporary Southern Gay Men edited by Jay Quinn

Metes and Bounds by Jay Quinn

The Limits of Pleasure by Daniel M. Jaffe

The Big Book of Misunderstanding by Jim Gladstone

This Thing Called Courage: South Boston Stories by J. G. Hayes

Edge by Jeff Mann

Trio Sonata by Juliet Sarkessian

Bear Like Me by Jonathan Cohen

Goneaway Road by Dale Edgerton

The Concrete Sky by Marshall Moore

Through It Came Bright Colors by Trebor Healey

Elf Child by David M. Pierce

Huddle by Dan Boyle

The Man Pilot by James W. Ridout IV

Ambidextrous: The Secret Lives of Children by Felice Picano

Men Who Love Me by Felice Picano

A House on the Ocean, A House on the Bay by Felice Picano

Bear Like Me

Jonathan Cohen

Southern Tier Editions
Harrington Park Press®
An Imprint of The Haworth Press, Inc.
New York • London • Oxford

Published by

Southern Tier Editions, Harrington Park Press®, an imprint of The Haworth Press, Inc., 10 Alice Street, Binghamton, NY 13904-1580.

© 2003 by Jonathan Cohen. All rights reserved. No part of this work may be reproduced or utilized in any form or by any means, electronic or mechanical, including photocopying, microfilm, and recording, or by any information storage and retrieval system, without permission in writing from the publisher. Printed in the United States of America.

PUBLISHER'S NOTE
This is a work of fiction. Names, characters, places, and incidents either are the products of the author's imagination or are used fictitiously, and any resemblance to actual persons, living or dead, business establishments, events, or locales is entirely coincidental.

Cover design by Marylouise E. Doyle.

Library of Congress Cataloging-in-Publication Data

Cohen, Jonathan.
    Bear like me / Jonathan Cohen.
       p. cm.
    ISBN 1-56023-417-2 (alk. paper)—ISBN 1-56023-418-0 (pbk. : alk. paper)
    1. Bears—Fiction. 2. Authorship—Fiction. I. Title.
    PS3603.O476 B43 2003
    813'.54—dc21

2002070700

PART I

If you're goin' to be a bear . . . be a grizzly!

Gene Sturlin
The Mooncalf Rubicon

– 1 –

Some people get their lifetime wake-up calls silently, a thief in the night stealing peace with a quiet revelation. Others are confronted with the bare truth face on, a message shouting to be heard in the din. Peter Mallory heard his wake-up call to the theme of "I Will Survive."

The song clip startled him out of the usual midafternoon reverie between lunch and Internet porn. Peter turned Gloria down in the middle of singing about survival and tapped the keys that brought up the e-mail that had summoned the music. Of course, it was from Chester Valentine. A half-hour meeting request for 2:00 p.m.

Peter reacted out of Pavlovian habit; he started to sweat, and glanced around the maze of cubicles to make sure all of the other employees in the editorial department were still there.

All of the other staff writers were still in their seats, typing quietly. No security guard had appeared to haul anyone away, and the gilded sign that read "PHAG MAGAZINE" still hung over the watercooler. Peter's heart rate started to slow to the beat of Gloria's music. Then, just to be sure, he checked *Phag Magazine*'s parent company share price on the Nasdaq.

23½. Well, that was a relief. Peter stared at the Queermedia ticker symbol, but the only news item was the same one he'd seen yesterday—"First Publicly Traded Gay Media Conglomerate Signs Co-branding Deal with Major Electronics Firm." As if that was news.

So if *Phag Magazine* wasn't going down the toilet, it was one of the employees in the department, Peter thought. Maybe even him. A half-hour meeting was a harbinger of doom. Chester Valentine needed at least an hour to, as he put it, "get consensus" (where Chester badgered subordinates into giving up their opposing viewpoints). Forty-five minutes was enough for a birthday celebration or card signing. Thirty minutes was just enough time for an exit interview.

"Looks like this place is a morgue today," Caliph, the mailperson, said, rolling the mail cart down the hall toward Peter. "You ever see so many quiet people on a Friday?"

Friday! Peter thought. Yet another bad sign. Prevailing management theory stated that employees were less likely to get violent if happy hour was around the corner. "Bad news, I think." Then, looking Caliph up and down, he added politely "Nice dress."

Caliph (Peter had never figured out if Caliph was male, female, or one of the trend-gendered) smiled and put a hand on Peter's shoulder. "It's a sari, dear. All the rage in India." Caliph's brow furrowed and Peter saw the sight line from Caliph's eyes to Chester's e-mail on his screen.

"Oh my," Caliph said apologetically, backing away. "Speaking of India, I'd say you were about to become one of the untouchables. Best wishes, Peter. Send us an e-mail before they block your home address."

Peter got to his feet and stretched. Now that was ridiculous. Just because someone got a half-hour meeting request didn't mean they were automatically getting fired. He glanced at the clock: 1:52. Restraining himself from the urge to start cleaning out his desk, Peter made a few pen scratches on his article outline, "Subcultures and the Gay Community: Renewal or Reprisal?" He'd written the catchy title to appeal to Chester, but Peter felt he was on to something—if they'd even publish an article of this type anymore.

Why did he even stay on? he asked himself. But one look at Danny's photograph on his desk was enough for Peter. A one-income couple was hard enough to manage; a zero-income couple would be impossible to maintain.

Looking around the cubicles at the other staff writers of *Phag Magazine,* Peter decided to try a test. "Anyone seen the latest Signorile piece in *OUT?*" he asked, trying to catch anyone's eye. "The one where he confessed to all those murders?"

Dead silence. Bette Chambers, the entertainment columnist, coughed as delicately as she could and rattled a sheet of paper dramatically. Oh, the weather forecast was looking stormy, Peter thought.

The *Phag* offices were arranged as a hemisphere of cubicles converging on Chester's office. Peter had always noticed a marked improvement in the quality of the carpeting and wood paneling from his cubicle to Chester's office, but it had never rankled him quite so much before. Anything was better than . . . but this time Peter couldn't resist looking at the Hall of Shame.

Chester had installed a series of framed covers of *Phag Magazine* from the past several years on the curved outer wall of the offices, and Peter suspected that he wasn't the only one to call it the Hall of Shame. It wasn't so much a reminder of their glorious past as how far down they'd come. Ever since the Queermedia Group had acquired *Phag Magazine,* it had been on a downhill slide editorially. The headlines spoke for themselves.

Peter walked past "ACT UP: The New Activism" and "Where Do You Go from Out?" Halcyon days for the magazine, times when Peter felt he was doing a service by reporting on the gay community. Then there were "Short Circuit: Parties on the Edge of a Nervous Breakdown" and "Drag Queen Makeover: Ten Easy Steps." Peter remembered the endless arguments with Chester over the use of colons—"If they're good enough for e-mail, they're good enough for a headline."

He stopped just short of Chester's office and looked at the last two magazine covers. "All the Steroid Rage: Protease Chic on the Beach" and "Bareback Dilemma? Just Lie Back and Enjoy It." The cover models had also slid down the respectability ladder, from activists to beefcake activists, to beefcake, and then to *straight* beefcake, since Chester had proven that straight hunks sold more copies than gay ones, especially if they were willing to be coy about their sexuality.

The last cover model was Ben Affleck—"He's Not, but He's Cute!" Peter rubbed his temples and leaned against the cool polished wood inlay of the door to Chester's office. Oh, the humanity.

"I often stop here myself to admire the magazine's progress," Chester's smooth voice came from behind him. Peter forced a smile and opened his eyes, willing the throbbing pain in his head to subside. "It's been quite a journey, hasn't it?"

Chester was always gracious enough to provide him with an ambiguous out. "Oh yes," Peter said, turning away from "Best KS Cover-Ups" and rubbing the smudge that his forehead had created on Chester's door. "I can't believe how far we've come."

Chester put a delicate arm around Peter's shoulders and guided him into the office. "Don't worry about that; it'll come right off." Under Chester's voice, Peter tried not to hear the subtext—"just like your cubicle nameplate."

Peter slumped into the visitor chair, while Chester arranged himself in the far more comfortable leather captain's chair. Chester's desk was the only modern piece in the office. Solid Plexiglas, it mirrored reflections from the walls, the filing cabinet, the framed lithographs, the large paper shredder, and Chester's elegant frame. Chester crossed his spindly legs beneath the desk and waited until the anniversary clock on his desk chimed 2:00 p.m. "You have two options," he said suddenly.

Peter had heard of Chester's ruthless side, but somehow until now he'd been insulated from the hatchet because of his work. There were rumors that Chester had a thing for him, but Peter had dismissed those out of hand; Chester's tastes ran to men of ethnic minorities, preferably at a financial disadvantage.

"What are those?" he asked calmly.

Chester steepled his thin fingers over a pile of proofs on the desk. "What was the last article of yours I approved for publication?" he asked quietly, his gaze never wavering.

Peter thought back. "The one about the year's best upcoming writers. Which you rewrote."

"Well, those writers were all so *old*," Chester said, brushing away an invisible speck from the pile of proofs. "Upcoming writers need to fall into our demographic—nineteen to twenty-three. Our readers don't want to read about old lesbians in Nicaragua. Unless they organize Nicaraguan circuit parties, I suppose, and even then . . ."

"Your point?" Peter asked.

"Queermedia Group and *Phag Magazine*'s editorial direction has . . . diverged from your writing direction," Chester said, drawing his hands apart. "Now as I said, you have two options. We'd love to work with you to mold your writing in a more contemporary direction, if you'd like."

Peter thought of Danny. What would Danny want him to do? To give in, to buckle under. Not in the sense of surrendering, but of doing what he had to do in order to survive. The moral distinctions weren't lost on Danny, but his boyfriend had a simple ethical system—survival came before what he called "posturing."

Their apartment, Danny's tuition, food for MacGuyver the cat— everything rested on Peter's decision. "And if I disagree?" he said, unable to bring himself to make the choice. "You give me my severance pay and wash your hands of me?"

"Never!" Chester said, looking aghast. "There's no need for us to pay severance. I consider your work these past few months as a form of constructive resignation, and our legal counsel backs me up."

That did it. "Then let me make it crystal clear for you," Peter said, standing up and grabbing the sheaf of proofs off of Chester's desk. "Pretend this is my latest overly academic article." He pushed past Chester and slid the proofs into the shredder.

The grinding was music to Peter's ears, as was Chester's horrified gasp. "Those were for the S&M on Campus issue!" he shrilled.

Peter collected the strips from the shredder and deposited them back in a heap on Chester's desk. "Who knows—they might even read better this way."

"Goodbye, Peter," Chester said, not even bothering to meet his eyes. "Maybe you can write a book. One of those horrible academic pieces that ends up on the remainder table." Peter sauntered toward the door, feeling an incredible weight lift. Everything would be all right; he'd tell his co-workers what he'd done, he'd send e-mails to his colleagues at the other magazines, and he'd have a new job in no time.

A burly, bearded security guard who had "hired thug" written all over him was waiting for him outside Chester's office. "Sir, please come with me."

Peter sighed. "I guess making a dramatic speech to you wouldn't have much effect."

"Sir, I've heard them all before. But if it makes you feel better, you can give it a try." The guard fastened his hand on Peter's elbow. "We're going to go clean out your desk now."

Fine, Peter thought. He'd give Bette and the others a piece of his mind while he was packing, and he'd drag it out . . . every paper clip would get packed separately.

The editorial cubicles were deserted. Peter caught a glimpse of Bette's e-mail program. An e-mail from Chester informed the staff that there was free cake in the break room.

The bastard! Peter thought. Then he thought back and realized how conveniently cake had materialized during the departure of his previous co-workers. So there hadn't been a Lesbigay Mothers Against Drugs Week after all!

Peter's enthusiasm had nearly evaporated, and the rest of it disappeared when he saw the file box on his desk. It was already half full. "You packed the paper clips already," he told the security guard accusingly.

"Sir, anything that's sharp or could serve as a weapon has been sealed away in plastic." The guard indicated the photograph on the bare desk. "There's still that to pack."

Peter picked up the photograph and cradled it in his hands. Danny would understand. He'd make some wonderful meal, they'd cuddle on the couch and talk until dawn, and everything would be all right.

Peter rolled his eyes and tossed the photograph into the box. Danny would kill him. "I still have a few things in the drawer."

Breath mints, a sticky note with Eric Rofes's e-mail address, an emergency chocolate bar (one of several from the past month, used up in various "emergencies"), and a worn Judith Krantz novel. It was amazing how few personal items he actually had in the office.

The security guard sealed the box, and they were about to go when Peter heard Gloria's voice one last time. "I will survive . . ." His hands automatically went to the keyboard, but the security guard stopped him.

"Sir, don't make me use the pepper spray."

The guard walked him to the service elevator, and his last view of *Phag* was the guard's broad shoulders blocking the way, and what looked like an empty cake plate peeping out from the break room.

Sunlight blinded Peter when he stepped outside, and he put up a hand to shield his eyes. He'd expected everything to stop, somehow, but pedestrians and traffic continued, unheeding. Peter started to walk, then stood still. For the first time in years, he had nowhere to go, nothing to do. He felt as if a long game of tug-of-war had ended suddenly when the person at the other end had let go.

Despite his better reason, Peter glanced back up at the *Phag Magazine* offices. An elegant shadow that looked like Chester was silhouetted against the window. Peter gritted his teeth and prepared his middle finger for one last visual assault when the file box's contents shifted and the corrugated cardboard came apart in his hands.

Papers, books, and the remaining contents of his desk drawer crashed to the sidewalk. Peter bent over, refusing to look up. He picked out Danny's photograph and put it in his left pocket. He took the breath mints out of the pile and put them into his right pocket. Last, he collected the chocolate bar, tore off the wrapper, and started down the street, eating as he went.

After a few yards, Peter found his voice, and he started humming "I Will Survive." Maybe Chester was right, after all. He *would* write a book.

– 2 –

"Tell me everything will be all right," Danny said.

Peter tried not to grit his teeth, or at least not to let it show. They were sitting at their nook two weeks after his departure from *Phag Magazine*. Peter had one hand on the Saturday paper and the other one restraining MacGuyver, who was purring hungrily and sniffing the omelets.

"If I tell you everything will be all right," Peter asked, "will you believe it?"

Danny hesitated, then grinned boyishly, one of the main features that had attracted Peter in the first place. "All I want is a little reassurance. Say it like you mean it, and I'll believe it."

Peter had lost track over the past few months, but their domestic life seemingly slipped into made-for-TV movies with increasing frequency. The old made-for-TV movies, not the ones these days that were about family members killing each other. While Danny was distracted by the cat's antics, Peter subtly slid the long bread knife out of his boyfriend's reach and underneath the newspaper.

"I'll do my best," Peter said. "With my savings we can get by for a few months, if we cut some corners."

"Does kitty want some cheese?" Danny said, holding a bit of cheese just out of MacGuyver's reach. "Does he want some nice cheese?" Then he yelped as the cat leapt up and nipped his fingers, grabbed the cheese in his mouth, and ran off. Danny frowned as he sucked on his injured fingers. "What kind of corners?"

"Nothing major, just the expendable luxury items. You know, movies, plays, new clothes, expensive haircuts, and cable."

Danny looked about to purse his lips in a pout, but Peter's expression brooked no argument. "Well, I'll let you make those decisions. I trust you." He got up and kissed Peter on the lips. "Now, do you want to make a start on saving money by showering together?"

Peter smiled and shook his head. "I've got to get ready to meet Mac," he said, then added hastily, "and Mac's paying for it."

"All right," Danny said, clearly disappointed. "Maybe when you get home . . . if we're allowed to take more than one shower a day." He grinned and moved out of the way as Peter aimed a swat at his butt with the newspaper.

Peter waited until he heard the sound of water running, then started to pick up the dishes that Danny had forgotten to clear. MacGuyver was back in a flash, rubbing himself against Peter's legs, purring like an overheated engine, and then howling bloody murder.

"You're a little slut when it comes to food, aren't you?" Peter asked, scratching the cat under the chin and patting his flanks. "No more catnip for you for a while, either."

MacGuyver sat back on his haunches and looked at Peter reproachfully. "That look won't work on me," Peter said. "Danny already tries it whenever *he* wants something."

The cat emitted a mew, then licked his paw and started washing his face. "Easy for you to say," Peter replied, scraping the remains of brunch into the food disposal. "I'm the one that has to make the tough decisions in this family."

He put down the plate and scrubber and looked fondly toward the bathroom. It was always so easy to pick on a relationship, to find the flaws. Part of it was his training; as a writer, he was expected to critique. *Phag Magazine* would never run any piece called "Gay Life: Just Great and Doing Fine."

Danny was five years younger than he, and Peter shared and encouraged his enthusiasm. They were great in bed, loved staying up late talking and watching videos, and yet . . .

Peter flicked on the food disposal and MacGuyver fled in abject terror from the noise. And yet, in a crisis Peter was the one who had to be the adult, and Danny got to be the little boy.

It was only when he caught sight of the clock on the stove that Peter realized he was going to be late. He got dressed with a minimum of interference from the cat, who was busy exploring the mystery of the space under the sheets.

"I'm going!" Peter called out to Danny, who was still in the shower. The water bill, Peter thought, and winced.

"Still time to join me!" Danny called back, and Peter smiled wearily. Maybe he'd feel like it once money was coming in again.

Instead of the taxi he usually took, Peter was stuck taking the bus. Jostling against the other passengers, hanging onto a strap while a demented woman tried to tell him her life story, he tried to use visualization to picture himself in the back seat of a comfortable cab. Stale cigarette smoke, foreign-accented English . . .

"Were you even *listening* to what I was saying?" the woman demanded, poking him in the chest.

Peter sighed. "Sure, sure. Government conspiracy, UFOs, et cetera, et cetera." He took a closer look at her; she had the disheveled, anonymous look of someone who had fallen into the crack between suburbia and reality. "Did you ever consider trying plastic wrap instead of tinfoil on your head? It's microwave safe."

Unfortunately, that only prompted her to reminisce about her discovery that Saran Wrap was actually impregnated with sarin gas, and Peter got off a block before the restaurant to escape her. He was afraid for a moment that she might pursue him, but she'd found another victim.

It was a crisp fall day, and Peter pulled his jacket tighter around him, enjoying the contrast of the warm sun against the cold air. All writers have to suffer, he reasoned. He was hardly indigent, or even poor. This was a momentary setback. When his book wound up on the best-seller list, they'd all see . . .

Peter drew himself up abruptly. Any more thinking like that and he'd be the one wrapping his laptop in tinfoil. He had to focus, concentrate on the problem at hand: finding a story idea.

"Where do you get your ideas?" people would always ask him when they found out he was a writer. Peter didn't know; they dropped from heaven or bubbled out of his subconscious. All he had to do was think.

Think gay, Peter thought. Think gay!

As he approached the restaurant, he fought the urge to skip down the street, humming and waving his arms. "Fired Writers: When Insanity Attacks." It wasn't a matter of thinking gay, it was more thinking about the gay angle in everyday situations.

Then Peter saw him.

The man was putting up posters for the local lesbigay community center—on lampposts, bus shelters, and anywhere that he could tape them. Peter didn't need his advanced gaydar to get a read on the man, but still . . . the man looked out of place for the gay ghetto.

He was just over six feet tall, easily 200, 250 pounds, Peter estimated, with a gut hanging out shamelessly over his jeans and encased in a plaid shirt jacket. No hair on the head (of course—membership in the gay community came with a lifetime subscription to Nair these days), but he had a thick beard and what looked to be a forest of hair sprouting from his T-shirt—front and back. Yikes!

Peter watched the man surreptitiously. He'd seen men of the fat/hairy/bearded type in the ghetto before, but they had always seemed like interlopers, airlifted in from a Dan Haggerty mountain movie. He supposed that he'd passed them many times on the street, but his eyes had simply glossed over them, as they did with any man he wasn't immediately attracted to.

"Here's where your anthropology degree comes in handy," a voice behind him whispered, and Peter jumped. It was Mac.

Peter looked at him quizzically, but Mac waved a hand. "Look and learn. I call this the Mating Dance of the Urban Bear."

Mac ambled over to where the hirsute man was doing his best to affix a poster to a bicycle rack. Now that Peter thought about it, Mac sort of resembled the other man; he had the bald head, the goatee, and probably more chest hair than was acceptable in the gym. Mac, however, took care of his body. Peter sucked in his own stomach and thought about going for a workout.

He couldn't make out every word, but what was going on was obvious. Mac smiled, put an arm on the hairy man's shoulder, and carried on in his usual way. Then Peter watched with increasing amusement as Mac chucked the other man under his beard, and in return got a belly rub, a hug, and what looked to be a phone number.

Mac glowed and giggled until they were in the restaurant and settled in a booth, waiting for their espressos. "So, dish already," Peter said. "A friend of yours?" He and Mac slipped easily into the conversational style they'd honed over the past ten years.

"A new friend, maybe. Or at least a fuckbuddy." Mac held up the scrap of paper with the phone number on it. "Not bad for five minutes' work, eh? I really have *got* to start framing these."

Peter sipped at his espresso. "Oh come on, give it up already. This is some kind of secret club, right? Handshakes, stomach rubs, initiations..." He grew thoughtful. "A gay scientology thing would be fascinating, on many levels."

Mac chuckled. "Oh, it's a cult all right. Man, you are so behind the times. Haven't you ever heard of the bear community? The bear movement?"

"There was something in *Phag* a few years ago. Wasn't it one of those fringe groups, like the chubby chasers?" Peter felt uncomfortable, treading the line between sexual banter and actual fetish material.

"I forgot about *Phag*'s target audience," Mac said dryly. "It's all about this." He pulled back the sleeve of his jacket.

"Really tacky Swatches?"

Mac flicked Peter on the nose with his finger. "Hair. Body hair. Well, that's simplifying it a bit, but picture big hairy guys. Most of them with beards."

Peter imagined hordes of men like the one outside, marching in lockstep, hair bristling from every clothing opening. "So they get together because nobody wants them?" he asked, dreading the answer.

"This, coming from a man who wrote 'My Genitals, Myself'? They get together because they find it hot!"

Peter couldn't help himself. "Ewww! That is *so* gross!"

"Really." Mac arched a thick eyebrow. "You didn't say anything about my body hair when we were going out together."

Peter kept his eyes on the espresso and away from Mac's hairy wrist. "You're not like... that guy. You're not a walking carpet. And my God, you've got muscle definition."

"It's all a question of degrees. First you sleep with a guy who has a treasure trail, then you sleep with a guy with a hairy chest... next thing you know," Mac said smugly, "you're buying a replacement filter for the shower drain."

"No!" Peter cried out, then looked around in embarrassment. Fortunately, nobody in the restaurant paid either of them the slightest bit of attention—probably because Mac was famous for breaking up with two-week boyfriends at brunch on a regular schedule. "I mean," he said more quietly, "it's some fly-by-night trend, like the Macarena or using female condoms."

"No," Mac said emphatically. "It isn't. And I bet there's a book idea in there somewhere."

Peter laughed. "Okay. If there's a bear community, I'll write a book about it. And if there isn't, you shave your chest."

"Deal." They shook hands, and Peter felt the hair on the back of Mac's hand rub against his fingers. He glanced outside, but the man with the posters had left.

Bears. The very idea was silly, totemic. It smacked of the gay community's tribal desperation in the mid-1990s. "Lions and tigers and bears, oh my," Peter murmured.

"What's that?" Mac asked, bemused.

"Thinking out loud. So, is everyone as caring and sharing as they are in the gay community?" Peter asked, already mentally drawing up a tentative outline.

"Oh dear," Mac grinned. "You have no idea. But you soon will, I promise."

– 3 –

"Can I help you with something?" the librarian asked.

Peter looked up from the library's card catalog terminal. "Probably not. Do you ever have anyone who comes in looking for something before anyone knows about it?"

The librarian, a stout woman in her midfifties, smiled. "People come in all the time asking for books on strange subjects. I remember when the magazines started covering the sexual revolution back in the sixties. The number of young men and women who came in asking for some kind of guide or handbook . . . as if it required an instruction manual." She shook her head. "I'm wool-gathering again. If there's a book out there on it, I'll know. Try me."

Peter drummed his fingers on the keyboard. "Bears," he said finally.

"Polar? Black? Brown? Teddy? Roosevelt?" the librarian reeled off almost automatically.

"Gay sexual fetish."

She furrowed her brow for a moment. "You do realize you're in the Animals and Natural Life section of the library, right?"

"Well," Peter hedged. "The Biology and Human Behavior section seems to be stuck back around when STDs were still known as *social diseases*. Their idea of a sexual fetish is probably anything not involving marriage."

The librarian nodded, then set her shoulders. "We'll try the Internet. We're lucky that way—one of the local colleges donated a computer and modem access to the Web."

She directed him to another computer, and they sat down. Peter was only familiar enough with computers to type out his stories, and he watched as she typed in various commands, finally entering the terms "bear" and "gay."

The stillness of the library was shattered by a loud beeping, followed by a red blinking box on the screen that read, "You have just been protected from seeing harmful Internet content. God bless."

Peter sighed. "That college wouldn't happen to have been the Baptist one, would it?"

The librarian shook her head. "God bless, indeed. Let me try something." He watched as she typed in "female ministers." Once again they were assaulted with the beeping and the blinking red box, only this time it added in a verse from the Bible.

"God loves us," Peter said, "but not enough, apparently, to let us use the Internet."

"Sociology!" the woman said suddenly, snapping her fingers. "I should have thought of it earlier. That's the only department that has any autonomy in this library. Go ask them if they can help." She smiled slyly. "You might even find you have something in common with the librarian there. They even have some alternative lifestyle magazines."

She rubbed her chin with the fingers of her right hand, and Peter wondered if this was some secret librarian code. The mention of magazines, though, caught his attention.

"Do they have *Phag Magazine*?"

"You could ask," the librarian said, then paused. "I guess it's probably not the best time to ask you to make a donation to the library."

Peter got up and dug a $20 bill out of his pocket. "Promise me you'll buy something kinky with it."

Walking over to the Sociology section, Peter marveled at the change in the library. Back in the 1970s, it had prided itself on having the most complete, up-to-date collection of avant-garde books. With the cutbacks of the 1980s and 1990s, they'd clearly finally buckled under to the major sources of money available . . . each of which came with their own strings.

It was even more surprising that *Phag Magazine* was headquartered in this town. Living in the gay ghetto and working at a gay publication had effectively insulated Peter from what the other 90 percent of the world was doing.

He shuddered as he remembered an incident when a car full of teenagers had sped by, shouting "Faggot!" at him and tossing eggs, which had fortunately missed him. Maybe that "bear" Mac had flirted with had come up with his own strategy—assimilate by dressing completely different from most gay men. Interesting . . .

When Peter reached the Sociology librarian's desk, he realized what the woman had tried to tell him. The Sociology librarian sported the universal early 2000s sign of gay camaraderie—a goatee. Mac had a theory for telling a straight goatee from a gay goatee. The really close-trimmed, shaped, and beautifully manicured goatees belonged to straight guys; the circle beards and thicker goatees were, for whatever reason, gay as all get-out.

Peter peered at the man's goatee, trying to decide whether the spaces in the hair under the lower lip were accidental or deliberate. Nature or nurture, he wondered?

Then he realized that the man had been staring at him in consternation for the better part of a minute. "May I help you?" the librarian asked in a lilting tone that automatically gave him away.

"I was checking out your goatee," Peter said and blushed.

"Oh!" The man smiled. "Well, I've been trying to grow it out for months now, but it simply won't cooperate. Something about me shaving it all these years; now it's decided it's not worth the bother to poke its follicles up."

The mention of body hair reminded Peter of his conversation with Mac over espresso and made him slightly queasy. Then again, he was never one to turn away from a potential flirtation. Even though I'm monogamous, Peter reminded himself. Strictly monogamous.

"I'm George. Is there anything in particular you're . . . looking for?" the man said, dipping his eyes just as he paused for the last two words. Sweet, Peter thought. But that wasn't why he'd come.

"Do you have anything on bears?" Peter asked. "Not the animal kind, the gay kind."

George wrinkled up his nose. "Those fat hairy apes. Well, that's not a fair description. How's this: Those large undertrimmed Sasquatches. Now really, why on earth would you want a book about *them?* Surely there's something . . . more interesting you could find to read about." Again with the eye dipping, Peter noticed.

"I'm doing research," Peter said, feeling oddly defensive. And after all, *he* wasn't the one wearing the goatee.

"Well I can tell you right now, we don't have any books on *that* subject," George said, folding his arms. "There was some book that came through ages ago, but it had all these boring articles talking about Foucault and Baudrillard, and I figured we had enough of that already with Camille Paglia."

Better the "bears" than this man, Peter thought. "But let me guess," he said easily. "You have the latest copy of *Phag Magazine*?"

George brightened up in an instant. "Now there's a wish I can grant!" He disappeared into the stacks behind the desk, rummaging around on the shelves. "Good thing you didn't want the December issue—someone always steals it."

"Oh yes," Peter said dryly. "The Swimsuit Issue."

"Andrew Sullivan looked *so* cute in that thong last year, but I think he's a closet Republican," George said, returning with the magazine. "Here you go."

Peter started to flip through it. "Don't you want my library card or something?"

George shook his head. "All I want is a kind word."

"Holy motherfucking, cocksucking love child of Jesus' money changing whores!" Peter cried out loudly as he spotted Chester Valentine's editorial.

He only had time to read the headline—"*Phag* Writer Leaves Under Cloud: Editor Regrets"—and see his name mentioned before George snatched the magazine away.

"Just go!" George said, trembling and shaking his head. "I may be a librarian, I may have heard it all, but that doesn't give you the right to abuse me in my own department!"

Peter was of the opinion that George's department hadn't been abused in a long time. "At least let me make a photocopy?"

"If you don't leave, I'm calling security," George said emphatically. "Let's see what kind of potty mouth you have once they're finished jackbooting all over you."

Peter considered arguing, but it was pointless. He turned on his heels and walked away, his Doc Martens clicking on the marble floor. He thought of the other librarian—she must have believed that any two gay men, once introduced, were bound to fall in love and settle down together.

But you did flirt with him, a part of Peter's brain said. The other part replied automatically: But I'm monogamous! Strictly monogamous!

Peter didn't feel his disquiet ease until he was back in the ghetto and had picked up a copy of *Phag Magazine* from the gay bookstore. He was supposed to meet Mac for a shopping spree, but he still had a few minutes before declaring his day officially wasted.

Peter settled into a park bench and scanned the editorial. Phrases such as ". . . carefully orchestrated strategy to strike at the heart of the magazine . . ." and ". . . a once-renowned writer sadly declining in quantity and quality of output . . ." made him wish he hadn't bothered paying the $7.95. This was close to libel, or at least as close as Chester could come without sending up warning flags from the legal department. Chester couldn't prove anything, but then Peter probably couldn't either, and without the money for legal bills, he'd die trying.

That was it, Peter thought, tearing the flimsy magazine in half with some difficulty. He'd see *Phag* and Chester Valentine ruined, if it took him years. There had to be something he could do to get back at them.

He was still pondering the problem when Mac came along, dressed in a plaid jacket and earmuffs. "So tell me what's on your mind," Mac said, sitting down next to him. "I saw that cloud hanging over you from three blocks away."

"I'm sitting here having revenge fantasies about the magazine."

Mac put his arms around himself and made a "brrr" sound. "They say revenge is a dish best served cold, but don't you think we'd be better off inside, spending money?"

So Peter followed Mac along, pretending to try on clothes, while Mac pretended that Peter could afford the things he was looking at. As usual, Mac only bought the plainest, butchest clothing. Peter didn't want to ask if it was a "bear" thing; he was afraid to find out that it was.

"Did you have any luck at the library?" Mac asked after they'd done three underwear stores and one sock mart. Peter recounted his story, and Mac shook his head. "You know what the interesting thing is, though?"

"The Religious Right now controls our library system?" Peter asked.

"I'm wondering why you were flirting with this guy. You keep going on about being monogamous any time anyone brings up the subject."

Peter pursed his lips and examined a sequin-encrusted tiara in a shop window. "Danny and I made a commitment. You know, the way traditional couples do. I'm not defensive—I'm proud of it."

"That tiara's a bit too small for your head," Mac commented. "The leather tux, on the other hand . . ."

"Oh God, don't get me started. Remember Danny in the leather tuxedo at our commitment ceremony?" Peter asked. "I kept thinking, just lie back and think of Martha."

They went into the store so that Mac could try on a heavy link key chain. "There you go again," Mac said after declaring the key chain to be too shiny. "It's commitment ceremonies, ring exchanges, monogamy, Martha Stewart, and your cat that's a perfect substitute for the child you two can't have yet. When we were going out, you were much more adventurous." Mac smiled ruefully. "I guess if I haven't changed, I don't want you to change either."

Peter tried the key chain on, but he could never remember if it went on the left or the right, and he suspected that sitting on it for a few hours would give him neuralgia. "Oh, I just followed the trends," he said sarcastically. "Swept along by the tides of gay history." He assumed a dramatic pose. "I partied when I came out, eased up on the sex during the start of the epidemic, experimented with the sex parties and J/O clubs when they came up as a *safe alternative,* and then . . . well you know. I settled. I mean, I settled down with Danny."

"Want to hear a bit of alternative history?" Mac asked. "You know, like those books where Zsa Zsa Gabor was born a man?" Peter shrugged.

"There was a gay community that never went through that crisis," Mac said. "Or at least it went through the shock of the plague, but it had a totally different reaction. Instead of everyone sealing themselves off, they had sex like crazy, swapped partners, and never looked back."

"This is the bear thing again," Peter said. "And let me guess . . . everyone accepts everyone else, and there's a lot of caring and sharing going on."

Mac looked serious. "Okay, that's the Disney version. But yeah, the whole thing was based on a lot of acceptance of who people were. Lots of affection and inclusion."

"Like a Ziggy cartoon with body hair." Peter ducked out of the way to avoid Mac's foot connecting with his butt.

"You'll never understand," Mac complained. "Not sitting out here on the sidelines. You can't write about it like it's some dead tribe of Incas."

"Then take me to one of these bear things," Peter said, feeling adventurous. "Maybe I could see what goes on for myself." As long as I stay monogamous, he thought.

Mac shook his head. "They'd see through you in a second. Bears are pretty accepting, but a lot of them are suspicious of . . . let's call them nonbears."

They stopped in front of a store for transvestites called The New You. Peter looked at all of the equipment and contrivances that existed solely for the purpose of convincing the world that a man was a woman.

"There must be a way," he said uncertainly, not liking the idea that was forming in his mind.

His eyes met Mac's in the reflection of the store window. "Oh my," Mac said, grinning. He took off his black earmuffs and held one end of them up in front of Peter's mouth as if it was a goatee. "I do believe we have a solution."

Peter looked at his reflection, turned quickly away, then looked back again in curiosity. Kill two birds with one stone, he thought . . .

That night, Peter started a journal to keep notes for the "bear" book.

To know the bears one must become a bear, he wrote with some trepidation. Tomorrow, I become a bear.

– 4 –

What is a "bear"?

It's the simplest question when you're first confronted with the notion of a "bear community," and the hardest one to get an answer to. Ask any ten "bears" and you'll get ten different answers.

Oh, they'll say that being a "bear" has to do with a certain group of attributes—the body hair, the beard, the extra weight, maybe even some personality-related characteristics. But one man will say a beard is essential, while another will insist that a thin man can never be a "bear."

"Bears" are like chronic fatigue syndrome sufferers, with less whininess and more self-righteousness. CFS sufferers see twelve out of eighteen potential symptoms and identify themselves with their particular malady; some "bears" will call themselves a bear even if they're not hairy, bearded, or overweight—just so that they can belong.

Like Judge Bork, they don't necessarily know what a "bear" is, but they know one when they see him. And of all the men they believe to be "bears," the person they consider that most embodies "bearish" attributes is the one staring at them in the bathroom mirror.

My friend "M" pointed out a young man who could have passed for a typical "scene" gay man, except for the teddy bear pin he was wearing. "He thinks he's a bear?" I asked, incredulous. "I'm more of a bear than he is!"

"Bear is a state of mind," M replied. "If you think you're a bear, you are one. At least until ten other bears get together and tear you to shreds."

Mac looked over Peter's shoulder at his laptop and harrumphed. "I said I wanted you to use a fake name instead of mine, but can you come up with something instead of "M?" I feel like James Bond's boss. Give me a butch name."

Peter thought about it. "Okay, how about Bruce, Lyle, or Oscar?"

Mac bapped him on the head and shut the laptop case. "That's enough out of you, Clark Kent. You've been putting this off long enough. Time to turn you into Superbear."

They were sitting on the couch in Mac's living room. It was much as Peter remembered it: lots of leather and chrome furniture, African masks on the wall, and rugs by IKEA. "Do we slide down a pole into your Bear cave?" Peter asked, turning the laptop off.

"I've got everything set up in my bedroom," Mac said, gesturing Peter in that direction. When Peter hesitated, Mac shook his head. "You don't really think, after all these years, I'm putting the moves on you?" Mac chuckled. "Peter, dear, I don't go for twinks anymore."

Peter had heard the term before, but he had to admit he didn't know what it meant. "What's a twink?"

Mac pushed him into the bedroom. "Anything nonbear. Hairless, thin, often blond guys with bubble butts and bubble brains. Just the opposite of what we want to turn you into."

Peter was about to object to the characterization when he caught sight of the contents of Mac's bedroom. "Oh, you are *not* serious!" he gasped.

> The term "bear" is not only a metaphor for how these men see themselves; the animal itself is a totem for them to anthropomorphize and assimilate. Certain pretechnological tribes believed that the consumption of an animal's carcass (or, in some cases, a human enemy's remains) would give them the characteristics of that animal—strength, speed, or bravery. That primitive "law of equals" still holds true in the bear community, though in a different form.

"Now what?" Mac asked, going over and opening up the closet.

Peter waved his arms around at it all. "You didn't have to go to all this trouble just for me, you know."

Mac turned around, puzzled. "Trouble?"

Peter stood back and took it all in. More than two dozen teddy bears, some in fetish wear, stood at attention on the bookshelves. A hirsute model with a glandular condition pointed his cock outward from a poster on the wall reading "Grin and Bear It!" The bedspread was covered with more teddy bears, and Peter could have sworn the night light was shaped like Dan Haggerty's head. "You mean it's like this all the time?" he asked, the realization slowly dawning on him in horror.

Mac laughed. "Oh, yeah. Bear kitsch. Some people really get into it. You like it?"

"Are there stores that actually sell this stuff?"

"Would you believe there's a store in town that only sells bear things?" Mac asked, returning from the closet with a full-length mirror. "It's in the ghetto. We'll have to go someday . . . when you're ready." His expression turned serious. "Time to start your transformation."

"You know," Peter said, picking up the nearest teddy bear, "this looks like a Steiff . . ."

Mac plucked the bear out of Peter's hands, readjusted its tiny jockstrap, and placed it back on the bookshelf in exactly the same position it had been in. "You want to become a bear, or not? You can stall all you want, but the time is *now*."

Peter examined himself in the mirror and waved a silent goodbye. "Be gentle."

> Maybe the accumulation of bear kitsch is as strong a sign as any of the intense identification of the "bear" with bears and the bear movement. Long considered outcasts in the mainstream gay community because of their weight, body hair, or general misfit nature, the "bear" finds enthusiastic acceptance in a hedonistic world where all the brakes are off . . .
>
> But I'm getting ahead of myself. Long before that man takes the first step into a "bear meet" or a dim sum, there is a crucial moment of self-recognition; the moment where the man realizes that he is a bear. There are parallels to the self-recognition that occur when one realizes one is gay, but the lines between gay and straight are far more clearly defined than the murkiness of "what is a bear."
>
> Thinking back to my own childhood, I remember my first gay role models—Paul Lynde, Charles Nelson Reilly, and Mr. Humphries from *Are You Being Served?* I remember wanting to hug and kiss the other boys, but not understanding why or what had made me different.
>
> And the "bear"? Had he idolized Mr. French from *Family Affair*? Any number of hirsute actors in the 1970s? Or was it simply a leap into a community where he'd be accepted, nay, revered for the physical attributes that others had rejected him for?

Stripped to his briefs, Peter felt uncomfortable in the cold air, but even more uncomfortable with Mac's examination. Not that there was anything sexual to it; it was Mac's clinical analysis that unnerved him.

"Toned muscles, mostly. A bit of a pot belly," Mac remarked, poking it gently. "Too much beer?"

Peter sucked in his stomach. "Beer, God! Give me a wine cooler any day. No, I need to get to the gym more."

Mac rolled his eyes. "Exactly the type of thinking we need to get rid of." He continued his examination. "Thick armpit hair and crotch hair, hairy calves . . . wait a minute." He looked up and eyed Peter. "You've been holding back!"

Peter blushed and covered his groin with his hands. "I don't know what you're talking about."

Mac grabbed a Bear Club Calling Card off of the dresser and rubbed the edge over Peter's bare chest. It made a scraping, scratching noise; Peter twisted away from it.

"You've been *shaving!*" Mac cried.

"Danny likes me to be smooth," Peter said defensively. "I shaved it once, a long time ago, and I liked how it brought out my muscle definition. Is that so wrong?"

Mac eyed him thoughtfully. "We're not starting from zero, at least. Get dressed. We have a lot of work to do."

Their first stop was a workers' clothing supply store. Peter looked around while Mac compared various patterns of plaid. "Construction workers buy their clothes here! . . . Construction workers!" Peter burst out when he couldn't contain himself any more. "Construction work!"

"Has anyone ever called you a snob?" Mac asked, holding up a suspiciously large shirt jacket in front of Peter's chest.

Peter pushed the bulky clothing away. "I'm no snob. But that doesn't mean I'm going to dress up like a lumberjack."

"But you'll look so *cute!*" Mac said. Eventually he persuaded Peter into trying the whole getup—shirt jack, jeans, and hiking boots. Peter felt swaddled; his arms hung at forty-five degree angles from his shoulders, and it looked like he was wearing a muffler. "You don't think I should get this in maybe two sizes smaller?" he asked.

Mac just smiled. Peter sucked in his stomach and shook his head. "No," he breathed. "It's the final betrayal . . . the final insult. I won't."

Mac led him from the store, carrying two large bags. "You'd think," Mac mused, "that after all this time I'd hate playing devil's advocate. You *would* think that . . ."

The scene of Peter's temptation was the food court at the local mall. Peter tried to find a decent salad on the placards in the various restaurants, but everything seemed fried in grease, dipped in chocolate, or, scarily, both.

"It won't work," Peter said confidently. "I've had thirty years of conditioning in gay eating habits. My body's trained to eat only food that's good for it."

"Denial is such a terrible sin," Mac said.

"Not denial, just eating in moderation," Peter corrected him, blocking the view of a french fry stand with his hand.

Mac's voice had dropped into the murmur Peter remembered from their late nights together. "Moderation, then. You go through life balancing yourself on the very middle. Just enough, never too much." Mac closed his eyes. "But just enough isn't enough, really. Is it?"

"I don't know what you're talking about," Peter said stubbornly, resisting the food smells assaulting his nostrils.

"Don't have casual sex," Mac said. "Get a steady job. Be a good role model for gay men. Make your bed every morning." He opened one eye. "But there's a part of you that says, 'I want more.' That little part of you that's so tired of being good."

Peter tensed his hands. The smell of the Chinese buffet behind him was intoxicating. "Aren't you tired of being good?" Mac asked quietly.

Peter screamed, "Aaaugh! I can't take it anymore!" and raced over to the buffet. Before Mac could stop him, he'd buried his face in the chow mein.

"Easy there, cowboy," Mac said with some alarm, then took out a $20 bill and handed it to the confused man behind the counter. "You'll have to excuse my friend," Mac apologized. "He's been starving for too long."

Finally, Peter rose from the buffet, sated. Bits of chow mein fell from his face.

"Oh God," he said. "I'm not sure if I want to throw up or smoke a cigarette. Is this what it feels like to be a bear?"

"No," Mac said, walking him toward the rest of the mall, "that's what it feels like to be a glutton. Of course," he added thoughtfully, "there is the occasional overlap."

"Am I done yet? Am I a bear?"

"Well, I don't have a source for topical Rogaine, but your chest hair is going to grow back. Still, this is only the physical stuff. There's one more thing we have to do, but it'll come in time . . ."

> Becoming a bear, just like coming out of the closet, requires a certain shift in perception. What you find attractive, what you find acceptable, what you deem important, all changes. In a way, you become an outsider, but in a way, you become part of a small, select private group. Usually, this is a long process that accompanies repeated exposure to the bear community. I, however, didn't have the luxury of time.

A week later, Mac came for dinner at Peter and Danny's apartment. "Are you sure you want another helping of potatoes?" Danny asked Peter delicately at one point.

Peter looked at Mac, who nodded. "Yes, dear," he replied. "And can you get me some more bread sticks while you're up?"

"I've been saving the hardest part for last," Mac said when Danny had retreated into the kitchen, holding up a pack of note cards, and a rolled-up magazine. "Are you sure you're ready?"

Peter nodded, feeling the stubble of his chest hair rub against his shirt. "I've come this far."

"Is he okay with all this?" Mac asked, gesturing toward the kitchen door.

"Danny? Sure," Peter said. "We talked about this already. He's behind me one hundred percent. He told me he'll love me no matter what."

Mac looked at Peter for a few seconds. "There will probably be some adjustments."

"He loves me," Peter said. "Now let's get to the last part of all this."

Danny returned and spooned a small amount of potatoes onto Peter's plate. "What are you two doing now?" he asked.

"I'm going to say a word," Mac said, holding up the cards, "and Peter's going to say the first word that comes to his mind."

"Sure!" Danny said brightly. "Word association. Like we do in psychology class."

Mac eyed him sideways. "Yes, sort of . . ." He looked at the first card. "Body hair."

"Gross!" Peter said, then yelped as Mac struck his head with the rolled-up magazine. "What the hell was that for?"

"Call it attitude adjustment," Mac grinned. "How about *bear?*"

"Minority." *Bap.* "Ow, that hurts!"

"Try again."

"Uh, group?"

Mac flipped cards. "Beard?"

"Richard Simmons' wife?" *Bap.* "Ow!"

"Stop it!" Danny cried. "You're hurting him!"

"No," Peter said, gritting his teeth and rubbing his head. "Let him continue."

"He'll make you bleed!" Danny said melodramatically.

"Fat chance," Peter muttered.

Mac hit him with the magazine again. "What was that for?" Peter asked.

"Never use fat in a negative way," Mac admonished, and flipped to the next notecard.

Peter had trouble falling asleep that night; he felt hampered by the extra weight, and the regrown chest hair itched and chafed him. He rolled over and put his arm around Danny's back.

"You're all hairy," Danny complained.

"Hairy is a good thing," Peter mumbled in his semisleep.

"That's what Mac wants you to believe. It's brainwashing. Like they did in *The Manchurian Candidate.* Or that episode of *Wonder Woman.*"

Peter regained a measure of consciousness. He propped himself up on a pudgy elbow in the darkness. "Does it really bother you?"

"It reminds me of how we get accused of converting little boys," Danny said, offended. There was a moment of silence.

"I meant me," Peter said gently. "The whole weight thing . . . the body hair. The goatee . . ."

"That's a goatee?" Danny giggled, touching it with a finger. "I thought some crème brûlée got stuck on your chin from dessert."

"You are a silly cub," Peter admonished, then felt the words stick in his throat. "A silly boy, I mean."

"You're allowed to have your voyage of self-discovery," Danny said. "We all are."

Peter rubbed Danny's hairless, taut stomach. "Now it sounds like you're reading from one of your psych textbooks. How do you really feel?"

In a more sober tone, Danny said, "I wonder why. I read somewhere once that the way you look ends up changing the way you feel. The way you are. And I wonder who you're going to end up to be."

"Just me," Peter said, rolling over onto his back and trying to sleep. "Just me."

But as the days passed, Peter started to wonder himself. That cute guy in the Starbucks, whose eyes always used to linger on his, now was curt and abrupt, and the steamed milk had less than its usual head of foam. Peter felt ignored when he walked down the street; on occasion, other people would even bump into him.

"It's all part of the process," Mac said. "Just a few more days, and you'll be ready to join the bear community. Remember, when God closes a door, he opens a window."

"Does he also let out jeans?" Peter asked, trying to squeeze into a pair of 501s that had fit him only three weeks before.

The next day the man at Starbucks mixed up his order, and Peter spent the morning in the Emergency Room with swollen eyes and a swollen nose from the hazelnut allergy he'd had ever since he was a child.

"You might want to consider losing some of that weight," the nurse counseled him helpfully.

"I'm not overweight!" Peter protested. "Well, not that much."

She looked him up and down. "If you're having problems finding housing, we have some programs here for indigents." Peter fled.

She wasn't entirely wrong, he reflected later. Although he only looked like a construction worker, his bank balance was slowly declining, and Danny was coming up on the next semester of his degree, which meant another few thousand dollars in tuition and books.

Peter had tried to find some writing gigs, but there weren't really that many openings for gay gadfly columnists. Mac suggested he try technical writing, but Peter barely knew how to operate his computer.

"Too bad," Mac mused. "I know a lot of bears in high tech."

Finally, Peter gave in and went to his bank for a cash advance on his Visa, the day before his "coming out" at the next bear meet. The First National Gay Bank was tastefully appointed, but that day Peter was more concerned with his credit limit than the orchids on the teller desks.

He stood in line for half an hour, behind an opera fan chatting glibly into his cell phone and in front of a surly lesbian, who seemed to be resentful that he had more body hair than she did.

"Next?" the teller asked when Peter was at the front of the line. "Next? Next? Anyone?"

"I'm right here," Peter said, standing in front of the teller.

"Oh," the teller said, surprised. "I didn't think you were here to do *banking*."

"You thought I was the plumber, maybe? I'd unplug your toilet," Peter replied politely, "but it seems like you have the plunger stuck right up your ass."

The teller served him in mutually bitter silence. As Peter left the premises, he caught sight of a burly, hairy (handsome?) man through the glass of the front of the bank. A bear at First National, he marveled. At least he wasn't the only one willing to brave their ridicule. Someone to talk to for his book, perhaps.

Then he rounded the corner and the realization brought him up short. There was no other man. He'd only seen himself in the glass.

Peter straightened his plaid shirt jacket and looked at his reflection. It was about time he met the other bears in this town.

"In for a penny, in for two hundred pounds," Peter murmured, then walked away.

– 5 –

"What do you mean you can't make it?" Peter said into the pay phone.

"I mean," Mac said patiently from somewhere downtown, "that I'm caught up at work and I can't make it. You go ahead."

Peter gathered the collar of his plaid shirt jacket closer around his neck. "I can't go in there *alone*. God only knows what they'll do to me. It's like being thrown into a lion's den. And what are you doing at work on a Saturday?"

He heard Mac sigh on the other end. "Calendar shoot deadline. We only have so many weeks before December thirty-first. Now you go and get your little Camryn Manheim legs to the beer bust. Just remember what I told you, and you'll do fine. I'll be there as soon as I can."

Peter was about to hang up when Mac said, "Oh, a couple more things. Remember that *woof* can be used as a noun, verb, adjective, and adverb. And if someone growls at you, that's not a bad thing."

"Woof? Growl?" Peter said into the receiver, aghast. "You're sending me into a foreign country without a Berlitz Guide! How can I get by if I can't even speak the language properly?"

Another sigh. "The printer's on the other line," Mac said. "Gotta go. Think of it like the Smurfs. They used the word *smurfy* for everything—you can use the word *woofy* for almost everything."

"Almost?" Peter asked, but the line had gone dead. He slammed the phone onto the hook and growled. "Well, this is just a woof-ful state of affairs," he said sourly, and headed down the street to the bar.

The Eagle bar was at the periphery of the gay ghetto, and as far as Peter remembered, it had been there forever. Maybe its patrons had been involved in the Stonewall Riots in the 1960s; rumor had it that they looked the part. The Eagle was a long-standing joke in the mainstream gay community, a place where trolls and hustlers hung out, the bottom rung of gay society. And now bears.

Peter ducked into a doorway and paused. Sure, he'd read enough serious essays to know that trolls were outcast (unfairly) from the gay community because of their age and looks, and that hustlers were merely sex trade workers empowering themselves while participating in victimless consensual crimes. It was always so easy to compartmentalize dissimilar people into negative stereotypes, Peter thought. Or, even worse, politically correct stereotypes. But still—the Eagle!

A gust of wind passed through the shirt jacket, flannel shirt, and thermal undershirt like a knife, and Peter shivered. Time to take the plunge. He sprinted across the street, acutely aware of the flab on his thighs jiggling slightly, and went into the bar.

Peter hadn't been in a bar since he and Danny had decided to settle down together, and the last he'd remembered of bar life was Grace Jones, disco lighting, and the crush of warm, sweaty bodies. The Eagle was mostly empty, and the few customers sat at tables instead of at the long bar, chatting sullenly and sizing him up.

He saw the expected forty-year-old leatherman with grizzled face to match his jacket, and the cherubic young hustler standing by the pool table, rubbing chalk on his cue with a predatory look on his face, but no bears. In fact, everyone looked perfectly normal—for a bar.

"He's one of *them*," Peter heard someone say. "You know . . ."

Peter turned around, but he couldn't make out who'd said it; everyone was hidden behind their drinks. "Why don't they stay in their part of their bar?" another voice asked. "They have their place, and we have ours." Even the hustler lost interest, and Peter blushed.

The bartender, a burly man with a shaved head and beard, smiled in a vaguely kindly way. "You looking for the bear beer bust?" he asked, polishing a mug with a cloth that didn't look particularly clean.

Peter felt all eyes on him. "Yes," he admitted.

The bartender pointed to a hallway at the end of which was a short flight of stairs. "Down there. You might find some more friendly folk in there."

"Thanks," Peter said and followed the man's directions. He tuned out the rest of the patrons' comments and walked down the steps, then stepped without warning into a small, dark bar full of bears.

His first thought was that he'd somehow walked into a demented redneck version of *The Stepford Wives*. Nearly everyone had the same buzzed hair, goatee, or beard; jeans, boots, and plaid flannel shirt. Peter now understood why Mac had been so meticulous in his makeover.

A large-framed man with a bushy beard and a wide smile came over and clapped Peter on the back. "Hi there!" he said, offering a big hand ("paw," Peter thought) to shake. "You look like you're new here."

Peter straightened up from the backslapping and tried to grip the man's hand as hard as his was being gripped. "Oh yeah," he managed. "First time."

The man grinned, exposing not fangs but a long set of white teeth. "I'm Jason—Jason Smith. President of the bear club. Pleased to meet you."

"Thanks. I'm . . ." Peter said, then realized that he'd have to use a pseudonym. He tried to think of bear-related things. "Dan. Dan Karn."

"Great, great!" Jason continued grinning and focusing his eyes on him. Peter wondered if he'd somehow be able to see past the thin facade to the twink within. What then? He looked around, but the exit was blocked by big bearded men. "You'll find all of us friendly and accepting. Mostly," he added, then guffawed. "You have any problems, come see me."

Peter relaxed a bit. Jason seemed like a friendly sort, even though he could probably demolish a quart of Ben & Jerry's without pausing for air. Maybe this wouldn't be as painful as he thought. Peter remembered the list of questions he'd prepared earlier. Jason was the ideal first "interviewee."

Jason's eyes suddenly veered away from Peter's. "You'll have to excuse me," Jason said absently, then pushed past him. Peter wondered if he'd done something wrong, but when he turned to follow Jason's path, he saw the man chatting up what would no doubt be considered a hunky bear. Ah, Peter thought. Even in the bear community, there were bears and there were *bears*.

He went over and bought a beer at the bar, wincing at the taste. I'm not that bad-looking, Peter thought, miffed, looking at himself in the mirror behind the bar. Not even for a bear.

"You won't catch many bears looking away from them," a mellifluous voice said behind him. It surprised him; Peter had expected every bear to have a working-class rough burr, or at the least Mac's endearing whimsical lilt. Peter thought it might be another interloper like himself, but the voice turned out to belong to a typical-looking bear with aquiline features.

"How's that?" Peter asked, sipping his beer and trying not to gag.

"If you're going to meet a mate, you have to get out there and introduce yourself. Be friendly. Show them what you've got." The man extended a hand. "I'm Sasha, by the way."

Peter smiled and shook it. "Thanks for the tip."

"You remind me a lot of how I was when I came to my first bear event. Not quite fitting in, not quite understanding how the game was played." Sasha sighed. "It was so long ago. Maybe I can offer you a pointer or two."

"Oh, that'd be useful," Peter said. And maybe this would be his first unofficial interviewee.

"You see that handsome bear by the pool table?" Sasha asked. Peter nodded, looking at a man who resembled nearly every other man in the room. "Well," Sasha said, "he's the guy I'm planning to get my husbear to do a three-way with." He winked at Peter. "Now, even though you're nowhere near as cute as me, I'd keep your hands off of him."

"I'll keep it in mind."

"That's so sweet of you!" Sasha said, rubbing Peter's goatee for a split second, then sweeping off to the other side of the room. *Husbear?* What the hell was that? Peter wondered.

Jason came by, arms around the man he'd been chatting up. "This is Will," Jason said, offering introductions. "Don't grope Dan here," he said, winking at Will, "he's not used to our ways yet."

Peter smiled demurely and matched Will's bone-crushing grip. "I see you were talking to Sasha," Will said in a gruff voice that matched his appearance.

"He was talking at me," Peter said dryly.

Will chuckled. "Nothing to worry about with that one. His woof's worse than his bite. As long as you don't get in his way, he's an adorable cub."

"And speaking of woofs," Jason added, "did you see that new bartender? Or should I say *beartender?* He's definitely husbear material."

Will groped Jason in a way that made Peter blush. "You're not ready to settle down yet," Will said. "There's probably dozens more otters, bears, and cubs for you to maul before you finish sowing your wild oats."

Both of them looked expectantly at Peter. "Woof?" he said at last.

"You said it, bro," Jason sighed contentedly, resting his head on Will's chest. "I think you'll fit in here fine." He rubbed Peter's head with his free hand. Peter relaxed. That was close . . . too close. If he didn't get his terminology in order, he'd be unmasked for sure.

"Looks like I didn't even need to come today at all," Mac said, coming up to the three of them. "I was going to introduce Chris here to you guys, but he did it all himself."

Jason frowned. "Chris?"

Peter felt a chill. "Uh, my middle name. Dan Chris Karn." He glared at Mac, daring him to say something. "We go way back, Mac and I. Nobody calls me that anymore."

The edges of Mac's lips quivered dangerously. "Looks like you're in good hands here . . . Dan." He hugged Will, kissed Jason, and rubbed Peter's head. What am I, Peter thought, a good-luck charm? He tried to smooth down the hair, but the buzz cut refused to flatten. "You know," Mac said after the ritual greeting was complete, "Jason here is a writer."

"Dan's a writer, too?" Jason asked. Peter was afraid his head would get rubbed again, but Jason had his hands full of various bear parts. "Anything published?"

"Not yet, but he's trying to find work," Mac said, interrupting Peter's attempt to say anything. "Maybe you two can get together."

"He could come work for me," Will rumbled. "We can always use some fresh meat at Bear Necessities."

Peter looked puzzled, and Mac explained. "That store that sells all the bear stuff in the ghetto. Bearaphrenalia, I call it. Thanks, Will, but Dan's more of a thinker bear."

"Looks more like a little furry cublet to me," Will boomed, tweaking Peter's left nipple through the shirt jacket. Peter yelped, then forced a smile after a sharp look from Mac.

"I'm going to use the facilities," Peter said, getting up and extricating himself from the bear mass. He went into the bathroom and washed his face, rubbed his sore nipple, and tried to smooth his buzz cut into some kind of order. From bear to cublet, he mused. Then he heard a familiar voice from just beyond the bathroom door.

"What do you think you're doing here, woofer?" Sasha's soft voice said. Peter couldn't hear the response, but his hackles (and the new hair on his chest) rose in protest.

"You stay outside the community," Sasha went on, "then you show up one day and we're supposed to drop everything to be your friend? I think not."

Peter came out of the bathroom and saw Sasha talking to a bear who was dressed in jeans and a shirt, but without the plaid or flannel.

"Putting out the welcome mat again, eh, Sasha?" Peter asked.

"You're so sweet," Sasha said smoothly, "for a newcomer who doesn't know anything about our little group."

Peter realized in a flash the meaning of the word that he hadn't understood earlier. He assumed a pose of mock horror. "I think I hear a dingo eating your husbear!" he cried.

The other man giggled, and Sasha growled at both of them in an unfriendly way, eyes narrowing.

"I think my drink needs refreshing," he said, and left them alone.

"That was priceless," the bear said, extending a hand. "I'm Frank."

"Dan," Peter said. They shook hands. "What was he going on about? Is there some reason you're not allowed in the club?"

Frank shook his head. "I don't really hang around the bears. It's not my scene, but I do some work for Will over there. All these clothes, the bars, the attitude—it's not me. So Sasha and some of the others get pissed off with me because I'm profiting off of the bear community without contributing to it."

Peter shook his head. "That's pretty silly."

Frank dug into his pocket. "Well, you showed him. It doesn't matter if we're in the scene or not. We're all bears underneath, right?"

"Uh, that's right," Peter said uncomfortably.

Frank put a key chain into Peter's hand. "Here, take this. My gift." It was a tiny teddy bear with a black leather outfit. "We bears have to stick together." He waved awkwardly. "Gotta go."

Peter sat down in a chair at one of the empty tables, nursing his foul-tasting beer. The edges of the chair cut into his love handles and he fidgeted, trying to find a comfortable spot. The designers of the chairs clearly had had another body type in mind.

"You having fun?" Mac asked, coming over.

"Well, I passed the undercover test," Peter said. "Nobody suspects I'm a twink."

Mac laughed. "You know, it's funny. When I first came in, I didn't see you there. I mean, I saw you, but I didn't realize it was you. You look totally different."

Peter put a hand on his padded hip uneasily. "This will come off, right? After I finish the book. I can lose the weight, shave the goatee and the chest hair, go back to being me. Right?"

"The weight will probably come off," Mac said. "But the way you think about things is probably going to be changed for good."

"You knew this would happen, didn't you!" Peter hissed.

"Oh, please. I thought you'd be a twink in bear's clothing," Mac said. "But you look completely convincing—like a real bear. Sooner or later it's bound to start getting under your skin." He grinned. "Chalk one up for our side. You're a member of the bear fraternity now."

Before Peter could say anything more, Mac had pushed through a group of bears and was embroiled in a discussion and groping. Fraternity, Peter thought. Support group was more like it.

Someone clapped Peter on the back, and Peter already knew enough about the various bears to know it was Jason.

"Sasha can be a pain in the ass," Jason said. "Nice to see that some people won't put up with him. Nicer still to see you sticking up for your fellow bears."

"Everyone's an outsider at one time or another," Peter replied.

Jason wrapped his paws around Peter and grabbed him in a tight bear hug. "Seems like a furry fella like you wouldn't be an outsider anywhere for long," Jason said and growled softly.

Peter was aghast. He tried to catch Mac's eyes, but his friend was off buying raffle tickets. Peter stiffened, and a moment later Jason let him go.

"Sorry, man," Jason said easily. "Didn't mean to scare you."

Peter straightened his shirt jacket. "You startled me," he said semi-truthfully. "I'm not used to all this."

"Okay," Jason said. He took a business card out of his pocket and pressed it into Peter's hand. "Call me and maybe I can find you a job." He grinned. "And no strings attached, I promise. You seem like a nice bear—we should be able to find you a writing gig, no problem."

Peter looked at the card, musing. Maybe being a member of the "fraternity" wouldn't be so bad after all . . . if it landed him a job before the rest of his money ran out.

– 6 –

A few days later, Peter was in the local megabookstore, shopping for computer books. He wandered down the aisles in a daze, marveling at the marble floors, Doric columns, and neatly arranged bookshelves. With the seating, it was more of a library than the public library, and a better-organized one. The local library would never let him drink a cappuccino while reading the latest Armistead Maupin. There was only the little matter of the price . . .

Peter and Danny had had their first fight in a long while over his shopping expedition.

"I have to prepare for this interview," Peter had explained patiently.

"You have to get groceries," Danny replied, with only a hint of the full-blown petulance that was threatening to explode. "What are we supposed to serve guests? Triscuits and cheese slices?"

"How *dare* you mock my canapés!" Peter had said in mock horror, but Danny wasn't placated. Only by promising to buy a single book and no more had Peter managed to avoid a larger confrontation.

One book. In the world of the megabookstore, that was equivalent to eating one potato chip and putting the bag away for later. Peter had already passed up the . . . *for Beginners* computer books, the . . . *for Dummies* books, and the . . . *for Idiots* books. The lower he sunk toward the moron level, the more Peter wondered who bought these books. Was there a book in the health section called *Losing Weight for Fat Pigs Who Lack Self-Control*?

Peter sucked in his stomach and tugged at his belt. If there was a book like that, he'd need it soon. No matter how carefully he tried to control his eating, his weight slowly crept upward. Similarly, not only had his chest hair grown back, but it was sprouting in new areas. I'm in crisis, Peter thought dejectedly, and my body's saying "Woof."

He came to the last bookshelf in the computers section and, incredulously, picked up a book titled *The Gay Dolt's Guide to Computers*. It used a large typeface and friendly text to explain its topics, helped along by Charlie Cocksure (a shirtless muscular man whose thought bubbles were sprinkled evenly with "girlfriend" and "Mary"). Peter read the other titles in the series: *The Gay Dolt's Guide to the Internet, The Gay Dolt's Guide to Finding a Boyfriend Online,* and *The Gay Dolt's Guide to Slimming Down and Bulking Up.*

Peter was about to pick up the last book when he heard a familiar voice. "Can you help me?" the woman said behind him. "I was looking for an introductory book on the Internet."

Bette Chambers! Peter's blood ran cold. He'd worked next to her at *Phag Magazine* for five years; what would she say when she saw what he looked like?

"Over there," he mumbled, covering his face with the *Gay Dolt* book.

"I need you to show me. With your own hands. They don't pay you minimum wage to stand there, face buried in a book." Bette pulled him around with a firm hand and uncovered his face.

Peter said nothing. "Do I have to call the store manager?" Bette asked imperiously. She didn't recognize him. He didn't know whether to laugh or cry.

"I don't work here," he said, trying to imitate Jason's booming voice.

Bette twirled her rattail with a finger and cocked her head at him. "Have we met before?" she asked suspiciously.

"I dunno," Peter said, scratching his crotch with one hand and rubbing the book along his forearm with the other. "You ever get down to the Harley meets?"

Her face squinched up into an expression of distaste. Without another word, Bette maneuvered herself around him and started examining the contents of another bookshelf. Peter looked at her over the top of the *Gay Dolt*'s book. It wasn't an act—she truly didn't recognize him. He could walk through the front doors of *Phag Magazine* without anyone knowing who he was . . .

Peter shook his head. Probably it was just Bette. To her, all men looked alike. He watched her pick up *A Feminist's Guide to the Internet,* and his thoughts of infiltrating *Phag* were replaced with a more important consideration: Why was Bette looking for a book on the Internet?

He cast his mind back nearly five years ago, when *Phag* was finally switching from the old green-text terminals to brand-new Macintosh computers. Peter, fresh from university and a left-wing education, was eager to get on Bette's good side. "You have to be pretty excited about these new computers," he said to her one day as they were waiting for the coffee machine to brew.

Bette made a face. "Computers are computers . . . another tool of oppression."

"But I read somewhere that graphical computers are more woman-oriented," Peter said. "The whole left-brain thing."

The coffee machine sputtered. "Men design computers, and men make them," Bette said with finality. "Men can't have power over *everything,* so they create an artificial version inside a computer they can control."

"Is the coffee machine an instrument of male oppression, too?" Peter couldn't help asking.

"Of course," Bette said brusquely. "The first person to take coffee while it's brewing gets the strongest coffee. You can't perpetuate the hierarchy any more clearly." Then, before he could reply, she whisked away the coffee pot, took the first cup, and left the break room.

She'd eventually made the switch to the Macintosh, but she'd griped about it for the next five years. Peter couldn't imagine her suddenly wanting to learn more about the Internet . . . unless there were changes underway at *Phag Magazine.*

The megabookstore had one long wall devoted to magazines, and predictably the gay magazines were in one dark corner marked Alternative Lifestyles. Alternative Lifestyles also encompassed cat lovers, knitters, and Seventh-Day Adventists, apparently, but Peter decided that the magazine jobber had just been lazy.

Aside from *OUT, GENRE, XY,* and the like, there was a rack devoted to the offerings from Queermedia Group, *Phag*'s owner and one of the newer publishing conglomerates that had sprung up with the publishing consolidation of the 1990s. With titles like *Biker Trash, Lesbian Moms,* and *Trans-Formation,* they were mostly slapped-together quickies created to capitalize on buyers hungry for any kind of glossy gay content, and designed to drive readers to Queermedia's Web sites, an uneasy mix of pornography, banner ads, and wire stories masquerading as content. But in the middle of all the trash stood *Phag Maga-*

zine, like a beacon in the dark. Still a model of editorial integrity, if only barely.

Phag Magazine looked even glossier than usual, with a cover piece on "The New Lesbian Fashion: When Same-Sex Meets Plaids and Checks." When Peter picked the magazine off of the shelf, the usual torrent of insert cards fell out. He knelt down to pick them up and noticed one that was quite unusual for *Phag.*

"Need any help?" a gruff voice asked. Two thick-fingered hairy hands started picking up the insert cards. Peter followed them up to what Mac would call a "cuddly daddy," with kind blue eyes and a salt-and-pepper buzz cut and goatee.

"Thanks," Peter said, and blushed. "Seems like there's more cards than magazine these days."

"Well, then, there you go," the man said, handing him the rest of the cards. "You need any more help, I'll be over there, keeping an eye on ya." He chucked Peter under the chin, grinned, and wandered off.

Peter felt himself blush even more deeply. What was wrong with him? A man twice his age made a clever comment and rubbed his chin, and his knees were weak as water.

He put the magazine back on the rack and turned to find a cashier. Out of the corner of his eye, Peter spotted a handsome, preppy young blond man reading *GENRE* magazine. Okay, Peter thought, not the best choice in reading material, but . . .

"Anything interesting in that issue?" he asked the man slyly.

The man looked at him once, said "Nothing you'd be interested in," and went back to reading.

Peter thought a moment, nodded, and took his *Gay Dolt*'s book to the checkout. While he was waiting in line, he examined the insert card that had fallen out of the copy of *Phag Magazine.* "Get 40 hours free with your first month's subscription to America Online!"

Peter knew that Chester had only upgraded the computer system because he liked the way the Macs looked, and because it had been a great tax write-off. But there was Bette reading up about the online world . . . and now this. If *Phag* was making a move onto the Internet, along with the rest of Queermedia's properties, it could only be fate that he was about to enter the world of computers.

Charlie Cocksure turned out to be a better-than-average tutor, but Peter did get tired of the "social commentary." As he explained to

Mac on the telephone, "I don't think I need to be reading about barebacking while I'm learning about computer viruses."

"Jason will hire you even if you can't turn a computer on, dear," Mac said. "He thinks you're cute."

Peter balanced the book on his stomach and ate another handful of chips. "The last thing I want is to get the job because I'm cute." He shook his head. "Because he *thinks* I'm cute."

"Everybody does it," Mac said sagely. "We use whatever we have to get where we need to go. Maybe you're feeling guilty because of Danny."

After he hung up, Peter scratched MacGuyver behind the ears and thought about what Mac had said. He'd always been obsessed with one thing or another—the job at *Phag Magazine,* the bear thing, and now the bear book. Danny had always been the one to keep the relationship going when things started to flag, but it wasn't fair when he had his own issues to worry about.

Peter sprang out of the couch, and MacGuyver ran off and hid behind the television. "Baiting the Trap: How to Give Him a Welcome-Home He'll Never Forget," Peter said, remembering a headline from *Phag* about a year ago. He'd never bothered to actually read the article, but the *Cosmo*-style, self-help *Phag* articles only had two centers to revolve around—food and sex.

Danny was on one of his diets, probably as a less-than-subtle hint to Peter, so food was out of the question. Sex, on the other hand . . . Peter smiled as he remembered how Danny used to greet him naked at the door when he got home from work in the early days of their relationship. Back then they would jump into bed right away and wouldn't get out for a few hours, or sometimes all night.

Peter changed into his housecoat, which fortunately still fit. He spent another half hour reading up on how to find a hunk who was a computer programmer, and how to work in a software company without becoming a geek. Then, when he heard the elevator door open, he slipped off the housecoat, switched off the light, worked his cock up into an erection, and pressed his eye to the peephole in the front door.

Moments later, Danny came into view. When Peter was sure his boyfriend was alone, he flung the door open and leapt at Danny, wrapping his naked legs around Danny's hips and planting a kiss on his lips.

Danny uttered a muffled curse, staggered backward under the weight, and fell flat on his back. Peter rolled off sideways, banging his head on the floor. He shook himself and looked up.

"You must be Danny's study partner," Peter said to the woman who had just come out of the elevator with a pile of psychology textbooks in her arms.

Dead silence. Danny grabbed one of the woman's books and put it over Peter's crotch, then got to his feet and pulled Peter up.

"How about some Triscuits with cheese slices?" Peter asked.

Later that night, Peter lay in bed reading his *Gay Dolt*'s book *(How to Appear Smart When Asking Dumb Questions)* while Danny did his ab crunches at the end of the bed.

"Vicky seemed nice," Peter said lamely after a few minutes of silence.

Danny's head bobbed into view. "She told me she wants to write a paper about you."

"Hey, you're helping a fellow student," Peter said and put the book aside. "Maybe you'll get extra credit."

When Danny didn't reply, Peter slid out of bed and sat next to his boyfriend. Danny lay on his back, perspiring, eyes closed.

"Was it so wrong?" Peter asked.

Danny smiled without opening his eyes. "Okay, it was kind of cute. And kind of a turn on, even."

Peter noticed some activity in Danny's shorts. "Reminds you of the good old days, maybe?" He rubbed the bulge a bit.

Danny rolled over onto Peter and kissed him passionately. "Yeah," he murmured in Peter's ear, licking his earlobe and biting him gently.

"Let's get into bed," Peter whispered.

"Oh, I got an even better idea," Danny said.

In the shower, they lathered each other up. Peter leaned back and pushed Danny's head down on his cock, then turned him around and worked his dick up Danny's ass as the water poured down around them. It was all over in thirty minutes . . . but they were great thirty minutes, Peter thought when they were relaxing in bed, still damp.

"Mmm," he said, snuggling up to Danny's chest. "That was great." It was wonderful. Just how their relationship should be.

"Yeah," Danny said, playing with the hair on Peter's chest. "Like the good old days." A moment later, his fingers stopped moving. "So how do these bear relationships work?" It seemed to take him an effort to pronounce the word *bear*.

Peter thought about it. "Like regular gay relationships, I guess. They sleep around a lot, but some bears are monogamous. A lot of them are in open relationships."

"You mean, they have sex outside the relationship?" Danny asked, sounding interested.

Peter tried to snuggle closer and closed his eyes. "Sure," he mumbled. "Different culture, different mores. Sex is almost like a handshake to some of these guys. Sleeping around expands their social circle . . . I should write that down."

"Hard to imagine what it would be like not being monogamous," Danny said in an odd tone that made Peter snap wide awake.

"Is that what you want?" Peter asked quietly.

Danny patted his head. "No. Of course not. Everything's fine like it is now, right?"

"Yeah." Peter stared up at the ceiling until he felt Danny go through his usual set of twitches and body positions that indicated he'd fallen asleep.

Peter tried to sleep, but he was still horny. His mind kept returning to the guy at the bookstore. The kind blue eyes, the goatee . . .

He sat bolt upright. That was the old guy, not the cute blond one! Danny, sensing his distress, flopped an arm over Peter's chest, and Peter relaxed again. The guy had to be twice as old as him.

But those eyes . . . that brush cut . . . that grin. Peter's hands drifted to his crotch. He stopped himself. That would be unfaithful to Danny—wouldn't it?

He lay next to his boyfriend, arms rigidly at his side, dick hard as a rock. All he had to do was get through the night without jacking off. Without thinking of that daddy bear.

He didn't make it.

− 7 −

Peter sat in the reception area of *Time to Compute! Magazine,* tugging at his collar, fidgeting nervously on the edge of his chair, and waiting for his interview with Jason.

It wasn't all in his mind; his neck had expanded just enough to make the shirt collar uncomfortable, and the top button kept catching his chest hair ("chest fur," he corrected himself) whenever he tugged on his tie. To make things worse, the chair had arms that reached around and grabbed at his love handles. He had tried sitting back in it, then ended up grabbing his briefcase with both arms and looking like a passenger on the *Titanic.* Peter tried slouching down, but his belly slumped forward and outward until he felt like he was in danger of oozing over the end of the chair and onto the floor. Finally, he settled on perching himself on the edge of the chair, which hurt his butt and strained his calf muscles. Peter compensated by grabbing his briefcase between his knees and pretending he was in Lamaze class.

He tugged at his paisley tie again and wondered if he'd been too formal in his choice of wardrobe. The receptionist was wearing jeans and a sweater, and the other employees he'd seen come in and pass through reception were all dressed in either jeans or khakis. Peter was wearing his interview suit and favorite tie, although he had to admit that neither seemed to fit as well as they had five years ago.

Five years ago, *Phag Magazine* was *the* gay and lesbian magazine of ideas to work for—as Peter's thesis advisor had put it, "Like *The New Republic,* but without all that icky conservatism." Business wear was still formal wear, and Peter had set back his bank account several mac-and-cheese dinners with the purchase of his suit, but it made him feel confident and forceful. The salesman assured him that he looked like someone out of a Calvin Klein ad.

"Not Dolce and Gabbana?" Peter had said, turning around slowly in front of the three-way mirror and admiring the way the suit fell along his lean lines. Having a clotheshorse body had its advantages when it came to buying clothes.

"No," the salesman said after examining him. "You've got the whole androgynous, beachside, don't-give-a-damn look. That's what everyone's wearing these days—that and the paisley ties. Do you like rainforest or puce?"

The salesman hadn't lied. When Peter strode into *Phag Magazine* the very first time, he felt as if he belonged. The puce swirls in his tie complemented the oak paneling in Chester Valentine's office, and sitting in the high-backed chair, recounting tales of his education, Peter knew he was going to get the job.

Now, with a small pop, the front button of Peter's suit snapped off and rolled into the center of the reception area carpet. Peter sighed and gathered the two sides of his suit together over his belly. Had his decision to work at *Phag* really been that superficial? he wondered. Had their decision to hire him been equally as superficial?

The reception area carpet was a dazzling white; the brown suit button looked like a spot of dried blood in the middle of it. Clothes make the man, Peter thought defensively. As he leaned forward in a futile attempt to pick up the button, he saw the sleeve of his suit ride up, exposing his hairy forearm. Peter leaned back and sighed. There was more to a man than his outward appearance. There had to be.

And with that he once again recalled Bette Chambers' face in the bookstore, no sign of recognition on her features. Well, to hell with her, he thought, getting down on his knees to pick up the button. I could still get the job at *Phag* again, if I tried again today.

"Lose something there?" Jason rumbled above him, and Peter snatched up the button, blushing. He got to his feet and brushed himself off, then shook Jason's hand. "Looks like you lost a button, fella," Jason commented and grinned.

Peter slipped the button into his pocket and followed Jason into his office. He was almost surprised that it lacked any bear paraphernalia; only a discreet Native American sculpture of a dancing bear on one foot attested to Jason's affiliations.

"Sit down, Dan," Jason said, motioning him to a chair.

Peter perched on the edge of the chair and took out his résumé. He and Mac had worked on the résumé for hours; creating a past for Dan Karn was harder than either one of them had thought. "Dan's a dreamer," Mac had said dreamily, "moving from town to town . . . leaving dozens of broken hearts in his wake."

"That's your fantasy, not mine, or Dan's," Peter had retorted. "Give him some menial jobs. Nobody would check on those."

"And a Harley," Mac had said. "We'll make him a Web designer . . . they're notorious for being unstable and going through jobs like nobody's business. Especially porn sites."

Each of them had won a partial victory, and Jason's raised eyebrow as he perused Dan's résumé concerned Peter. "I know I've had a lot of jobs in the past few years," Peter said, trying to fill the growing silence. "You know . . . Web designers," he added helpfully.

"Our Web designer's been on staff since 1995," Jason said, making a note on the résumé with a red pen.

Peter didn't like the look of that mark. "Well, most of those sites were porn sites. Usually they folded in a few months." He winked.

Jason made another mark. "We're looking for a writer, not a Web designer. They're a dime a dozen." He smiled, the first break in his stone exterior since the start of the interview. "No offense, Dan, but this résumé looks like it's telling the story of a man who doesn't know who he is, or what he wants."

Peter felt a chill, then realized that Jason wasn't questioning *him*, but *Dan*. I'm a drifter, Peter thought. What do I want? "Did I mention I was on the road, breaking hearts a lot?" he said in desperation.

Jason narrowed his eyes and put down the résumé. "Look, I like your writing samples, even though they're about anthropology, not computers. I don't know what's going on in your personal life, and I don't want to know—although if we hire you, you can join the company's MC Club in your spare time."

Before Peter could interrupt, Jason waved a cautionary paw. "I don't like the whole flakiness bit you're giving me in this interview," Jason went on, "but I'm willing to cut you some slack because Frank Adams said you're good people."

Frank Adams? Peter remembered the man he'd rescued from Sasha's clutches at the beer bust.

"We're short of good writers, so I'll give you a chance," Jason said. "You know the computer convention going on in town now?"

"Sure," Peter said, completely unaware of any convention.

"Write up a fifteen-hundred-word piece about the up-and-coming trends. Let me give it a read through on Friday, and then we'll see." Jason stood up, indicating that the interview was over.

"Thanks for giving me this chance," Peter said, shaking Jason's hand and flashing him his best smile. Jason nodded and turned Peter's résumé over onto a pile of papers.

"On a nonwork topic. . . . There's a bear meet coming up before Christmas," Jason said. He grinned, breaking a smile across the stone face he'd had through the interview. "You planning to be there?"

Peter hadn't considered it. "Sounds like fun," he said. He gathered the lapels of his suit together and turned to go, then paused at the door.

"You would've given me the chance anyway, right?" he said uncertainly. "Even if I hadn't been a bear?"

Jason put down his pen and looked into Peter's eyes. "I probably wouldn't have given you the assignment if you'd come on to me any more strongly," he replied, expression stony once again. "How's that for an answer?"

"See you Friday," Peter said, chastised, and backed out of Jason's office.

Later that afternoon, he and Mac drank steaming cappuccinos at the café while Peter pored over the promotional material for the computer convention.

"I can't believe you," Mac said. "Coming on to your interviewer!"

Peter shook his head. "I didn't come on to him." He bit his lip. "Okay, maybe a little bit. You know, the whole charm thing. Everybody does it."

"No, everybody doesn't do it. Only people like you," Mac said. "The good-looking ones who don't realize they're good-looking. You think it's your birthright."

"Now that's just envy," Peter protested.

"Probably," Mac said, sipping his cappuccino. "But let me tell you something, so you don't get the wrong impression. As a bear, you're no A-Bear."

"A-Bear? What is that, some kind of hairy superhero?"

Mac simply smiled mysteriously. "You'll find out soon enough. Then maybe you'll come down from your high horse and join the rest of us mortals."

"I'm about to meet a whole new breed of them," Peter muttered, shoving some of the flyers across the table to Mac. "Looks like the convention's infested with geeks."

"I think you're in for another surprise," Mac said. "And one fashion tip before you go? If it's not wash-and-wear, you're not going to fit in. Let me know how it goes, and I'll let you know how I did in Mexico."

Peter didn't go that far, but he substituted a plaid flannel shirt and khakis for his interview suit. He knew that his intuition had paid off when he entered the noisy convention hall and caught sight of the masses of men passing among the aisles. With all the plaid moving back and forth, Peter felt as if he was watching some bizarre test pattern.

It was only on closer inspection that he realized the bulk of the plaid wearers were hairy, bearded men. There was the occasional nonbear, typically a salesman handing out promotional pens and Frisbees, or a saleswoman who looked like an extra in a Greek gladiator movie.

"It's bearadise!" Peter exclaimed. "I've come home to Tara again!"

"And the interesting thing," an urbane voice said behind him, "is the large percentage of the men here who are gay."

Peter came face to face with a relatively slim bear (an "otter") outfitted in preppy clothes and with frameless glasses and a heterosexual-leaning goatee.

"I saw you at the beer bust the other week," the man said, offering his hand, "although you seemed to be busy being the fresh meat. I'm Richard."

"All of them are gay?" Peter asked in amazement, watching the burly men move through the aisles of computers like lumberjacks who'd decided to take up software development.

"The ones we'd consider important are," Richard said lightly, "and the ones we don't consider important, well, who cares?"

"That sounds like an epigram," Peter said.

"Epigrams belong to a lost time," Richard remarked. "I rely on other amusements these days." Peter thought that Richard belonged to a lost time as well—the poised, elegant type without the usual sharp-tongued malice. The old term came slowly to him, but he thought of it at last: a *bon vivant*.

"I'm covering the convention for a local computer magazine," Peter said, showing Richard his leather-bound notebook and pen.

"Then you must learn the two words that make any computer-related article indispensable," Richard pronounced. "If a technology is interesting, it's *intriguing*. If a technology has potential, then it's *compelling*. When you hear of something truly remarkable, such as e-mail or a virtual Steve Kelso, then you can say it's *compelling and intriguing*." He cocked an eyebrow at Peter. "Don't mock me. John Dvorak started with as much."

"Didn't he invent that weird backward keyboard?" Peter asked.

"That's the level of analysis I'd expect from an adorable cub like you," another voice said behind him, equally as elegant but with the edge missing from Richard's delicate tone. "The Dvorak keyboard, which was *not* invented by John Dvorak, by the way, had the capability to overcome the problems of the QWERTY keyboard, if it hadn't been for the military-stenographical establishment."

Sasha was carrying a batch of pens in one hand and several Frisbees in the other. "You two know each other, then?" Richard asked.

"We've had the pleasure of meeting," Peter said, feeling his voice patterns slip into the rarefied zone Richard and Sasha inhabited.

"Then maybe we can all have a bit of lunch together," Sasha said, putting his arm through Peter's elbow. "Richard and I are dying to know what you think of the convention. I'm writing a little piece for the weekly gay newspaper."

Fortunately, Peter didn't find himself on the spot during the greasy lunch. "You know," Richard started off, "Esperanto was such a lost cause, in much the same way as the Dvorak keyboard."

Sasha ate a bite of the limp Caesar salad, grimaced, and pushed away the plate. He doodled absently on a piece of notepaper. "On the other hand, you're forgetting that Esperanto was a manufactured language. QWERTY did not evolve naturally, but was a response to the technical limitations of the time . . ."

Peter looked from Sasha to Richard, then back again. It was the final horror—droning encyclopedic robots come to life, with no way to shut them off. "I took a couple of years of Spanish once," he tried to interject at one point, but that only set them on a further tangent dealing with cultural imperialism, voice recognition technologies in foreign languages, and the problems of software internationalization.

Thankfully, at some point Sasha's pager beeped. He checked the display and smiled. "You have to excuse me," he said, getting up. "Time to go to some backroom demonstrations."

Peter smiled back. "I'm sure you'll find some interesting backrooms, Sasha."

"I take it the two of you don't get along," Richard said, pressing his napkin to his lips and folding it as if it were damask.

"Don't you think he's a pompous fraud?" Peter asked, then blushed.

"Oh, I've been accused of being the same."

Peter shook his head. "There's a difference. He's just mean-spirited."

"And I'm merely pompous?"

"That's not what I meant. He tries his best to hurt people. You don't." Peter struggled to articulate his thoughts. "Why do you hang around with him?"

Richard sighed. "When the other bear boys were off chopping down wood and going camping, I was in the library reading. Sometimes I crave intellectual stimulation—even if it's from Sasha."

"There are other bears who might have something to say besides Sasha," Peter said defensively.

"And one day, maybe you'll write a discourse on the ontological meaning behind the word *woof*." Richard tipped an imaginary hat at Peter. "Take care." He disappeared into a crowd of flannelled bears.

Peter drummed his fingers on the tabletop, thinking. Then he noticed the piece of notepaper that Sasha had left behind. Looking around to make sure nobody saw him, he slid it over and read it.

The list of scrawled terms was puzzling, but Peter slipped the notepaper into his pocket anyway. That evening, after he'd left the conference, he spent hours in the library going through old computer magazines reading up on the trends that Sasha had spotted.

All he had to add was "compelling" here and "intriguing" there, and the article practically wrote itself. After reading over a few John Dvorak columns, Peter changed his style to be more argumentative and added in a few predictions for the coming year. He came in at 1,750 words, but removing half of the occurrences of "compelling" and "intriguing" in the word processor brought the count down to 1,550. Good enough.

Peter sat on the edge of the chair in Jason's office that Friday, more in anticipation than discomfort. Jason skimmed the article, making notes in the margin with his ever-present red pen, then went through it again more slowly, doodling on a Post-it note.

"What did you think?" Peter asked.

Jason set his pen down gently. "This piece would be great . . . if it was written about five years ago. Push technology? Pen computing? Internet appliances?" He shook his head. "I don't know which vendors you were talking to, but this is all yesterday's news."

Peter thought back suddenly to the computer magazines in the library. Sure, they'd all been old, but things didn't change that quickly in the computer industry. Did they? "How about the style of the piece?"

Jason shrugged. "It's fine, nothing wrong with that. But our readers want the very latest. You're rehashing things we published ages ago. That's not cutting edge." Jason looked him right in the eye. "I'm sorry, Dan. We can't hire you. We can't even buy this piece."

Peter nodded. "Okay," he said, trying not to let his voice choke up. "Thanks for the chance, anyway. See you at the bear meet?"

Jason took out a pager. "Good thing you reminded me. Let me set a reminder." The pager beeped.

"Did you make it beep like that?" Peter asked with growing suspicion.

"Sure. One of those features, if you want to get out of a meeting early." Jason smiled. "Not that this is one of those times."

He'd been set up by Sasha. The lunch meeting, the notepaper, the beeper. Maybe even Richard, although Peter couldn't believe it. But Sasha—damn him.

Once he was alone in the elevator, Peter checked his last ATM statement. Not even enough money to pay the upcoming rent. And there were Christmas presents to buy, and Danny's tuition check.

Despite himself, he leaned his forehead against the cool wall of the elevator and let the tears flow. Now what was he going to do?

– 8 –

"Dear <FIRSTNAME>: You are cordially invited to attend *Phag Magazine*'s annual seasonal holiday party this December 20th from 7:00 p.m. to 10:00 p.m. We'd love to share the successes of the past year with you and <SIGNIFICANTOTHERNAME>, as well as share our exciting future strategy for the coming years."

Peter turned the invitation over, but the other side was blank. At first he thought it was a practical joke, until he examined Chester Valentine's signature at the bottom of the heavy linen card. The black ink, the odd loop in the "L," and the faintness in the "H"—it could only have come from Chester's signature ink stamp.

"You have a choice," Danny called from the kitchen. "Wrap gifts or write cards. Don't sit there watching TV all night."

"I got an invitation from *Phag*," Peter called back. "Seems like they still have me in their database. Sort of, at least." He gazed into the crackling logs and the dancing flames.

"Are you going to go?" Danny asked, appearing in the doorway. With the elf hat ($1.50 on sale at the dollar store) cocked at a jaunty angle, he looked more like a satyr than one of Santa's helpers who had taken growth hormones.

Peter rolled his eyes and passed him the invitation. "Their computer wants me to go. If you're so interested in going back to the company that utterly humiliated and degraded me, I'll RSVP for SIGNIFICANTOTHERNAME."

"At least the computer magazine didn't degrade you," Danny said, and winked. "Now come on. I got over my holiday blues and bought all the gifts. Less napping, more wrapping!"

Peter cast a longing eye at the burning logs, then followed Danny into the kitchen. Danny had set up a mini production line on one end of the kitchen table: gifts, paper, tape, scissors, and bows.

"This is all so . . . organized," Peter said, amazed. He sat down and started to wrap the first gift.

"Your answer to stress is to turn into a bear," Danny replied. "Mine is to organize." He frowned. "No, wait, you're doing it all wrong! The red bows go on the green wrapping paper, not on the red wrapping paper. It's red overkill!"

Peter looked at the gift label. "It's for the landlord. Do you think he'll really notice?"

"I'll notice," Danny said. "Put a green bow on that gift. All I want is a *traditional* Christmas."

"Here's something to consider," Peter said, peeling the back off of a green bow. "We're men who sleep with men. We're not involved in the reproduction of our species. Charles Dickens would have cast us as villains if he could've written about gay men back then. Linus and Charlie Brown would probably lynch us from that spindly frond they called a tree. And *you* want a traditional Christmas?"

"I'll write the cards," Danny said, grabbing the stack of cards and envelopes. While Peter wrapped the gifts, Danny used a calligraphy pen to fill out each card with a flourish. Besides the crackling and popping of logs from the living room, Peter heard Danny grumble once or twice about coal.

It was probably harder on Danny, Peter admitted as he cut yet another length of wrapping paper, only to realize it was half an inch too short to fully go around the gift. Peter had been in charge of the household finances, while Danny had relied on him for food and shelter. Danny had always been at the mercy of Peter's employment, and it didn't surprise him that his boyfriend's response in the face of crisis was to snatch at something he'd never had much of—control.

Peter sighed. Last year at this time, they'd been cuddling on the couch watching Christmas specials on TV and talking for hours. This year they'd had to cancel the cable, and everything they bought was on special. Which reminded him . . .

"Did you take a look at that cookbook I brought home from the library?" he asked Danny. "The three-ingredient one?"

Danny stopped writing in midflourish. "Oh, yes. A main dish with only three ingredients. I'll give you a hint what's for dinner. The first ingredient is macaroni and cheese mix, and if you guessed salt and pepper for the other two, you wouldn't be too far off."

They continued wrapping and writing in silence. When Peter had finished, he put away the wrapping materials and was about to put the gift wrap scraps into the recycle bin when he spotted a newspaper inside.

"Is this today's?" he asked casually.

"Mmhmm," Danny said absently. "I already checked it for writing jobs."

Peter flipped through the classifieds with an already-practiced eye. It was like reading the personals, only the people submitting the ads had all the power and most of the time didn't really want to hear from you anyway.

He ran a finger down each column of the classifieds, and when his finger stopped with a *screek!* on the counter, it was loud enough to scare MacGuyver out of a sound sleep.

"You find something?" Danny asked, looking up.

Peter couldn't believe what he'd just read. It was nothing short of amazing; he felt equal parts dread, shame, and excitement. "There's a sale on at Barnes and Noble," he lied. Quickly, he tore out the newspaper ad and put it in his pocket.

Danny sealed the last card and smacked his parched lips. "There's always a sale on somewhere. Wait until the twenty-sixth—I bet we can get a great deal on a Christmas tree."

Peter put his hands on Danny's broad shoulders and started kneading the knots out. "I told you a friend of mine has connections. Frank said he can get us a beautiful one, and cheap too."

"He's one of your 'bear friends,' right?" Danny asked.

Peter kneaded harder. "Does that bother you?"

"I always hoped we'd have the same friends," Danny said. "That bear meet you keep talking about—you know it's the same night as Irving's Christmas party, right?"

Peter sat down across from Danny. "That tired old queen," he sighed. "The bear meet's an all-day thing, but I'll only go for a couple of hours. I'll go to Irving's from the meet."

"He may be a tired old queen," Danny huffed, "but he's a friend . . . a friend of both of us."

"You could come to the bear meet," Peter said hesitantly.

He saw Danny draw back, emotionally as well as physically. Even in his boyfriend's irritated mood, Peter saw a great deal of affection in Danny's eyes. At least he hoped he did.

"When I wanted to go back to school that was a really big change," Danny said, "but you told me you'd follow me." He shook his head. "Maybe you're going somewhere I can't follow you."

The conversation was over. Peter nodded and pushed himself away from the table. "But promise me one thing?" Danny asked.

"Sure," Peter said, rubbing his belly and wondering if there was any leftover pie in the fridge.

"Don't wear those flannel and plaid things to the bear meet. Wear something nice. That way you can be presentable when you show up at Irving's."

The trap was set. If Peter refused, he would be cementing Danny's view of their relationship and his one-sided deviation from it. "All right," he said at last. "I'll be presentable."

Peter's promise came back to haunt him the day of the bear meet. "I'm in a panic," he said to Mac on the cordless phone as he tore through the contents of his closet. "I never thought I'd say this, but I don't have a thing to wear!"

He heard a crash and some laughing in the background. Mac chuckled. "You have to get over here," Mac said. "Jason just got onto the dim sum table to do a dance, and it collapsed!"

Anything plaid was out, and most of the nonplaid items didn't fit him anymore. "I don't think you heard me," Peter said, holding up a rayon shirt that he wondered why he'd ever bought.

"Gotta go," Mac said suddenly, and the phone was filled with masculine giggles before the line cut off. "Think butch!"

As if *that* was a help. Peter settled on khakis, a starched white shirt, and plaid tie. Let Danny criticize him for that one lapse. With an overcoat, he felt more respectable than he had since starting the whole bear experiment. Even the bus ride to the bear meet was tolerable. Peter sighed with relief as he passed through the doors to the meet. If anything, they'd be understanding.

"Dear, I thought you read the copy of *The Bear Handbook*," Sasha said out of nowhere. "You simply can't show up here like you're interviewing for a job—and I'm telling you this as a friend."

"Now, Sasha," Jason rumbled, coming from the opposite side of the room, "just because Dan isn't dressed like one of us doesn't mean we have to fall on him like a ton of bricks."

Peter blushed. "Not like one of us"—the bear club president couldn't have said anything crueler. Jason was the last person Peter wanted to talk to, except of course for Sasha. Peter paid his entrance fee in change, then did an end run around Jason and Sasha and made a beeline for the bar.

"Oh, the health inspector's making a sneak visit!" the bartender said in mock horror. "What'll you have?"

Peter examined the change he had remaining. "Give me a soda water," he mumbled.

"I didn't hear you, honey," the bartender replied, grinning. "I think that tie's strangling your vocal cords."

Peter grabbed the bartender's leather suspenders and pulled him toward him until their faces were inches apart. "I *said* I wanted a soda water!" he shouted, just as the song on the PA system stopped, leaving his last words to break the sudden silence.

The room erupted in laughter. "I want a soda water, too!" Sasha said, coming up and clapping Peter on the shoulder. "Oh please, before they're all out!"

Peter snatched up his drink and headed away from Sasha. Mac was talking to someone, but even he was chuckling. "I thought you were my friend," Peter said, hurt.

"I'm sorry," Mac said, pressing his lips together. "Okay, I'm not. It's a social thing, like an initiation. We're all so used to being ostracized, as soon as someone deviates from the norm, it's open season. Sort of like a pack mentality."

Peter turned away from Mac and headed into the one dark corner that wasn't crowded with bears. Anywhere far from Jason and Sasha was a good idea, he thought.

"Do you mind if I sit down?" Peter asked the grizzled man who was the only occupant of the dusty table in the corner.

"Be my guest," the old man said, rubbing his mustache. "Sure you don't want to get out there and mingle?"

Peter took a long sip of his soda water and shuddered. "They all think they're better than me," he said bitterly.

The old man waved his hand vaguely. "Nah, they're too busy comparing themselves to the others." He looked around.

"The others?" Peter asked.

The man leaned over and said in a whisky whisper, "The A-Bears."

Peter remembered Mac using the term a while back, although he'd never received a proper explanation. "What's an A-Bear?" he asked.

"The ones who run the whole show," the man said slyly. "The ones behind the scenes. They set the standards, and the rest of those poor souls dance to their music."

It was a horribly mixed metaphor, but Peter's curiosity got the better of him. "Some kind of secret conspiracy?" he asked, amused. "Like the Freemasons?"

"Nobody knows," the old man said, taking a swig of his drink. "I think they run everything out of San Francisco—that's bear headquarters, you know. There's only a handful of them . . . most of them do bear porn or hire themselves out as escorts."

Peter tried to imagine a secret society made up of hustlers. "Are there any A-Bears here tonight?" he asked, looking around.

The man laughed a sharp, short laugh. "Nah. You'd *know* if one was here. Everyone else stops talking; they all stare at him." He smiled dreamily, exposing one broken tooth among the rest. "It's like standing in the sun. You don't look right at it or you go blind. You just get warm."

The man was a lunatic, Peter decided, but there was nowhere for him to go except leave the meet, and he wasn't about to waste $3.00 for the cover charge and another $1.50 for the watered-down soda.

"Gotta go drain the lizard," the grizzled man said after he finished the last of his drink and slammed his glass down on the table.

He fixed Peter with a steely gaze. "Trust no one." Then he corrected himself. "Well, unless they're really hot." He staggered off to the bathroom.

A conspiracy? Peter drew an "A" with his finger in the liquid on the tabletop. It was nonsense. A secret group might want to control the gold supply or dictate the top TV sitcoms. But who in their right mind would want to tell a group of hairy, big men who dressed the same what to do?

A manicured hand came down flat on the "A," wiping it out. Neat trick, Peter thought. He looked up and saw Richard leaning against the table.

"This section is typically reserved for the wallflowers and the drunks," Richard said with a smile.

"The rest of the bears don't seem very playful tonight," Peter said.

Richard shrugged. "They're like crows. Give them a shiny thing to look at and they're distracted; five minutes later, they're all digging at the soil for grubs."

"That's a pretty negative view," Peter said, sipping his soda. Pack mentality, he thought, then saw the letter he'd drawn on the tabletop in his mind. "Usually, when everyone acts the same, there's some reason behind it."

Richard smiled. "You've been talking to Bill," he said, indicating the old man, who was now trying to play a game on an unplugged pinball machine. "He's the type who sees Bolsheviks around every corner."

"He's pretty fixed on those . . . A-Bears."

The dance music segued into another piece of identical dance music, and two bears broke off from the pack to do a herky-jerky number that reminded Peter of bad Japanimation.

"An A-Bear," Richard said in an insinuating tone, "is simply a bear that everyone pines after, and nobody ever gets. Every culture or subculture has them—that class of people that is at once intensely desirable and completely unattainable. Beyond that, the A-Bear is a myth."

His expression looked almost wistful, and when Peter said nothing in reply, Richard glanced back from the dance floor. "I watched *The X-Files* with everyone else," he said lightly, raising his glass. "The truth may be out there . . . but I'd rather have another Tom Collins."

Peter saw Sasha approaching, and with visions of the Esperanto conversation from the computer convention in his mind, he nodded at Richard and backed away toward the center of the room. Richard was nice, but he mixed together with Sasha like baking soda with vinegar—an interesting science project for about twenty seconds, but ultimately a messy, fizzled paste.

Peter took one last step back and found himself enfolded in a strong pair of arms. Jason, he thought. Then he felt another pair of arms wrap themselves around him, one hand on his chest and another moving toward his groin. Before he could utter a startled "woof," a third pair of hands were moving over his brushcut and butt.

Help! Peter thought—I'm being attacked by an East Indian religious sculpture! But he couldn't speak; one hairy forearm was over his mouth, and a goatee delicately nuzzled his right ear. He got hard instantly, which only urged the hand at his groin to rub more firmly.

Peter blushed deeply and felt a stiff cock pressing against his ass. I've got to get away, he thought, and instinctively pressed himself back against the man behind him. As two hands alternatively pinched and rubbed his nipples through his shirt, Peter felt a wet pre-come spot start on the front of his khakis. His khakis!

Peter gently detached himself from the grope circle, which he now saw included Jason and Will. Waving an embarrassed thank you, Peter went into the bathroom and checked his appearance.

He sighed. Not only did he have a stain on the front of his pants, but his hair was a mess. Even his tie was rumpled and askew. There was no way he could go to Irving's party like this. Not without a major fight with Danny.

"Leaving so soon?" Jason growled when Peter made his way to the exit.

"I've got to go home and change," Peter said.

"Looked like you were having a lot of fun back there," Jason said, "even with the way you were dressed. Can I get a rain check?"

Jason's bulk towered over him. It was all a bit too much to handle at once. "I have to go," Peter said again. "Have a woofy Christmas."

"Woof!" Jason said and gripped Peter in a tight hug. Peter felt two shirt buttons pop.

On the bus ride back home, Peter was acutely aware of other passengers looking at him. He felt like an earthquake victim—or, more accurately, a victim of a bear mauling. And he was still half hard.

After catching a glimpse of the clock, he strode through the apartment with a renewed sense of purpose. He probably had another clean shirt in his closet, and even if the tie had to go, there was always the top button-buttoned look.

Peter flicked the light on in the bedroom. Danny's nearly vertical legs cast odd shadows on the far wall. Irving was poised over him in an acrobatic position, thrusting and grunting.

"You like that big dick, don'tcha?" Irving muttered as the light hit them.

Utter silence. Peter shook his head and started taking a pair of jeans, flannel shirt, and underwear and socks out of the closet and dresser.

"Aren't you going to say something?" Danny asked Peter from beneath Irving. "Anything?"

Peter held up the plaid flannel shirt. "And *you* said *I* had bad taste," he said, then walked out of the bedroom and into the living room. He pulled on his jeans awkwardly and abruptly, and struggled with his shirt until he realized that he was, after all, furious. He cast the burning logs a last glance, then clicked the TV remote. The fireplace videotape they'd got from Wal-Mart faded to black.

He didn't remember anything more until he was standing in the street. Where could he go? Not back to the bear meet. Not to Mac's— Mac was probably getting laid or groped. Peter decided to take a cab to the café.

When he fished in his wallet for a $20 bill, he came up empty-handed. Not a bill in his wallet, and all of his credit cards were maxed out. He still had his bus pass, though. Peter knew what he had to do.

The burly security guard looked at him oddly when he knocked on the door at the back of the office building. Peter had never seen it from this side before. "You here about the janitorial job?" the guard asked.

Peter nodded. "I saw the ad in the newspaper," he said, taking the crumpled scrap of paper out of his pocket.

"Come on in and fill out an application," the guard said.

Peter followed the guard into a crowded mail room. His eyes strayed to a mail slot with a familiar label. "*Phag Magazine,* Sixth Floor."

"Here you go," the guard said, passing him a set of papers. "You can sit down over there." Then the guard narrowed his eyes. "Wait a second. Do I know you?"

"No," Peter said after a long moment. "No, I don't think you do."

PART II

A kiss without a beard is like an egg without salt.
                                            Dutch Proverb

– 9 –

When I could no longer study bears from the outside, I became a bear. But that was not enough. Bears may share the same physical characteristics, but something clearly differentiates them from lumberjacks and other roughnecks. There's a parallel to the gay community in terms of levels of commitment. When a bear decides to join the bear community, he can simply attend the occasional beer bust, he can become a regular member, or he can immerse himself in the "bear lifestyle."

In some ways, gay men have it easier in terms of living the "gay lifestyle"; they can work at gay companies, eat at gay restaurants, shop at gay stores, and consume gay-only media. Bears, on the other hand, are a small minority of the gay community, and face one of two choices: create their own venues, or co-opt traditional bastions of heterosexual masculinity (think The Home Depot) for their own purposes.

When circumstances forced me to leave the trappings of the "gay lifestyle," I decided to follow my friend M into the bear lifestyle. He was willing to put me, or rather my pseudonym "D," up for a few months, and continue in his role of mentor.

To that end, I am journaling "a day in the life of a bear"—a day in my new life.

10:00 a.m.

Peter rolled over, fell off the couch, and landed on the carpet with a muffled groan. Going from a queen-sized bed to a sofa that didn't fold out was playing havoc on his back.

"I heard that!" Mac grumbled from the bedroom. "Keep it down—I have the hangover from hell."

Peter got up and shook his head to clear the muzziness. He stumbled over a teddy bear, and then another that he'd knocked off of the coffee table. He picked them up and put them on top of the coffee table book *A History of Body Hair.*

"How many wine coolers did you have last night?" he asked as softly as he could.

Mac poked a tousled head out of the bedroom. "Beers! Not wine coolers!"

Peter ran a hand over his buzz cut. "I saw the bartender pouring wine coolers into beer bottles for you. Don't even bother lying."

"Oh God," Mac said, rubbing his eyes. "Those things are a yuppie plot. And how many beers were *you* drinking?" He looked at Peter suspiciously. "Or were those beers?"

Peter waved a hand in truce. "Never," he mumbled, "never drink margaritas from a beer bottle. It's like watching a Latino porn movie set in Beverly Hills."

He walked into the kitchen and shielded his eyes from the blinding glare inside the fridge. Then, getting an idea, Peter pressed down on the internal switch with his finger and the fridge light went off.

"What do you have for breakfast usually?" he asked Mac, who had on a teddy bear-patterned houserobe over a jockstrap.

"Fruit Loops, Count Chocula, or Fruity Pebbles," Mac said, opening a cupboard. "And there's chocolate milk to wash it down with."

"Gah," Peter replied, peering into the fridge. "Anything with a bit less sugar?"

A few minutes later they were settled at the kitchen table, Mac eating Count Chocula ("he's a vampire, but only for chocolate") while Peter squeezed a tube of chocolate chip cookie dough into his cottony mouth. "Uh, don't you have work today?" Peter asked.

"I'm photographing bottles," Mac said. "It's not like they're on a schedule. I'll do it tonight, while you're at work."

Peter grimaced. "Don't remind me."

"Does it really bother you that much?" Mac asked. "Doing manual labor?" He shook his head. "Didn't you ever have jobs in high school like that?"

"I worked in offices every summer," Peter said. "No, being a janitor doesn't bother me. What bothers me is having to go back and clean the offices where I used to work. I feel so . . . degraded."

Mac licked the bowl and looked over the edge of it at Peter. "You think blue-collar work is beneath you, don't you?"

Peter reached over and wiped off the milk mustache from Mac's mustache. "It's just not what I want to do," he said at last.

"You think," Mac said, getting to his feet and collecting the dishes, "that because it's not intellectual, like writing or computer work, that it's of less value."

Peter sat back in his chair. "You're a pretty good debater for a hungover drunk." He considered Mac's comment. "I was brought up in a left-wing household—every job has value, and every job needs doing."

Mac ran water over the dishes and left them in the sink. "As long as you're not the one doing it." He grinned. "Let's hope a few months of hard labor gives you a bit of a real social conscience."

Peter smiled uneasily. A few months? He couldn't even imagine a few weeks, judging from his first days on the job so far.

"I'll make it my New Year's resolution."

They looked at each other. "New Year's!" they both said at the same time. "That's what we were doing last night, wasn't it?" Peter asked.

Mac glanced at the calendar above the telephone. "No, that was two nights ago. Then there was the New Bear's Day Party and the New Bear's Resolution Party. I think that's it."

"You're blinking," Peter commented.

Mac rubbed his eyes. "Nervous twitch, I think."

Peter shook his head and pointed to the answering machine. "You have messages."

Mac pressed a button. "Hi, it's Jason," the answering machine said. "See you at dim sum for lunch? Will and I and Steve and Jack are getting together. If you're not on time, we'll eat your stuff. Later!"

"Hi, Will here," the next message said. "Drop by Bear Essentials this afternoon if you get a chance. I need to get your opinion on our latest flyer. See you there."

"Hi, it's Steve," the next message said. "Jack and I broke up, so we won't be going to the dim sum, but if you want you can catch me at the café tonight—it's bear night, if you didn't know."

"Hi, it's Jack," the next message said. "I have *got* to talk to you about Steve. He thinks we're broken up, but I'm not going to break up with him until we have our three-week anniversary. Call me."

The last message was from Jason. "Okay, Steve and Jack are back together—problem solved. They had a three-way with Will, and that did the trick. Dim sum is at three instead of noon."

Peter just stared at Mac. "You should hear it on a busy day," Mac said. "Sometimes a guy can go through two boyfriends before I get a chance to return all the messages."

Then Mac's expression turned serious. "Have you heard anything from Danny?"

Peter avoided Mac's gaze. "He called the other day. We had a bit of a . . . chat."

Mac grabbed Peter by the wrists. "Tell me you didn't give him any money. Tell me!"

Peter sighed. "Look, it's so hard. I feel like we went through a divorce, like I owe him some kind of support."

"After he supported you by throwing up his legs for the first guy who came in through the door?" Mac bit his tongue. "Sorry, that was pretty cheesy. But you shouldn't feel guilty for something he was responsible for. How much did you give him?"

Peter said nothing. "Five hundred dollars?" Mac asked. "A thousand?"

Peter stuffed more cookie dough into his mouth and mumbled, "The tuition for next September." When Mac looked like he was about to explode, Peter added, "but it's in installments—I gave him a series of postdated checks. It's almost nothing."

Mac just sighed. "A bear with a heart of gold—like I've never heard that one before. At least Danny's already out of your life. Who knows how much more money he could drain out of you if you guys were still living together." He smiled and clapped his hands. "Come on—we have a busy day ahead."

> The bear community tends to have a few spots where everyone congregates. In this city, it's Bear Essentials, the local bearaphernalia store for shopping, the Eagle for drinking, and the café for nondrinkers and alcoholics. The small nature of the community means not only that you know everyone's business, but you're forced to know everyone's business. You can and will run into the same five bears over and over again. This leads me to one theory as to the supposed friendliness and camaraderie of the bears. They all see each other so often that they can't afford to be at each other's throats.

12:00 p.m.

Peter tried to keep track of all the bears that Mac was saying hi to on the way to Bear Essentials, but he lost count after Wolf, Bruce, Mark, Weaver, Stone, and Trent.

"Does every bear have a butch name?" he asked at one point while they were waiting to cross the street.

Mac rubbed some frost from his goatee. "Don't worry, *Dan*. Some guys take their own bear names, others shorten theirs or use their middle names. Stone is a good example. You want to know what his real name is?" He giggled. "Nathaniel!"

Bear Essentials had a narrow storefront on a side street in the heart of the gay ghetto. Peter had been past the street a dozen times, but he'd never seen the store, or thought to check it out. Only an odd earth-toned version of the pride flag gave any hint as to the store's contents, aside from the name.

"What's that flag all about?" Peter asked.

"Bear flag," Mac said. "See the paw print?"

Inside, the store was warm and packed with bearaphernalia. Peter had expected a porn shop or a curio shop, but Will, the owner, obviously had a fondness for retro kitsch. At the front of the store stood a life-sized cardboard cutout of Dan Haggerty, with an erect penis extending out of his jeans made from a broom handle; various sets of handcuffs dangled from the broom handle, and a dialogue balloon from the cutout's mouth said "GRAB A BARGAIN!"

"I have to go talk to Will," Mac explained. "Steve and Jack are his best friends."

Peter nodded understandingly. "You want to make sure he's all right after all that breakup/reunion thing?"

Mac shook his head. "No, I want details about the three-way! Man, you sure are slow sometimes. Look around the store. Don't touch anything."

While Mac went off to find the owner, Peter walked past bear flags, patches, and stopped in the leather department. The harnesses went from size XXL and up, and the largest set looked as if it could hold a Clydesdale.

"My God," Peter murmured when he spotted a dildo with the requisite paw print logo as large as his forearm. Danny would have enjoyed this place, he thought with a pang.

He walked over to the next department, which had an assortment of kinky teddy bears and one leather dildo that looked entirely ordinary. "I don't see what's so bear about this," Peter said to himself, and picked the eight-incher up. "Woof!" the dildo intoned. "Woof! Woof! Woof!"

"They're not toys," a voice behind him growled. Peter put down the dildo and it stopped woofing. He turned to face a red-haired man who was even taller than Jason, and even wider, with a heavy full beard and the hint of a scowl beneath.

"Actually," Peter pointed out, "they are."

The man put the dildo back exactly where he'd found it. "Not until you buy it and take it home."

More bear attitude, Peter thought, sighing. There had to be some connection between testosterone and bitchiness.

"Do you work here?"

"No," the man said. "I'm a jobber."

"Of course you are," Peter nodded, then tried to get past the man. The red-haired man was wide enough to block the aisle, and even when the man tried to let him pass, there wasn't enough room.

"Go back the way you came," the man said. "I have work to do."

Peter mentally stuck his tongue out at him, and as he backed away, he deliberately knocked over the dildo onto the floor. "Woof! Woof! Woof!"

He saw Mac and Will talking together. Will seemed to be using his hands to demonstrate various sexual positions, and Peter was in no mood for juicy gossip. He walked around the bear T-shirt collection, the bear books *(Bears Who Love Cubs and the Cubs Who Love Twinks)*, and ended up in the porn video section.

It was a good thing that most of these videos were filmed recently, Peter thought, perusing the titles. Otherwise, it'd be hard to tell where the performers left off and the shag carpet began. Most of the recent titles seemed to be movie parodies. He rifled through *The Bear Up There*, *Con Bear*, and *Bear: The Musical*, and was just about to take a video off of the rack when Will came up.

"See anything you like?" he asked Peter.

"This one looks interesting," Peter said, pointing out a video cover that showed several hairy, sweaty men in a daisy chain. "The one called *Bear Tea Party*."

Will pulled off a price tag. "It's *Bear Tearoom Party*," he said, offended. "The director, Canis Major, is a genius."

"Is that his real name?"

Will smiled and pulled a pen-sized recorder out of his pocket. "Note to self," he dictated. "Remove price tags from video covers where they block titles." He put the pencorder away. "You cubs were put here on earth to try me, that's what I say." He shook his head. "Now where are my manners?"

He engulfed Peter in a hug. Peter returned it as best he could, then stepped back and caught his breath. "Nice selection of things you have here," Peter said.

"They come from all over the world," Will said proudly. "Did you see the carved bear totems from Madagascar?"

Peter shook his head. "No, but I saw the plastic bear tikis."

"They're on the same shelf." Will made way for Mac, who joined them in the aisle. "Did you have a look at the flyer?"

Mac showed Peter the sheet of paper. "I'm impressed," Mac said. "The detail reproduction on Carl Hardwick's chest hairs is pretty good for a photocopy."

"Scott at the copy place helped me out—he owed me a favor," Will said, smiling slightly. "What do you think, Dan?"

Peter kept looking at the paper until Mac stepped discreetly on his foot. "Oh," he said. "Looks good. Do you have a pen?"

"Why?" Will asked, handing one over.

"Well, it should be *your* with no apostrophe or *e*, and *ass* only has two esses, not three," Peter commented, reading over the text with an experienced eye. "And Free Gift is redundant. You can just say Free Offer. But I'm nitpicking," he added hastily, when he caught sight of Mac's expression. "Looks good."

"That's so kind of you," Will said. "I'll get Jason to make the changes on his computer, and I can run them off while we're at dim sum."

He patted Peter on the head. "Such a sweet cub," Will said to Mac as he left them. "Why on earth is he single?"

"Note to self," Peter said. "Avoid sticking foot in mouth."

"Nah," Mac said. "He likes you. Probably wants to have sex with you, too. Just remember that a lot of bears have a history of being criticized, so they're not always going to like it."

Peter held the pen up. "I miss writing for publication," he admitted. "Even if it's correcting someone else's work."

Mac put a comforting hand on his shoulder. "And you miss Danny too, don't you?" He sighed. "My friend, you've gone through so many changes in the last few months, I don't know how you do it."

"Danny and I are still friends," Peter said. "We don't live together, that's all."

Mac nodded, looking unconvinced. "Let me show you my favorite part of *Bear Tearoom Party* before we go. They're working on a sequel, you know."

Peter looked around. "Show me? Do they have a screening room or something?"

Mac dragged Peter to the back of the store and through a beaded curtain into the dark. "Sometimes you can be *so* naive."

> The web of relationships that characterizes the bear community also contributes to the nearly uniform way that bears look. It's a far subtler form of the peer pressure that exists within the mainstream gay community. While I, during research for this book, experienced some small measure of criticism when I acted outside of bear norms, I found that the carrot, not the stick, is far more often used to ensure compliance.
>
> Imagine this scenario: You have no media role models (aside from pornography) to emulate. Your friends, on the other hand, all dress and act the same. Through a form of osmosis, you take on the external characteristics of a bear, and eventually the internal ones as well.
>
> The interesting aspect comes with the migratory patterns of the bears. It's not uncommon for bears to move across the country, for a boyfriend, a job, or simply a new adventure. There is a whole segment of bears, particularly high-tech ones, that wander the country seemingly endlessly, sure that whatever they're searching for can be found over the next horizon. And each place they settle down in, the bear meme continues to propagate.
>
> It's a lot subtler than the sledgehammer conformist approach the mainstream community takes, but just as powerful.

3:00 p.m.

The informal dim sum was held at Fuk Hing Restaurant. "You're sure this isn't some kind of gag?" Peter whispered to Mac as they passed through the ersatz golden gates into the restaurant.

"Mr. Hing swears it's his first name," Mac replied, "but I think he caught on a long time ago. Either way, it can't hurt business." He pointed into the crowd. "Ooh, there's Will and Jason."

The large airy room was full of two readily identifiable groups of people: Asians and bears. Mac waved at several bear couples as they passed, and neatly dodged the waiters pushing carts with assorted steaming delicacies.

"You didn't tell me this was a bear hangout," Peter said as they approached Will and Jason's table.

"There's something about bears and dim sum," Mac mused. "You'd think it'd be sushi, with the bear-fish connection, but sushi's not filling enough. Dim sum means comfort food."

Peter took in the array of empty plates around Will and Jason. Dim sum was also clearly a way to avoid tracking how many calories you were consuming, he thought. Leaning forward to let a waiter pass behind him, he felt his belly press against the edge of the table. If he didn't watch out, he'd outgrow his new wardrobe.

Mac hugged Jason, then Will hugged Jason, and Jason and Will hugged each other for good measure. Then they fell upon Peter, squeezing him front and back in the middle of the restaurant, apparently indifferent to the glances of the nonbear customers.

"That's some good huggin'!" Jason rumbled, sitting back down and signaling a waiter over.

Will grinned at Peter. "Gets your insides all ready for some quality dim sum. It's the best in town."

The waiter uncovered a bamboo steamer full of dumplings. "What's that?" Peter asked. The waiter replied in Chinese.

"Sticky buns," Jason explained. Then he reeled off a series of orders in fluent Chinese, to which the waiter bowed politely and retreated. "Mac says it's your first time here. Don't worry, we'll make sure you get a good meal."

As other waiters approached, Peter had a frantic fantasy of the musical number "Be Our Guest" from *Beauty and the Beast,* complete with fried rice, chopsticks, and uncontrollable gorging. "Oh, I'll stick with a tea and some steamed rice, if that's okay."

Jason glanced at Will. "We've got to put some meat on his bones."

Will nodded. "Dan won't last through hibernation without a good food store."

Peter hurriedly changed the subject. "So, you guys hang around other bears a lot," he said, unfolding the napkin and placing it in his lap.

"Well, sure," Jason said in his deep voice. "It's our community."

The tip of a booted foot started to delicately explore the inside of Peter's right calf. "Don't you ever take a break?" Peter asked, squirming a bit from the sensation. "From the whole bear scene?"

All three of them looked at Peter blankly. "You know," Peter went on lamely, "do nonbear things? With nonbears?"

Will took out his pencorder. "Note to self," he said. "This boy needs to get out more." Then, facing Peter, he added, "Sure, I own a bear store, but I'm also part of the gay choir."

The mystery foot started to edge its way up Peter's thigh. "And I work at a computer magazine," Jason said. As if he didn't know. "And Mac plays volleyball in the summer. *Nonbear* volleyball. Seems like you have a weird idea of what being a part of the bear community is all about."

The foot rested for one lingering moment on Peter's crotch, then retreated. "I guess I'm new to all of this," he admitted. "Sometimes there's just so much . . . bear there."

Jason speared three sticky buns with the same chopstick and lifted them to his mouth. "Two things you have to understand about the bear community, Dan," he said, munching contentedly. "First, it's about living life—all aspects of it—to its fullest. And second," he said with a mischievous look in his eye, "once you're in the bear community, there's no way out." He pushed the plate forward. "Want a sticky bun? There's room for one more."

> The archetypal bear is an outdoorsman, or a manual laborer: the forester, lumberjack, or construction worker type. While most bears dress the part, I was surprised to find the majority of them work in the high-tech industry or at retail jobs. Like the yuppie who drives an SUV and dreams of off-road adventure, the bear "look" is usually more for play than any practical purpose. Class divisions still exist within the bear community, and it's odd to see a couple where the higher-wage earner is dressed more blue collar than the actual blue-collar worker.
>
> Maybe it's the Village People syndrome: we all wanted to have sex with a fireman, construction worker, or cop . . . but we didn't want to be one.

5:00 p.m.

"He's mine," Danny said on the other end of the phone. "You can't have him; you simply can't!"

Peter sighed and leaned against the cement wall. "I thought we talked about this. You don't even have a place to live yet, and Mac's apartment building has no restrictions."

"You're only going to harm him," Danny said. "The last thing he needs is to be put into a disruptive environment. After all, he's already endured our breakup. Do you think it's fair to put him in some situation where you might not even be able to feed him?"

"We're talking about a *cat,* Danny." Peter cursed the day that his boyfriend had convinced him to let him subscribe to Lifetime. "And the papers are in my name. MacGuyver's mine."

"He needs a stable home. If I had the money I'd hire a lawyer. . . . You did write those postdated checks for me, didn't you?"

The security guard tapped on Peter's shoulder. "Hey, we don't pay you to make phone calls. Back to work."

"I'll come over after my shift," Peter promised. "Make sure Irving's not there." He hung up before Danny could reply.

The security guard glared at him. "I'm sweeping, I'm sweeping," Peter said, pushing the heavy flat broom ahead of him. "You ever get tired of making me work?"

The guard waited until he had moved into the corridor beyond, then flicked the security monitor over to *Jerry Springer.* "Keep sweeping."

Peter trudged through the darkened offices, sweeping lackadaisically and stopping to lean on the broom when he thought he could get away with it. It was amazing what people in an office dropped on the floor: sandwich wrappers, money, and sometimes even used chewing gum.

As Peter made his way through the empty building, he went slower and slower until he reached his final destination: the offices of *Phag Magazine.* In the dark, with no snooty receptionist, the reception area looked abandoned. Peter indulged his fantasy that *Phag Magazine* had shut down, gone bankrupt; he was the last employee to turn out the lights.

But the wastepaper baskets were full of papers, and the floor had scuff marks that had to be wiped off with a scrub brush. Peter wandered down the curved hallway, looking at the framed magazine covers on the wall.

"I wrote that article," he said, pointing to an old headline. Nobody answered.

Chester's office was locked, of course; he clearly didn't trust the cleaning staff, and Peter couldn't blame him. Peter moved to his old desk, which was still vacant, and sat down. Even the Macintosh computer was in the same position . . .

An idea occurred to him. Oh, it couldn't work, could it? Not after all this time. Peter drummed his fingers on the desk and looked around. It couldn't hurt to try. Nobody was looking. Nobody would know.

Peter booted up the computer and waited for the familiar chime. When he saw the log on screen, he entered his username (PeterM) and password (Gloria). "Access Denied," the screen blinked. "Your Password Has Expired."

Peter shut down the computer and was about to leave when he looked over at Bette's desk. Bette had always had a habit of using the most obvious passwords. . . . He started her computer up, typed in "BetteC," and hesitated before entering a password.

"Password?" he mused. "Butch? Femme? DieselDyke? He glanced at the books on the hutch over her computer and got an idea. "FridaKahlo," he typed in and waited.

"Welcome, BetteC, to PhagNet," the screen displayed. Now what? Peter felt uncomfortable about his intrusion. His finger strayed to the off switch when he noticed a second line of type.

"You Have 3 New E-Mails."

This was too good to pass up. Peter opened up the e-mail program, and read through the messages. The first two were innocuous company memos about coffee breaks and pro bono work. The last one was from Chester. "Bette," it read, "*Boston Cream Pie Magazine* e-mailed me to let me know their advertising deadline's been moved up a day. Make sure you get the marketing manager to submit the copy by tomorrow at 6 p.m."

Boring! Peter thought and clicked on the button he thought would close the e-mail program. "Message Deleted," the screen said. Peter, panicked, started clicking at random. All he managed to do was delete the message from the Trash, then shut down the e-mail program completely.

Peter, panicked, looked around. Surely they'd know it was him. Surely they'd come for him.

"Hey there!" a voice shouted from the darkness. Peter shut off the computer, sprang out of his chair, and grabbed the broom defensively.

It was the security guard. "You get real slow when you reach these offices, you know that?" the man said.

"Must be the altitude," Peter muttered and returned to his sweeping, trying to ignore his heart, which was beating furiously.

> One last point about clothes and the bear. For most of this century, gay men have dressed in a way that subtly set them apart from their straight counterparts. The mustached-clone look of the 1970s gave way to the club kids of the 1980s and the ACT UP clone of the 1990s. Surely these uniforms were a way not only of forging an identity, but of flagging the wearer's gayness to other gay men. Eventually, though, the heterosexual world came to understand the clues and cues that identified a gay man . . . perhaps providing the impetus for the changes in fashion. The bear fashion code, however, stands in clear defiance to this model. Bears can go unnoticed, in the gay community and elsewhere. This has some definite advantages.

The next night, Peter entered the offices of *Phag* in dread, sure that he'd been found out. Was that Chester waiting behind the photocopy machine or Bette behind the fern (she'd been on a liquid diet recently)?

Silence. Nobody had found out. Peter relaxed and quickly went over to Bette's computer. This time, the violation didn't bother him at all. If she was using such an obvious password, didn't she deserve to have her e-mail read?

One new message. "Bette," it read curtly. "Since you missed my previous e-mail, we had to spend an extra $3,000 on the ad space to get them to extend the deadline. The expenses for your forthcoming trip to Venezuela to cover the gay rights trial fortuitously come to the same amount. Your trip has been canceled. Don't make the same mistake again. Ciao, Chester."

Peter raised an eyebrow and smiled faintly. This, he thought, could have some very interesting possibilities . . .

– 10 –

"You did what?" Mac asked, aghast.

"It was a mistake," Peter said, clutching the popcorn bowl to his belly defensively. He'd thought that Mac would be proud of his computer exploits, but dropping it into conversation hadn't had the desired effect. "I didn't mean to, but it worked out perfectly."

Mac hit the "Pause" button on the VCR. "Do you know they can track who logged into anyone's system on the network? And you logged in as yourself? With your old password?"

"Does this mean we don't get to watch the end of *Now, Voyager?*" Peter asked plaintively.

Mac shut off the TV and took the popcorn bowl away from Peter. "You don't deserve this. I don't know what you were thinking." Mac looked as if he'd just discovered a moth in his flannel closet. "Didn't you learn about computers in school?"

Peter glanced at the black TV screen regretfully. "Well, math wasn't my strong point. And there were all those punch cards . . ."

"You're thinking of *The Computer Wore Tennis Shoes,*" Mac said in exasperation. "When we went to school we had desktop computers." He put down the bowl and got to his feet. "Don't you realize we gay men drive technology?"

"I had a digital watch," Peter offered.

"In the late seventies, we all bought VCRs so we could watch gay porn without having to leave our apartments," Mac said, pointing at the VCR. "In the eighties, we all used phone sex lines so we could get off from home, and look where voice mail is now. And in the nineties, we all got online so we could hook up with other guys in the comfort of our living rooms."

"So the gay community's a bunch of Albert Schweitzers with agoraphobia?"

Mac ignored him, walking back and forth in the small area in front of the TV set. "There's a real pattern developing here," he said, ticking imaginary points off on his fingers. "You love to rush into things you don't understand, without preparation or research. Then, when you screw up, you have to get bailed out."

"In all fairness," Peter protested, "you were the one who got me into this bear thing."

Mac stopped pacing. "And it's finally catching up with you. You used to be able to get away with it because of your looks, but not now."

"Jason thinks I'm cuddly," Peter said, running a hand through his buzz cut self-consciously.

"Jason thinks everyone's cuddly," Mac said, then relented. "Okay, maybe you're cuddly in some quasi-bear way."

"I *am* a bear," Peter said.

Mac raised his bushy eyebrows. "Now there's something I didn't expect you to say. Let's get your bear buddies together to help you learn something about computers before you end up in jail. Those porn videos really glamorize it, believe me." He didn't elaborate.

Peter was prepared to object, but in the end he gave in. If nothing else, it was another venue of bear expression to explore and document. And he'd heard all about "chat rooms" and online pornography.

Frank, the Bear Essentials supplier that Peter had met at the bear meet, came over and installed a box between Peter's laptop and the telephone line. "Can I get pay-TV on this thing too?" Peter asked.

Frank looked at him as if he wasn't sure if Peter was serious. "It's a modem," he explained. "It sends information through the phone lines."

Peter tried to look interested. "Pornographic information?"

Frank blushed. "Well, sure. But first you have to get online. You know how to do that?"

"At work everything was point-and-click," Peter explained, wondering what was on TV. "Well, we also had a cute guy that came around to help me print things out when I finished typing them up on the screen."

"I could help you . . . get started. If you want," Frank said with a slight stutter. "But the porn—that's up to you."

"Sure, go to town." Peter pretended to watch Frank as the man's hands flew nimbly across the keyboard. Frank explained each step of what he was doing, using words that Peter remembered from the computer convention, and that still didn't make any sense.

"Fascinating," Peter murmured. "Compelling. Not to mention intriguing."

"Now all you have to do is click on this, then enter your username and password when it says so," Frank said at last. "Did you pick a username yet?"

"Uh, how about BearGuy?" Peter said. Frank typed it in and shook his head. "It's taken," Frank said.

"HairyDude?" Frank shook his head again. "HungBear? HirSuit? FurTher? ToSirWithBear?"

Peter nudged Frank out of the way. "They can't all be taken. Okay, how's this?" Frank blushed again. Peter entered his password and clicked OK. KarnAl was online.

"Ooh, I've got mail!" Peter exclaimed. "Is it porno?"

"Probably," Frank said resignedly. "Now do you want me to show you how to use the Web browser, and the chat, and your e-mail program?"

Peter thought that Frank was sitting uncomfortably close to him, but the desk was tiny as it is. "That's all right," he said equably. "After all, you got me this modem at cost." He paused. "By the way, do you know anything about hacking?"

"Oh . . . I have friends who do that," Frank said, shaking his head violently. "But not me. I try to keep my nose clean." He sniffed hard. "You sure you'll be all right?"

"I'll pick up the phone and give you a call if I run into any problems," Peter said. He picked up the phone to demonstrate, and dropped it when he heard a shrill squeal from the receiver. "Good Lord, it's Fran Drescher!" Peter said, then turned back to the computer. "And look, somehow I got disconnected."

Frank gave him an awkward hug at the door. "Let me know if you have problems," he added, pushing a lock of unfashionably long hair out of his eyes and smiling shyly.

"No problem," Peter said, easing the door shut, then dashing back to the computer. One hour, two at the most, and he'd be doing bear research on the Web. "Ooh, I have mail again!"

When Peter looked up again, the apartment was dark and Mac was walking in the front door. "Looks like Frank set you up," Mac said. "Are you computer literate yet?"

Peter looked up from the screen, bleary eyed. "Well, I found out that I can make a lot of money if I send this e-mail around, and then I got a whole bunch of e-mails from people who didn't like that e-mail, so I sent *them* e-mails, and then I think the system got overloaded or something."

"Good gods," Mac said, rushing over. "Did you major in running with scissors at college?" He clicked a few keys and sighed. "They canceled your account."

"Oh," Peter said, crestfallen. "I didn't even get a chance to download any pornography."

"No problem," Mac said. "We can create another one for you."

And KarnAl2 was born, and Peter saw that it was good.

Soon it seemed as if Mac was avoiding him, because every time Peter started the computer, his roommate had an errand to run or a videotape to return. Peter hated being ignorant, but he didn't have anyone else to ask questions of.

"Should I give out my password to tech support?" he called to Mac while Mac was preparing dinner the next night.

"No!" Mac said, rushing into the living room, trailing salad. "You didn't, did you?"

"Uhh . . ." And KarnAl3 came into the world.

"Let's hope KarnAl3 has more of a self-preservation instinct," Mac said dryly during one of the few times he agreed to sit and watch Peter use the Internet. "Are you on the BLS yet?"

"No, but I think I just ordered nineteen copies of *The Kama Sutra of Gay Sex* from Amazon.com," Peter frowned. "I shouldn't keep clicking that Buy button if nothing happens, should I?"

Mac growled. "If you want to find out more about bears, you need to sign up. It's called the Bear ListServ—it's a global mailing list for bears to discuss subjects that interest them."

Peter finished clicking "Cancel Order" nineteen times. "What kind of subjects interest them?"

"Knowing you, you'll probably hit all of them with your first e-mail," Mac said, and showed him how to sign up.

Every day or so, Peter received a new digest e-mail from the BLS, but it seemed full of people like Sasha and Richard talking, talking endlessly. Peter's postmodern journalism course had been more interesting, and less self-referential.

"It's important to remember," he read in one post, "that in the discussion of 'What is a bear?' KindBear shouldn't forget the sociocultural bias of his assumptions. Not only is KindBear a cultural imperialist, but he also has no idea what a real bear is."

"I'm a happy monogamist," he read in another post, "and all you polygamists are just sad. Can't you learn to love one bear, a single bear, and leave the others alone? P.S. I'm always interested in meeting new people—your pic gets mine."

"This post is a bit off topic," Peter read in one of the last BLS digests he ever bothered opening, "but did anyone see that woofy mass murderer they showed on CNN last night? I would LOVE to hiBearnate with him. And if you're on the list, Ray Vance, e-mail or instant message me!"

When Mac came home the next evening, Peter was shaking his head in sorrow. "I just asked a simple question," he told Mac. "One simple question . . ."

"You didn't," Mac said, squeezing some Squeez-a-Snak from the tube onto a celery stalk. "You didn't!"

"Subject: What is a bear? I know you guys have probably discussed this before, but what is a bear, really? I'm doing some research. And is it true that bears think polygamy is better than monogamy?"

"Oh dear," Peter said, looking at the "incoming e-mail" indicator. "I think KarnAl3 just died an honorable death."

KarnAl4 was more of a slut. "If I could," Mac said in exasperation the next night, "I'd put on the parental blocking feature, but I believe in freedom of expression." He eyed Peter warily. "Now do you remember the ground rules?"

Peter looked skyward, then recited from memory: "Online cocks are one and three-quarters times as long as real cocks. If someone thinks I'm woofy, he lives three-thousand miles away, but if he thinks I'm woofy and he lives in the same city, he's married and monogamous."

"And?" Mac asked impatiently.

"CBT does *not* stand for computer-based training."

"I'm so proud of you."

Although Peter was usually online during the day and very late at night, he was surprised to discover the gay and bear chat rooms were full at all hours. While the general conversation was typically nonsexual, he found himself the subject of various private messages and entreaties. "Age/sex/stats?" one message asked. "Slave 2 serve u," another whined.

Peter soon discovered the "Ignore" button, and once he'd applied it to everyone who'd messaged him with illiterate sexual solicitations, the chat rooms were eerily silent. From out of nowhere, a message window popped up. "Hi. Looking for some intelligent conversation?"

TheThinker was the man's username, and his profile looked promising. Bear, college graduate, writer, and in the same city as Peter. "Sure, though I'm just getting used to this whole thing," Peter typed slowly.

"I see you're a writer, too," the response came lightning fast. "Surely you can type faster than that! And I know the 'surely' joke, so don't try it :-)"

Peter was enjoying this. "Nice to talk to someone who doesn't have sex on his mind," he typed.

"Look, you want to get together for coffee? I could use some face to face."

"Sure," Peter typed, and gave his address. Now all he had to do was decide on whether to wear the blue or the green flannel . . .

He was checking his appearance in the mirror when Mac came home. "You have a date?" Mac asked, curious.

"I met a guy from the chat room," Peter said, straightening his baseball cap, then tilting it again. "He's a writer, and he lives in town."

Mac clapped a hand to his forehead. "Not TheThinker!" He looked around frantically. "Did you give him our address?"

When Peter didn't reply, Mac growled, a sound that was becoming increasingly familiar, Peter thought. "Get me a screwdriver, stat!" Mac bellowed, checking his watch.

Peter dug a screwdriver out of the gadget drawer and handed it to Mac. "Cover me," Mac said, handing him the pepper spray he always had on hand. "If you see a psychotic bear with a mohawk, spray first and ask questions later."

Peter's heart was racing. "What are you doing?" he asked.

Mac unscrewed the last digit off of the door numerals and held it up. "This goes on our neighbor's door, and *his* number goes on our door."

Peter helped Mac screw the neighbor's door number onto their apartment door. "And what happens when TheThinker shows up at his door?" he asked breathlessly.

They retreated into their apartment. "Remember what I told you about prison?" Mac asked. "My neighbor's the one who told me about it. They called him Whipsaw on the inside."

Once the police had left, Mac pointed a threatening finger at Peter. "No more Internet. Gods, I should say no more computers. You're like a bear in an activewear shop."

"I have one more alias left, right? What can possibly happen?"

Mac held up a loose door number. "Do I have to answer that? This time you'll probably get some kind of computer virus."

Computer virus, Peter thought. When Mac had gone to work, Peter guessed the password he'd put on the Internet connection program (as if "Hardwick" was so hard to figure out) and logged in. In the BearsDen chat room that he frequented, Peter considered asking for a virus, but discarded the idea. He needed someone who could create one for him.

Peter typed the word "hackers" into the chat room search. There were over 130 results. He chose the one with the least misspellings.

"Looks like we've got a common interest, dude," a message window popped up. Peter checked the nickname—3l33tB34R, whatever that meant, was on HackerParadise and BearsDen. A fellow bear? Peter wondered. "Woof," Peter typed. "Woof Woof Woof Woof!" Cut and paste was useful too.

"Yeah, that's all well and good for the pic traders," 3l33tB34R wrote. "You looking for some help?"

Remembering TheThinker, Peter hesitated. "Just checking things out," he typed.

"I think I know what you need," the reply came back. "Meet me at the gazebo in Stewart Park, 10:00 p.m. I'll be waiting . . . Dan."

Peter sat back, startled. At Mac's suggestion, he'd never used his "real" name at any point online. Maybe somebody could figure out he was Dan Karn if they lived in the same city, but still.

"How do you know my name?" he typed.

"I love a mystery," 3l33tB34R typed, then logged off.

Peter told Mac he was going to work, then stopped at a pay phone and called in sick. He felt an equal mixture of curiosity and dread—if this man knew he was Dan, could he know his real identity?

The park was deserted. Peter shivered as he stood in the shadow of the gazebo; a cold wind blew through his flannel jacket. His watch read 10:03 when he heard footsteps behind him.

"It's everyone's favorite computer hacker," Richard said, stepping forward. "Ah, Dan, I had figured you for an intellectual, not the type to get your hands dirty in . . . illegal activities."

"Frank told you," Peter said slowly, putting the pieces together. "That's how you knew it was me, that I was looking for hackers."

Richard spread his hands and shrugged. "We don't reveal our methods." He smiled slightly. "The prime motive for hacking is usually revenge. It's always interesting to find something new about someone, don't you agree?"

Peter had the disconcerting feeling that Richard was referring to something else entirely. "Can you help me?" he asked. "Call it a hypothetical hacking situation."

"Yes, that would certainly limit any collateral damage," Richard replied, seemingly unaffected by the bitterly cold wind. "Oh, I could give you any number of useful computer programs, if I wanted to. But that would be inelegant, not to mention making me an accessory." He fixed Peter with an intense gaze. "I'd suggest you try social engineering."

"Everyone wants me to learn something," Peter complained. "Computers, the Internet, now engineering. Can't you just give me a floppy disk?"

"Social engineering," Richard explained patiently, "means using the weakest link in the chain that holds computer systems together." He added, "The user."

"Get them to give me information?" Peter asked.

"People are careless and negligent. They make mistakes." Richard looked up into the starless sky. "Say someone leaves a password list around. Or a hacker calls someone else up, pretending to be the telephone company. Or . . . but you get the picture. Hypothetically speaking."

Peter thought back to guessing Bette and Mac's passwords. "I think I do." He drew in a breath and slowly let out white clouds of steam. "You always seem to be at the center of one thing or another, don't you?" he commented.

Richard drew his trench coat around him. "We all have our secrets. Even you . . . hypothetically speaking, of course."

He stepped backwards and melted into the night. Peter knelt down and gathered a snowball, then tossed it into the darkness, wondering if Richard was still there. Did he know who Dan really was? And if he did, was he going to tell the other bears?

A snowball came out of nowhere and caught Peter square in the face. He grinned. Time to start to plan his own "hypothetical hacking" situation.

– 11 –

A few nights later, Peter found the note in the garbage at *Phag*.

After his talk with Richard, he did some research on the Web about "social engineering." Apparently, the two best ways to get information about a "corporate opponent," as they so charmingly put it, was through anonymous telephone calls or by rooting through corporate garbage.

He'd considered the first approach, but Mac was quick to disabuse him of the idea. "Peter, we've been friends how long now?" Mac had asked.

"Uh, forever."

"Then let me tell you something I never told you before." Mac had looked around, searching for the words. This was extremely unusual; the only time Peter had known Mac to be at a loss for words was the day he'd learned that *Home Improvement* was finishing its run. "How can I put this? You have a . . . distinctive voice."

Peter had looked at him suspiciously. "A *queeny* voice, you mean."

Mac had sighed. "See Dan Haggerty, hear Julie Hagerty. What's the other option?"

The other option involved a pair of sterile disposable latex gloves (Bear Essentials had a two-for-one sale). When Peter kneeled down to poke through the first wastebasket in the *Phag* offices, he'd shivered and felt like he was going to throw up. Then, when he realized that most of the garbage was papers and plastic, he became more enthusiastic.

It was one of the few times that Peter was glad *Phag* had a policy prohibiting employees from eating lunch at their desks. Unfortunately, they also had confidential recycle bins and a shredder. When Peter went to empty the shredder bin, he discovered that it wasn't going to give up any secrets, unless Chester wrote really, really narrowly.

The first few nights proved fruitless; Peter learned that Bette had a craving for Butterfingers, and that someone from the office actually subscribed to the *Watchtower,* but this wasn't information he could use.

That fateful night, Peter was wandering from one desk to the next, emptying wastepaper baskets and practicing his butch voice. "Hello, is this *Phag Magazine?*" he said into the silence. "Hello, is *this Phag Magazine?*" Then, looking around, Peter tried, "You like that big subscriber list . . . don'tcha!"

He picked up Bette's trash and sifted through it, expecting the usual. The note he found was anything but. "Bear Essentials," Peter read as he stood in the darkened office. Before he could think that he'd misunderstood, he saw the telephone number. It was Will's store, all right. But what was Bette doing calling them?

The answer lay in Chester's office. Peter looked at the locked door. Now, if he was lucky, the door would open with the building's master key. Peter tried his skeleton key, but the knob wouldn't turn. He sighed. Maybe he could weasel the information out of Will somehow . . .

His key in Chester's lock, he heard a familiar click in the distance; someone was opening the front door to *Phag Magazine.* Heart racing, Peter pulled the key out of the lock and turned to go.

There was only one problem: the key wouldn't come out of the lock on Chester's door.

Peter pulled at it mightily. If an employee was coming this way, Peter could hide, but there was no way the employee would miss the huge ring of keys hanging off of Chester's door. The footsteps drew closer. Two people, Peter thought, tugging at the doorknob frantically.

It wouldn't budge. Maybe if he could get on the other side of the door, he thought, he could push it out from that side. Peter unclipped his security card from his shirt and tried to wedge it in between the door and the jamb.

At the last moment, the door popped open, and he heard a crack as his key snapped off in the lock. Peter had been applying his full body weight to the door, so he fell forward into Chester's office.

"Do we need to discuss it at this hour?" a voice asked, not far off. It was Bette.

Peter kicked the door shut and looked around in the pitch black. He tried to remember the layout of Chester's office, then immediately bumped his forehead against what felt like a filing cabinet. Hide under the desk, he thought!

"We're lucky to get him," Chester's voice came from the other side of the door. "I feel bad enough about the venue as it is."

Peter curled up in a fetal ball under Chester's desk and relaxed for a moment, until he heard the doorknob rattle and remembered that Chester's desk was glass.

"If your key isn't working, we can always have the meeting in the boardroom," Bette said hopefully. Peter was sure she just wanted to get out of there, and he envied her.

He scuttled over on all fours to the wall and found a door. Sliding it open, Peter crawled inside as the door to Chester's office opened and the light sprang on. He stood within the closet, breathing heavily. How appropriate.

"Now let's see," Chester said, flipping through his Day-Timer. "You're sure we can't use any of the big bookstores? Did you get back to all of them?"

"Every last one," Bette said impatiently. "Glad Rag Books is having Gabriel Rotello, Sunshine's is doing Alison Bechtel, and the People's Lesbigay Bookstore Collective . . . well, they're on strike because of the softwood lumber issue."

"Then Bear Essentials it is," Chester said, reading the words with distaste. "Did you confirm that they have enough room for the press?"

Peter imagined Bette rolling her eyes. "They said they have a large area in the back."

He nearly burst out laughing; Will must be clearing out the video booths from the backroom to make space. Peter clapped a hand over his mouth and shook with silent giggles.

"I'll get Caliph to fax out the press releases tomorrow," Chester said, making a note. "We'll get good coverage . . . it's not every magazine that can land Ted Dennison."

"He went to the highest bidder," Bette said acidly.

A pause. "Did I mention I'm sending him to Venezuela?" Chester asked. Peter heard footsteps, then the door slammed. "Poor loser," Chester said, clearly to himself. Peter waited another few minutes, and Chester finally left the office, turning out the light and closing the door.

Peter waited in the closet to give himself a margin of safety, but his mind was reeling. Ted Dennison was obviously his replacement, a columnist from back East who had first made a name for himself at a left-wing gay magazine, writing exposés on viatical companies, and then who had made a name for himself at a right-wing online magazine with articles about the moral bankruptcy of the Left. On the other hand, he was so *nice*.

The next morning Peter showed up at Bear Essentials. "Weird to see you around without Mac," Will commented, giving him a bear hug. "You two seem like you're joined at the hip."

"We're not in a relationship," Peter said hastily.

"No, I know. But sometimes," Will said dreamily, "I think about how things might be with me and Mac."

"You're going out with Jason," Peter pointed out.

Will waved a hand dismissively. "That's just a relationship of convenience. Now what can I do for you?"

"I could use some extra money," Peter said, which wasn't all that far from the truth. "Do you have any work I could do?"

Will balanced himself back and forth on his heels, thinking. "Chloe usually has things under control," he said at last. "But we have an event coming up in a few days. Do you know what you'd like to do?"

"No," Peter said thoughtfully, "but I'm sure something will come to mind."

Peter followed Will into the stockroom behind the store, where Will introduced him to a tall, graceful-looking woman with an easy smile and waist-length hair.

"Chloe, this is Dan," Will said. "He's going to help you set up for Monday morning."

Chloe shook Peter's hand firmly. "Ah, another member of the cabal," she said knowingly after Will had left.

"The cabal?" Peter asked.

"You know, the bears. The fraternity, the community—whatever you want to call it." Her words were bitter, but Chloe seemed more resigned than anything. "Help me uncrate these videos."

"It's not a secret society," Peter protested, opening a box marked *The Nad-Ooze Bears*.

"You're right," Chloe said. "As long as you're a man."

Oh no, Peter thought, another toxic lesbian. When she saw the expression on his face, Chloe apologized. "It's a sore point," she explained. "I've worked here for two years, but I always have to stay in the stockroom. And away from the bear events."

Peter examined the cover of *The Nad-Ooze Bears.* He doubted that Mate-em O'Feel was the actor's real name.

"You can always go to a bear event." He had to admit, though, that he hadn't seen any women at any of the bear events he'd been to.

"Sure," Chloe said, "they'd let me in. They're too PC not to. But they'd let me know I wasn't wanted. It cramps the guys' style."

Peter wondered how Jason, Will, and the others would react if they knew a twink had infiltrated their cabal. "I understand."

Chloe looked him over and shook her head, smiling. "No, you don't. You look the part and you talk the part. I'm a straight woman, and for a bear that means I have to be a fag hag or one of the guys. I can't just be *me*."

There really was nothing he could say. They were saved from an increasingly awkward silence by the appearance of Frank, who stuck out a hand for Peter to shake.

"I hear you're working here now," he said.

"For now," Peter replied.

"Wow, that makes us co-workers, almost." Frank looked at the counter. "So what are you working on?" He blushed as he saw the video cover. "Oh, no."

Peter felt an odd vibe from Frank, and he was more interested in talking to Chloe than in a halting conversation with the other man.

"There's rimming *and* fisting!" he pointed out on the box cover copy.

Frank fled. "Nice guy," Chloe said. "He needs to find someone and settle down."

Peter glanced at the Bear-of-the-Month calendar on the wall. "Don't we all," he said absently.

Between his janitorial work and Bear Essentials, Peter found himself exhausted. The morning of the press conference, he and Mac had a rare shared breakfast together.

"Did you get all the popper smell out of the backroom?" Mac asked, dousing his pancakes in syrup.

"Sort of," Peter said. "After a while, Will gave up and just told us to hang up a lot of room fresheners. We did this checkerboard pattern on the wall."

Mac shook his head. "More to the point, do you have some kind of evil plan ready?"

"Yes," Peter said enthusiastically. "Let me demonstrate."

Mac watched as Peter organized the condiments and forks and knives into a complicated pattern. "I don't suppose we could do a montage sequence?" he asked.

"Hush," Peter said. "Now, pay attention." He pointed at the salt shaker. "This represents Ted Dennison's plane, arriving from La-Guardia."

"Maybe that could represent Ted after Bette gets through with him," Mac suggested, picking up the salt and sprinkling it on his sausage links. "Use the syrup for the plane."

"No!" Peter said, taking the salt back. "The sugar substitute is the plane." He moved the salt into position. "I've had a lot of time to think this through . . ."

An hour later, Peter's own words were still going through his mind as he stood in the back of Bear Essentials, ignored among the crowd. The first step was getting a taxi to go pick up Ted at the airport. Next, the taxi would take him to the Winston Arms Hotel, not the Dunston Arms Hotel where he was supposed to be staying. At that point, Frank would become an unwitting accomplice in the plot . . .

"Hey, you're here early," Frank said, looking around the renovated backroom. "They cleaned a lot of stuff out."

Peter looked at Frank, aghast. "You were *supposed* to be at the Winston Arms Hotel!"

Frank looked confused. "No, you said go to the Dunston Arms Hotel, but Ted Dennison wasn't there."

The members of the press were already filing into the room. "Go back to the Winston Arms Hotel," Peter said, trying to keep his voice calm.

"Um, I don't have to," Frank said regretfully.

"And why is that?"

"Ted told Will he'd check in after he did the talk."

If you need to do something right, Peter thought, brushing past Frank, you have to do it yourself. He walked toward the stockroom as quickly as he could, until he bumped into someone and nearly knocked him down.

"Watch where you're going!" Peter growled.

"I would suggest the same of you," Chester Valentine said, brushing the lapels of his suit jacket with a manicured hand.

Peter turned his face away from Chester and rushed into the stockroom. He already had the airport's telephone number programmed into the speed dial.

"Can you page Ted Dennison for me?" he said, affecting a masculine Southern drawl.

"One moment, please." Peter checked the clock. Ted's flight had probably deplaned by now . . . there might still be time to catch him before he picked up his luggage and hailed a cab.

"Ted Dennison," the man said at the other end of the line. He had such a *nice* voice, Peter thought. "Who's this?"

"Officer . . . O'Feel," Peter said, thinking fast. "We're shutting down your press conference. Bomb threat."

"Bomb threat?" Ted asked mildly. "Do you take those seriously?"

Chloe came into the stockroom. "Yes, big bomb threat," Peter said quickly into the receiver. "Go down to the station and wait for further instructions." He hung up before Ted could say another word.

"The natives are getting restless," Chloe said. "And some of them are complaining about the smell of amyl nitrate."

"Should I send around the hors d'oeuvres?"

Chloe gave him a funny look. "Did Will really ask you to make processed cheese slices with Triscuits?"

"Now don't you start." Peter edged over to the stockroom door and smiled to himself as he watched Chester at the podium, fidgeting and checking his watch. "It'd be too bad if Ted didn't show up."

Chloe joined him in the doorway. "Maybe we'll sell some videos."

After fifteen long minutes and several cell phone calls, Chester finally gave up. "It seems like Mr. Dennison is delayed," he said smoothly.

"Does that mean we came all this way for nothing?" one of the journalists asked.

"Just another *Phag* publicity stunt," a second journalist said from the other side of the room. This was working out better than Peter had hoped. "Do you have any real news for us?" the journalist asked.

Chester looked unprepared and ill at ease. "Well," he said at last, "there is one piece of news. I was saving it for another time, but you all were so kind to come out here this morning. . . ."

Nobody said anything. Chester straightened his tie. "Queermedia is expanding the *Phag* brand onto the Internet."

"Been there, done that," another journalist said. "None of the gay offerings online are making any money, even the other Queermedia properties. Are you going for e-commerce, the portal thing, or just online porn?"

So, Peter thought, he'd been right. "We'll be announcing our full plans at Queermedia's Annual General Meeting in February," Chester said, "but you can be assured that we'll be at the forefront of a new era."

Not if I can help it, Peter thought.

"Peter?" an ambiguous but familiar voice asked. Peter turned around before he could stop himself. It was Caliph, dressed in a blouse and harem pants. "Peter, is that really you?"

– 12 –

Peter drew Caliph into the stockroom. "Yes, it's me," he said in a low voice, "but I wish you wouldn't tell Chester I'm here."

Caliph looked around with large, liquid brown eyes. "Oh, this is *so* Secret Agent Man! Are you going to tell me what's going on, or do I have to get out the truth serum?"

Peter sighed. In fact, Caliph usually used heavy doses of vodka martinis on his victims—make that confidantes—to get them to spill their secrets. Caliph was easily the biggest gossip at *Phag Magazine,* which was a pretty big accomplishment.

"Nothing like *that's* going on," Peter said offhandedly. "It's just that ever since I left *Phag,* I've been on a . . . downhill spiral."

Caliph snapped his or her fingers. "I knew it! That scruffy attempt at a beard, those Sally Ann threads. What is it? Drinking? Drugs? Religion? I promise I won't tell."

Peter leaned forward conspiratorially. The best lie, he remembered, was a partial truth. "I had something of a nervous breakdown after I left *Phag.* I even lost Danny. I was wandering in the desert, alone and afraid . . . metaphorically speaking."

"Oh, enough about the desert, dear," Caliph said impatiently. "I want to hear about the debauchery."

"I fell in with a bad crowd," Peter sighed dramatically. "Rough, hairy, burly men, some of them bikers." He searched around for a way to wrap up the story. "They made me dress like this, and I grew the beard and cut my hair so I could sneak through them and escape."

Caliph poked his chest with a long, thin finger. "Now you're playing games with me," Caliph accused. "But it's a good story."

Peter pulled the door to the stockroom half closed. "Promise you won't tell Chester, or Bette, or any of the others. Promise."

"Your secret, my dear, is safe with me." Caliph drew a finger across his or her lips and tossed an imaginary key into the garbage bin. Peter eyed the staple gun on the counter wistfully. "I probably won't tell

Chester about you, but I have *got* to tell you about Chester," Caliph said cheerfully.

"I'm sure he's doing fine," Peter said, trying to walk the thin line between encouraging Caliph and being the model of discretion. "After all, he managed to land Ted Dennison."

"That boy is so *nice*," Caliph murmured. "He'd make someone a good husband someday." A shake of the head. "But that's not the dish."

Peter snuck a glance at the crack in the door; most of the journalists had left, but he kept waiting for Chester to go by before he dared to leave.

"Surely there's nothing else," Peter ventured.

"Chester's had a constant parade of young men into his office, and even some women," Caliph sniffed. "Not the usual houseboy types he goes for, my dear. I thought this was some sort of new fetish involving black clothes, body piercing, and surliness. But I was wrong."

"Mmm," Peter said, hand edging toward the staple gun.

"Computers," Caliph said, smiling when Peter snapped his eyes open. "Oh yes, it's some sort of horrible conspiracy involving those dull machines. We won't even be using our old computers for much longer; Chester's about to replace them with ugly gray boxes." Caliph sighed. "Now how am I supposed to do creative work on something like that?"

"Lots of wires connecting them, I bet," Peter said lightly. "Must trip you up with them all over the office."

Caliph waved a hand. "No, no. We had some delicious young man from Ma Bell come in and put them all behind ceiling panels. Now *that* was a sight, let me tell you . . ."

The Internet, Peter thought. It was amazing what he missed, even though he was in the *Phag* offices most nights. He was about to ask Caliph about the software when he heard a shout that chilled him to the bone.

"You!" Chester Valentine yelled elegantly, flinging open the stockroom door. "What are you doing here?"

Peter clenched his fists, ready to fight or run, but the stockroom door hit him in the face and flattened him against the wall.

"You asked me to come, *boss*," Caliph said, lacing the last word with just the slightest edge of contempt.

"I asked you to get Ted Dennison from the airport to the press conference on time. What did you do, send over one of your camels to pick him up?" Peter had never heard Chester so angry, and he stifled a smile; clearly this had been an important event.

A long pause. "I'm sure that if he missed the conference, he managed to find his way to our ... inclusive ... offices, boss," Caliph said, barely disguising the hurt in his voice. "I gave him the right directions."

"Somebody screwed up," Chester said in a low voice. "And I'm not going to tolerate any more screw ups. If I find out it's you ... well, let me say that you can wait another year for a raise. *And* the gender reassignment surgery."

Peter heard Chester clear his throat; perhaps he knew he'd made a tactical error. "Now let's go do some damage control," Chester said, more placatingly. "What were you doing in here in the first place?"

Out of the corner of his eye, Peter saw Caliph give the slightest of hand waves in his direction. "Not a thing, boss."

"Then walk this way."

"If I could walk that way, I wouldn't *bother* with the surgery," Caliph muttered, and soon their footsteps trailed off into the distance. Once Peter was sure the coast was clear, he pushed the door away from his face and rubbed his sore nose. Now he probably looked butcher than ever.

Will and Chloe came into the storeroom a few minutes later, chatting excitedly. "What?" Peter asked. "What happened?"

"Note to self," Will said, dictating into his pencorder. "I'd call that a success!" Chloe nodded.

"Will," Peter said gently, "it was a disaster. Ted Dennison didn't show up." And, he thought guiltily, it was his fault.

Will shook his head. "*Phag* makes a big misstep on our front door! We couldn't buy publicity like that. Our name's going to be in every gay magazine in the state—well, except one, of course." He grinned and held up a stack of tags. "And what's more, we sold out of *Bear Tearoom Party*. Those journalists ..." He went back into the main part of the store, still dictating.

Peter helped Chloe feed the video tags into the stockroom shredder, which was clearly marked "For Bear Essentials corporate documents ONLY."

"Is there something wrong with us using this thing for personal documents?" he asked once they'd fed the last of the tags through.

Chloe scooped up the strips of paper. "Will loves gadgets. When he first got this thing, he started feeding in all sorts of things. I think he stopped when he tried to see what would happen if he put in his credit card. He made me put up the sign . . . but it's really for him."

Peter squeezed his nose; although he felt like Marcia Brady, it seemed to be back in place and the right size. "What now?" he asked.

Chloe unlocked a cabinet and took out a stack of pink and purple signs. "Now we start decorating for Valentine's Day."

"Oh, God," Peter said, pushing the signs away. "You better unplug the shredder."

Chloe bent down and took out a roll of tape from the supply cabinet. "That bad, eh?"

Peter took half of the stack and followed Chloe into the main part of the store. The first sign read "It's 14 Days Until Valentine's Day. Do You Know Where Your Husbear Is?"

"This isn't helping," he said, holding the sign while she taped it into position. "No, it's not that bad. Just that it's the first year I'm going to spend Valentine's Day alone."

The next sign said "Dildos Are a Bear's Best Friend—And You Don't Have to Spend Two Months' Salary on One."

"That can be rough," Chloe said. "Well, I've been single forever and a day," she admitted matter-of-factly, "so I'm not one to talk. But there's missing a relationship because you want to be in one, and missing a relationship because everyone else is in one."

Peter picked up a teddy bear with a heart on his stomach and the words "I WUV WOO" in fine embroidery. He smiled wistfully. "Sure, everyone in the bear community has a husbear, or wants one."

"If I was anticapitalist," Chloe said, taking the teddy bear out of his hands and slapping a price tag on it, "I'd say that love can become a commodity, especially when everyone wants it."

"But sometimes you want it, because you want to be with someone," Peter said simply.

"And what's all this talk about boyfriends?" Will asked, coming up behind them and rubbing his hands. "Am I getting a chance to play Cupid a bit early this year?"

"Peter was saying that he misses not having a boyfriend this year," Chloe explained, not missing a beat.

"Okay," Will said, biting the tip of his pencorder. "So what was the last one like? Body type, amount of fur, facial coverage, dick size? Let me know what you like, and I'm sure I can come up with something."

"This isn't Fur Fun Barbie," Peter protested, trying to get off the subject. "You can't find a boyfriend using a laundry list."

Will stared at him. "Mac told me you were on the Internet. Didn't you learn *anything*?" He sighed. "Now tell me about your last boyfriend."

"He was . . . sweet," Peter said, leaning on what he thought was a broom, then putting it down when he realized he'd picked up the Jeff Stryker special. "Young, but not naive. Innocent in some ways. Great sense of humor. Usually pretty quiet." He blushed. "Good in bed."

"Sounds nice," Chloe admitted. "What happened?"

Peter thought about it. "A bear came between us."

Will patted Peter on the shoulder. "No worries. We'll find you someone by Valentine's Day. Someone good in bed, because that's the only thing you've given me to go on." He clapped his hand to his forehead. "Did Fanny Brice ever have these problems, I wonder?"

He wandered off, and Chloe pointed to the remaining stack of signs. "Is he serious?" Peter asked, helping Chloe put up another one.

Chloe tore off the edge of the tape with her teeth. "Bright, shiny things get his attention for a while, but he gives up pretty easy."

Three days later, Peter found an envelope addressed to Dan in the mail slot when he opened up Bear Essentials for the morning. "Woof!" the note inside read. "I saw you in here the other day, and I think you're hot. Signed, an admirer."

"Not bad," Chloe said once she'd read it. "You should be flattered."

Peter rolled his eyes. "Oh wow! Maybe we can go to the prom if he talks to me during first period!" He shook his head. "But seriously, what kind of guy sends secret admirer notes?"

"Innocent, in some ways?" Chloe quoted. "Usually pretty quiet?"

"The neighbors always said he kept to himself . . . until they discovered the bodies," Peter retorted.

The next day, the thermostat went on the fritz and the store was as hot as an oven, even with both sets of doors open. Will and Chloe both begged off early, and since Peter had the night off from his janitorial duties, he offered to work overtime to get the backroom in order again.

Another note arrived, telling Peter that "I look forward to getting to know you better, soon." Peter shrugged and tossed it in the garbage, then dug it out again and held it to his chest for a moment, before shaking his head and tossing it back in the garbage.

That evening, he stripped down to his waist, sweat pouring off his body as he pushed the video machines back into their places in the backroom. There was something disturbing in how clean the spots underneath the machines were, as opposed to the rest of the floor. After manhandling the fourth machine into place, Peter stopped to rub his face and chest with his T-shirt. He sniffed his pits; God, he was ripe! There was something about excess weight and body hair that made him smell like a day-old pizza.

Peter caught sight of a reflection in one of the rear windows; someone had been watching him. Tossing aside his sweat-soaked T-shirt, he picked up a wrench and walked toward the back door. It was creepy enough getting secret admirer notes without having to worry about being stalked. Peter waited, then flung open the door and looked out into the alley.

"Hello?" he called. "Anyone there?"

"Dan," Frank said, coming out of the shadows, "what are you doing without your shirt on?" Frank blushed. "I was driving by with my other supplier, but I saw all the doors were open. I thought something might be wrong."

"Thanks, Frank," Peter said. It was sweet of him to worry. "I'm all right."

They stood in the alley, Peter increasingly aware of his shirtless condition. "Well, I should go back in and finish moving those things around," he said at last.

"Good night, Dan," Frank said. He waved awkwardly and headed around the corner of the building.

Peter shook his head and went back into the store. He finished hooking up the video machines and was about to close up shop when he noticed another envelope lying behind on the mat behind the front door. "From your secret admirer," it read.

He'd been by the front door only an hour earlier, and no note. Peter weighed the envelope in his hands and thought of Frank saying, "I was driving by . . ." "Oh dear," Peter said.

Il Duce was the only restaurant in the gay ghetto that was never frequented by gay men, and once Peter stepped over the threshold, he realized why. The pink-and-orange striped decor hadn't been changed since the 1970s, and combined with velvet paintings of Italian monuments, created an affront to any sensible gay man's senses.

It was the perfect place, however, to meet Frank for a "man-to-man" chat. Frank had been surprised and awkward when Peter had asked him to dinner, but Frank was *always* surprised and awkward. He was a sweet man, Peter admitted, but that was all there was.

As Peter sat at the table waiting for Frank to show up, he glanced around the restaurant. Happy couples holding hands, a few married couples with babies and one teenaged couple who couldn't keep their hands off of each other. How does it feel? he wondered.

"Sorry I'm late," Frank said, sitting down at the wrought-iron table. "Is the food good? I've never come here before." He looked around. "Weird choice of furniture."

Even Frank noticed it. "Well," Peter said delicately, "I didn't exactly ask you out to have dinner."

Frank looked confused. "Are we having appetizers? Or those antipasto things?"

Peter placed his hand on Frank's. "We need to talk."

Frank blushed. "Oh," he said. "Oh, no."

"It's all right," Peter said. "There's nothing wrong with admitting how you feel."

"No," Frank said with renewed strength. "No, there isn't. Even when you know it's impossible." He studied the menu.

Peter closed Frank's menu. "It's all right," he said. "You can say what's on your mind. I won't judge you."

Frank broke into a sad smile. "I'm sure you'll find someone, Dan. You're a really nice guy. Good boyfriend material for someone."

Peter blinked. "Excuse me?" He picked up his glass of water and gulped at it.

Frank ran a hand through his hair. "I really appreciate all this; the dinner, the sweet talk. But I'm taken. I thought you knew that."

Peter spat out a mouthful of water. "I'm sorry," he said at last. "What did you say?"

Frank smiled shyly. "It's flattering. Really. But I go for the leather, biker types. Lots of leather." He leaned forward and whispered, "I'm wearing a leather harness right now, under my clothes."

"Check, please!" Peter called to the waiter.

"Sir," the waiter said, coming over, "you didn't order anything yet."

"Then charge me for the breadsticks, goddammit," Peter growled. The waiter backed away.

"You'll find someone," Frank said consolingly. "Probably when you least expect it."

Peter forced himself to calm down. After all, who was he angry with, Frank or himself? "You're right," he said. "It was a mistake. Let's never speak of it again."

"Sure thing," Frank said, looking relieved.

Peter returned to Bear Essentials from the restaurant, chewing on the last breadstick furiously. He stormed into the stockroom, looking for something to shred. Peter grabbed the nearest teddy bear with "I WUV WOO" on its chest and turned on the shredder, then relented.

"He thought I was . . ." he said angrily to the teddy bear. "I thought he was, but it was really . . ."

Peter grabbed the teddy bear with both hands and advanced on the humming shredder. "Am I interrupting something?" a deep but surprisingly gentle voice came from the doorway.

Peter dropped the teddy bear onto the floor. The man who'd spoken had a bushy ginger beard and red hair, and his frame completely filled the doorway. The other jobber, Peter remembered. Frank's coworker. The smell of nicotine filled the air.

"Is there something I can do for you?" Peter asked angrily.

"I brought something for you," the man said.

Peter snatched up the teddy bear. "Everyone has something for me. Pity, concern, compassion. Everything except what I need. Jesus." He shook his head. "What is it now, chocolate dildos?"

The man furrowed his brow in anger. "No, those are on the shelves." He brought up his massive hand that had been behind the doorjamb. In it was a dozen roses. "These were for you."

Peter's anger melted in a second. "Look," he said, "what I was saying just now . . ."

The man barreled forward into the stockroom and shoved the roses into the shredder, which protested with a squealing, grinding noise. "That's clearly marked for company documents only!" Peter said.

"Go to hell," the man said, turning on his heel and walking out. Peter shut off the shredder, which whined mercifully down into silence. After he heard the front door of Bear Essentials slam shut, Peter went into the main area and picked up a silver-wrapped dildo. He slowly unwrapped the foil wrap, then contemplated the milk chocolate.

With a snap, Peter bit off the end of the chocolate dildo. "Happy Valentine's Day," he said to the empty store.

—13—

February 1—*Phag Magazine* ordered five binders with the company logo (a green "P" superimposed over a pink triangle), but five hundred showed up. There was no way to return them, because they were already printed, and besides, who else would buy them?

February 5—A scheduling mix-up caused Bette Chambers to end up in Paris, Texas, instead of Paris, France. Although she was able to salvage her reputation by reporting on "Diesel Dykes and the Religious Right in the American Heartland," Chester was unable to maintain diplomatic relations with *Gai Aujourd'hui,* a magazine that had been on the brink of signing on as *Phag*'s French co-venture partner. They didn't want any binders, either.

February 10—Ted Dennison had to go home early when he accidentally used poppers from the office fridge instead of his medicated eye drops. When the soap opera star who was planning to come out to Ted got his voice mail, he called *GENRE* magazine instead.

Chester's office was alternately too hot and too cold, and his orchids died. Bette's bike, which she kept by her desk, ran over a thumbtack. Even Caliph's favorite eyeliner went missing (although everyone suspected the accounting intern).

Peter's campaign was going even better than he'd planned. It was ridiculously easy to sabotage things at *Phag;* everyone blamed the computers, or the voice mail, or the poor communication. With all of the changes at the magazine already, the company was close to a chaotic state; Peter was merely helping it along.

He hadn't even switched the poppers with Ted's eyedrops—it had been a fortuitous coincidence. Apparently, when Chester had to come in early to deal with the binder problem, he didn't have time to go to change, and deposited the poppers in the fridge. Sweeping the offices that night, Peter could hardly keep from giggling. By this point, everyone thought that the company was cursed, and Peter wasn't about to disappoint them. He'd opened a service door into the elevator and tied one end of a vacuum cleaner hose to the elevator cable; the hose made eerie noises as it swung in the windy shaft.

Along with the increase in chaos had come an increase in tension; Peter could feel it palpably, even though the offices were empty when he went through doing his rounds. It manifested itself in a pile of Diet Coke cans on one person's desk, a pile of papers scattered frantically on another's, and dozens of Butterfingers wrappers in Bette's trash. The cause didn't escape Peter's attention either. He stopped his sweeping and looked up at the communal wall calendar and to-do list that Chester had installed recently.

February 28—Queermedia's Annual General Meeting, which of course included *Phag*. Although *Phag* was a subsidiary of Queermedia, Chester had given all employees (and, from the gossip, his string of houseboys) shares in the company several years earlier.

Peter's hands tightened on the broom handle. As an ex-employee, he still owned stock in Queermedia. "Well, I guess I still *am* working at *Phag*," Peter muttered. He reached up and erased a zero with his index finger. Bette would certainly have an interesting time finding wine for "$3 a bottle max!"

Peter continued sweeping, thinking of the Annual General Meeting. He sighed—these pranks were all well and good, but he needed *information*. Ever since Richard and Mac had come down hard on him about "hacking" into the office computers, Peter hadn't dared try anything computer related. Theoretically, he could do something else that would cause real problems for *Phag,* but that would lead to an investigation. Chester was relentless about tracking down leads.

He was about to leave the premises and lock up when he heard the main doors open. When nobody turned on the lights, Peter's curiosity was piqued. He pressed himself against the curved wall leading to reception and listened.

"If you want me to show it to you," Bette whispered to someone, "then you have to keep it quiet."

Peter couldn't quite make out the other person's response. "It's top secret," Bette said. "I'm one of the few that knows about it."

Their voices receded, and Peter followed them at a safe distance, down the hall toward Chester's office. Peter peeked out from behind the corner and saw Bette and another woman he didn't recognize, who was carrying a briefcase. He watched in amazement as Bette took out a key and unlocked Chester's door; he was even more amazed when the door swung open. Bette must have damn good connections, Peter thought. Access to Chester's office was granted to nobody but Chester.

Peter edged forward, hearing furniture being moved and the distinctive sound of a briefcase being opened. This had to be good. Even if he was caught, chances were that Bette wouldn't recognize him. Besides, he was the janitor; he had the *right* to be in the office. Bette's right to be in Chester's office was far murkier.

Rationalizations completed, Peter was about to make his move when he saw the door to Chester's office start to swing shut. Thinking quickly, he extended the broom handle so that the tip just managed to wedge itself between the door and the doorjamb. Peter sidled up to the door, ready to flee at any moment. He took a breath, held it, and listened.

"What's two plus two?" Bette asked from beyond the door. Peter furrowed his brow.

"Five?" the other woman asked querulously.

"Wrong!" Bette said, and Peter heard an odd zap. "Did you do your homework last night, Marie?"

Peter couldn't take it anymore. He peeked around the edge of the door. Bette was standing at a podium, dressed in a tight matronly suit with horn-rimmed glasses. "Marie," her charge, was in pigtails and a sailor suit, quivering in a chair. Bette had something long and dildolike in her hand, which was quite odd, until Peter remembered that Chester had bought a taser ages ago.

"Oh, teacher, I tried," Marie wailed, "Really I did!"

This was clearly no remake of *Stand and Deliver*. Peter shook his head and retreated down the hall. Then he had another idea. Ducking into the reception area, he surveyed the combination telephone and PA system. He pressed a button. "Welcome to *Phag Magazine,* a subsidiary of Queermedia Group," the receptionist's voice said. "You have reached the automated menu." Peter hit the button again, and the voice fell silent.

He pushed another button. "You're a bad girl," Bette breathed suddenly, "and you have to be punished!" Or at least dropped a grade point, Peter thought. He pushed two more buttons in succession, then watched a progression of lights.

Finally, Peter pushed the first button again. "You're a bad girl!" Bette's voice came over the voice mail system in a choppy techno remix. "A bad girl! Bad girl! Bad! Bad! Bad!"

Ah, revenge was sweet. Peter was still smiling on the bus home. Just another day in the decline and fall of *Phag Magazine*. He looked out the darkened window and saw a straight couple walking arm in arm. Then, when he turned away from the window, he spotted a gay couple pressing arms together as they sat on the wide seats at the front of the bus. Peter sighed and looked up at the overhead ads. A condom ad, a romantic restaurant ad, and an ad for a divorce lawyer. He stopped smiling. Revenge against *Phag* or revenge against Bette for having a relationship?

The question was easy enough to dismiss at 1 a.m. on a city bus, but Peter had a harder problem dealing with it the next day at Bear Essentials. The sign now read "There Are Only 2 Days Left Until Valentine's Day—Do You Know Where Your Husbear Is?"

Peter grumbled as he set out more of the chocolate dildos—the store's hottest-selling products. "You want to separate the red-wrapped ones from the green-wrapped ones," Will said gently, coming forward. "Don't mix them up, Dan."

Peter picked up one of the chocolates and looked at the bottom. "So the red ones are milk chocolate and the green ones are dark chocolate. Mind explaining why the green ones are larger?"

Will punched him playfully on the shoulder. "You really don't want to go there," Will said. "That's really not what's bothering you, is it?"

Peter was in no mood for Will's attempt at hands-on management. "After I get the dildos out, do you want me to straighten up the video aisle or clean out the backroom?" Peter asked, picking up a dildo that was wrapped in blue—he didn't want to know.

"I was hoping you'd *smile*," Will said. "Frankly, you're scaring off the customers more than Chloe does." He adjusted the one dildo that was slightly disarranged. "Maybe you want to hang around the stockroom until one of our . . . jobbers . . . shows up?"

Peter snapped the chocolate in half involuntarily. "Does everyone know?" he asked in a low voice, looking around.

Will took one half of the dildo and unwrapped it. "Ooh, nuts," he said, biting into the chocolate foreskin. "No, everyone doesn't know about it. We all feel bad about it."

"Who is *we?*" Peter asked, reluctant to hear the answer.

"Oh, me, Jason, Frank, Mac, Richard, I think," Will said, counting off on his fingers. "And Ben, of course." He tsk-tsked.

"Ben?" Peter asked.

"Ben Conaway. The guy who was sending you the notes," Will said, pointing. "There he is."

Peter ducked behind a display of leather accessories. "Oh God," he said. "Did he see me?"

Will chuckled. "Even if he didn't, Frank saw you, and he'll probably tell him." He pried Peter away from the squeaking leather harnesses. "Are you going to spend the rest of your life avoiding him?"

"Actually," Peter confided, "I was hoping he'd be hit by a truck.... So many bears drive them."

Will grabbed him by the shoulders and frog-marched Peter into his office. "You're not going to get anything done hiding behind cockrings and flails," Will announced. "So while he's here, you might as well help me with this flyer I'm writing."

Peter groaned inwardly, and the groan escaped audibly when he saw the ad copy. "A storeful of Bearish Goodness!" he read. "Mind if I do a bit of editing on this?" Peter asked.

"Sure, go ahead," Will said. Peter took out a red pen from the desk drawer, then glanced at the ad copy and took out another red pen. "You know, you're not the only one with relationship problems," Will confided, leaning on the edge of the desk.

"I'm *not* in a relationship," Peter growled. Was "butt fuck" hyphenated? Two words? One word? Did anyone care?

"Jason's father died a few weeks ago," Will went on. "He had a lot of money." He sighed and rubbed the bridge of his nose. "You'd think it'd be fun—well, aside from the dying part—having all that money."

"Isn't it?" Peter asked, giving up on the headline entirely.

"All of a sudden, Jason wants new clothes, he wants a new car, he wants a new house." Will shook his head. "He inherited some cabin up in the woods, wants me to go spend a month with him in the summer. *I* can't take the time off from the store, but he won't have to work anymore."

Peter finally sensed the distress in Will's voice and put down the pen. "My last boyfriend didn't have a lot of money," he said, careful not to let any details slip out. "But we managed to work things out as far as money was concerned. It doesn't have to tear you guys apart."

"And what if you were the one who didn't have the money?" Will asked.

"You're right," Peter said after a moment. "It's always easier to tolerate something than to be tolerated."

The door to Will's office opened and Ben walked in, filling the doorway with his broad frame. When he saw Peter sitting at the desk, his face darkened. "I got that last shipment in," Ben said to Will, brandishing a clipboard. "You want to sign for it?"

Will went over and signed the form, then stood there holding the clipboard. "Anything else I need to know about?" he asked, keeping the clipboard just out of Ben's reach.

Ben scowled and snatched the clipboard out of Will's hand with a meaty paw. "See you next week," he rumbled, stealing a glance at Peter and closing the door, hard.

"There's romantic tension in the air," Will said. "Can't you feel it?"

"I think he's waiting outside with a tire iron," Peter confessed.

Will clutched his hands to his heart. "It's something about Valentine's Day—my relationship radar starts working overtime. I can tell about the two of you. You're destined to be together."

"Destiny?" Peter laughed. "One of us is destined to murder the other, that's it. He might have the strength advantage, but I have the brains."

"Don't count Ben out," Will said. "He's pretty smart." He walked toward the door, then stopped. "Remember, you two have to end up together, or my psychic streak will be broken."

"How many couples have you predicted?" Peter asked.

"All fifteen of my relationships in the past year," Will replied. "It's a one hundred percent success rate!"

He left Peter to ponder that. After a few minutes of slashing away at the flyer, Peter got up and stretched his arms. In the reflection from the front door, he saw Ben leave the store and lumber down the street. Peter leaned against the wall and took out a piece of paper that had been folded and refolded many times. He slowly unfolded it, smoothing out the creases so that he could read the handwriting.

In his last note, Ben had quoted Yeats:

> How many loved your moments of glad grace,
> And loved your beauty with love false or true,
> But one man loved the pilgrim Soul in you,
> And loved the sorrows of your changing face.

He read it one last time, then smiled sadly and shook his head. Destiny, Peter thought. Unlikely. He turned on the paper shredder and fed in the poem. Goodbye, Ben Conaway. The shredder squealed and jammed, no doubt as a result of being fed a dozen roses earlier in the month. Peter carefully pulled out the poem.

It was intact.

– 14 –

Peter had been hoping to spend the evening of February 13 alone with a two-liter bottle of Coke and a copy of *Bear Sex Brawl* ("now in 3-D!"). Bear Essentials was out of 3-D glasses, though, and when Peter started pawing through the supply closet, Will presented him with an offer he couldn't turn down.

"Come on up to Jason's cabin," Will said. "We're all going up there to have a great dinner. It'll be you, Jason, me, Frank and his husbear, and Mac."

Peter fixed Will with a suspicious eye. "Not Ben?"

Will shook his head. "Dear, Ben wants to avoid you as much as you want to avoid him. This is going to be our cabin-warming party, and we don't want any petty squabbling. Did I tell you Jason is a gourmet cook?"

"Throw in a pair of 3-D glasses and you've got a deal."

The 3-D in *Bear Sex Brawl* was a gimmick, Will explained; the 3-D glasses only had a magnifying effect. And in any event, the cabin was rustic—no television, no VCR, not even a telephone. "How is Jason going to cook dinner?" Peter asked. "Over a fire?"

Will rolled his eyes. "Well of course there's a microwave and refrigerator. Probably even one of those gas ranges. Jason's set the whole thing up. He bought all the food and drove up last weekend to drop it off."

With that contradictory image of the cabin in mind, Peter set off alone in Mac's car ("I'm coming up with Frank," Mac explained. "Some soup cans at work thought I didn't capture their best sides."), driving through heavier and heavier snow along the highway. Peter didn't to know what to expect: a shack equipped with a high-tech kitchen, or an elaborate cottage that happened to lack the odd accessory.

He shivered and turned the heat up to the maximum position. Through the windshield, Peter could barely make out the glittering trail of orange highway lights hanging in midair. The yellow line separating the lanes drifted in and out of visibility with the blowing snow. A sudden gust of wind slammed into the tiny car, and Peter had to fight against the steering wheel to keep the car on the road.

Enough of this, he thought, and turned on the radio. "Do you have someone special you're spending Valentine's Eve with?" the radio announcer asked in dulcet tones. "Is there a special song we can play to commemorate your love?"

"Can you go fuck yourself?" Peter asked rhetorically, and hit the "Off" button. A flash lit up the sheets of falling snow, followed by a loud crash. He peered through the windshield. That's all he needed . . . a thunderstorm.

Peter looked at the passenger seat, where he'd laid out Will's carefully drawn map. Well, "careful" had to be measured in relative terms, Peter thought. Will was not a detail person, and in the infrequent flashes of light, Peter couldn't tell if the landmark he was supposed to turn right at was a boulder or a chocolate stain.

Finally, he steered the car slowly onto an unmarked road that according to the map led right to the cabin. Another loud clap of thunder crashed down, and Peter gripped the steering wheel tightly. Shouldn't the thunder be *after* the lightning? he wondered, looking around for the flash of light.

The road just ahead of him lit up, but it wasn't lightning; he caught a glimpse of a massive truck through the snow, coming straight at him.

"Get out of the way, you idiot!" Peter shouted helplessly, trying to hold onto the steering wheel as his car skidded and skewed sideways.

The truck driver must have seen his lights, because the truck picked up speed and started to veer in the other direction. Peter slammed on the brakes and his car spun faster, right into the path of the side of the truck. He screamed and brought up his hands to his face as the truck spun the other way and its headlights bore down on him.

The front of Mac's tiny car disintegrated in a groan of cheap foreign metal and glass, sparks shooting up from the engine block. Peter felt himself yanked forward, then slammed backward against the lumbar support. Thank God I had on the seat belt, he thought when he was able to think straight again. Peter looked down and realized that he had forgotten to wear his seat belt; only his bruised belly had managed to cushion the impact.

Peter forced his car door open and staggered out into the dark. The front end of the truck looked just as bad as the car; both headlights were out, and the grille was a tangle of metal.

"Are you all right?" he called to the driver, silhouetted in the starred and smashed window. No reply. Peter limped around the back of the car and climbed up to the cab of the truck. At that moment, the cab door opened, and a heavy weight fell onto him, spreading him out flat on the snow. Oh, I've fallen, and I can't get up, Peter thought.

"Are you okay?" the man sitting on him asked. Then their eyes met. It was Ben Conaway.

Peter pushed Ben off and got to his feet, wiping the snow from his jeans. "Let me guess," Peter said, "you were following me in the truck and you wanted to tell me how *woofy* I was."

Ben glared at him. "I was on my way to the cabin when I got lost. Then *you* crossed over into my lane."

"Lane? This is a one-lane road. If you weren't driving that . . . convoy," Peter started, then gave up. "Never mind. Let's see if we can get the car or the truck started." Of all the people, Peter thought. He got back into Mac's car gingerly and tried to start the engine. It wouldn't even turn over.

"Looks like the engine's cracked," Ben announced, looking under the crumpled hood.

"Looks like you cracked it," Peter said, pointing to the truck. "Get in there and start it up. I'm freezing."

He shivered and stamped his feet while Ben climbed into the cab. Peter listened to the truck engine make a few halfhearted noises, then sputter to a halt. "It's a goner, for now," Ben said, climbing out of the cab. "We better get to the cabin."

Peter pointed to the cell phone at Ben's hip. "Why don't you use that?" he asked.

Ben gave him a "duh" look and handed him the cell phone. The display read OUT OF RANGE. "I tried calling my voice mail for messages earlier," Ben said. "It's all this snow and the thunderstorm."

Peter grabbed the map out of the passenger side of his car and pointed down the lane. "Let's get moving before we freeze," he said.

"It's that way," Ben said, gesturing in the other direction.

"You were the one that got lost. We're going this way."

Lightning continued to flash as they trudged through the snow, but in the intervals between the thunder, the heavy snowfall muffled their footsteps and any ambient noise. It was eerily quiet. As they rounded a curve and came into sight of the cabin, Peter realized something.

"What are you doing here, anyway?" he asked.

"Will invited me to come up for a cabin-warming." Ben's eyes narrowed. "And he definitely said you weren't going to be there."

"I have a bad feeling about this," Peter said.

The cabin turned out to be small but well-appointed, with wood paneling and secondhand furniture, as well as the promised microwave and fridge. There was a note on the kitchen table, in Will's spiky handwriting. "Enjoy, you two!" Peter read. "Food's in the fridge, and dinner's on us."

"They must die," Ben growled, and Peter was about to agree when there was a final, blinding flash of lightning. The thunderclap split the sky nearly right above them, and the two men covered their ears.

Then the lights went out.

Peter and Ben looked at each other across the kitchen table. "I'll go check the fuse box," Ben said, looking uncertain in the last remnants of light. Peter just shook his head and shivered.

When Ben came back, the news was written all over his face. "Let me get this clear," Peter said. "We're stranded in the middle of nowhere, with no electricity, no transportation, and no phone." He walked over to the fridge and peered inside. Although he could barely see anything, Peter's hands confirmed his worst fears. "And the food's all frozen."

"There's canned food," Ben said, opening the cupboards.

"And an electric can opener."

Ben searched his pockets and pulled out something that Peter couldn't see. The dim light of a match flared up, then subsided as Ben lit a cigarette.

"Your answer to being a castaway is filling your lungs with cancer-causing nicotine?" Peter couldn't help himself asking.

"Do you have a better idea?" Ben asked, puffing away.

Peter took the box of matches out of Ben's large hand. "I think I saw a fireplace in the living room."

He got halfway there before the match burned his hand and he dropped it, cursing. Peter felt the rest of the way to the fireplace and was gratified to feel the outlines of logs and kindling. With a few attempts, he soon had a fire going in the grate, and both he and Ben stood in front of it, warming their hands.

Eventually the heat was too much for their fronts, so they turned around to warm up their butts. Peter's mouth dropped open when he saw the contents of the living room. There were hundreds of candles: tea candles, long-stemmed candles, colored and scented ones, placed strategically on every available flat surface. "What a fire hazard," Peter remarked.

"It was a good idea," Ben said, lighting a few candles from the fireplace, then placing them around the living room. He picked up the last lit candle and relit his cigarette, then puffed contentedly.

Peter watched this little ritual in disgust. "So we're stranded here until morning," he said. "Are you going to make dinner, or should I?"

Ben coughed a bit and looked at him apologetically. "I kinda grew up on the microwave school of cooking."

"Whatever." Peter went back into the kitchen and propped open the fridge doors to try to help the food defrost. "You can't fix an engine, you can't cook dinner. The least you can do is set the table."

Peter took a quick inventory of the fridge contents and started on a simple menu: cold greens, cold pasta salad, hot soup, lasagna, and popcorn.

"You like onions and tomatoes?" Peter called to Ben.

"Sure," Ben called back, "and carrots."

"You want carrots, you can come eat them out of the fridge." Peter shook his head. "Rabbit food." Or, he thought, a phallic substitute, like the cigarettes.

Ben came into the kitchen for cutlery. "Do you want the napkins in a standard trifold, or an origami peacock?" he asked.

"Just promise me you won't smoke at dinner," Peter said, waving the smoke away. He gathered up the food and brought it into the living room, brushing past Ben. The fireplace wasn't big, but it was big enough to stick a pan in above the logs, and Peter soon had the soup simmering while he sawed through the frozen lasagna with a knife.

"I'll stick to carrots," Ben said. "Love those crunchy suckers." He munched away happily in the background while Peter concentrated on dinner. Surprisingly, it didn't take Peter all that much longer than usual to put the meal on the table.

After the accident, the walk, and the cold, Peter was famished. He had lifted a spoonful of soup to his mouth when Ben asked, "Are you going to say grace?"

"There's nothing for me to be thankful for tonight," Peter said sullenly. Or tomorrow, for that matter, he thought.

Ben closed his eyes for a moment, lips moving. "Okay, let's eat," he said, then devoured the soup, the greens, and the salad. He slowed down when he got to the lasagna. "A little chewy," Ben observed through a mouthful of food, which he politely covered with his hand while he spoke.

Peter's jaws were working overtime to chew through the tough lasagna, which seemed to have hardened into rubber over the fire. "A little."

After the main course, they settled into the sofa in front of the fireplace while Peter shook a pan full of popcorn kernels over the fire. "Do you think they'll figure out what happened to us?" Peter wondered idly.

Ben looked at him sideways, then clasped his paws over his belly. "Probably find a couple of skeletons once the snow melts in spring."

The popcorn started to pop. "Probably find you alive and well fed, and my skeleton buried out in the yard," Peter said, shaking the pan back and forth as the popcorn popped faster.

"Nah," Ben said, shaking his head lazily. "I'd bury ya in the woods. Besides, there's not all that much to you—you're just a snack."

Peter withdrew the pan and set it down on the tiles in front of the fireplace. "You ready for dessert?" he asked.

Ben shrugged. Peter took the top off of the pan and dug in; it was hot and delicious. "Go ahead, it won't bite," Peter said.

There was a pop. "Ow!" Ben howled, clapping a hand to his eye. "I got a kernel in my eye, goddammit!"

He started howling and swinging around with his free arm, and Peter ducked, trying to avoid being hit. "Slow down a second and let me get it out."

"Christ, it *hurts!*" Ben said, hand over his eye. "Get it out, get it out!"

"And here I thought you were a religious man," Peter remarked, then shut up when he caught sight of the expression in Ben's good eye. "Now lean over this way and let me pull it out."

"Don't hurt me," Ben said, leaning over. He flinched as Peter pulled the eyelid gently back, looking for the kernel shell. "You're *hurting* me!"

"Sorry, let me poke around some more," Peter said dryly, locating the kernel. "I feel like I'm taking a thorn out of the lion's paw."

He withdrew it and showed it to Ben, whose eye was red and streaming. "You see, it was nothing, just a little flake."

"Like the chef," Ben grumbled, nursing his eye.

In the flickering light of the fireplace, they looked at each other without saying anything. "Isn't this the point where we're supposed to have wild sex?" Peter asked.

Ben nodded. "You know, I was thinking that, too. We're supposed to fight and fight and fight, then fall into each other's arms."

"I don't feel like having sex, do you?" Ben shook his head.

Peter folded his arms. "Well, *I* feel cheated. I watched *Moonlighting* for years, and this was their whole premise."

"Yeah, and *Remington Steele*," Ben said. "And *Cheers*. Wow—TV lied to us."

"Let me get you a washcloth and clean out that eye," Peter said.

Ben got to his feet. "Nah, I'll do it myself. You have stubby little fingers."

In comparison to Ben's broad hands, Peter was ready to admit his were stubby indeed. "Were you always that big?" he asked, looking up at Ben's massive frame.

"Nah," Ben said, heading to the kitchen. "I just grew that way."

They were too cold to do much else after dinner, so they decided to go to sleep on the sofa. "We'll freeze if we sleep in the bedroom," Ben explained.

"You think we're going to both fit on that sofa?" Peter asked, incredulously. "You're going to roll over in the middle of the night and turn me into a cub pancake. No, one of us sleeps on the tiles."

"Do we flip a coin," Ben asked, sounding very tired, "or do we keep on yelling at each other until we fall asleep standing up?"

Peter tugged at the couch, which did a flip, then a flop, and popped open into a small but serviceable sofa bed. "Problem solved," he said, just as tired. "I'm going to bed." He got onto the sofa and pulled several blankets he'd brought in from the bedroom around him.

Ben got into the sofa bed, and it creaked and groaned under the weight. He grabbed some of Peter's blankets, and they tussled briefly until they were both securely wrapped up like mummies. Peter closed his eyes and tried to sleep.

Fifteen minutes later, he was still trying. "You're not sleeping," Ben said sleepily.

"How can you tell?" Peter replied, looking at the patterns of light dancing on the ceiling.

"You're not twitching. When a guy falls asleep he twitches a bit."

"Maybe I'm not a twitcher," Peter said and yawned.

"Everyone's a twitcher."

A long silence. "So let me ask you a question," Peter mumbled.

"Sure."

Peter paused. "Why me?" he asked. "I mean, why were you interested in me?"

An even longer silence. Ben cleared his throat. "I saw you in the store one day. And I guess I was interested."

"More than interested," Peter said. "You sent me all those notes. You don't do that with everyone, do you?"

Ben propped himself up on one shoulder and looked into Peter's eyes. "Okay, I'll say this one time, then we don't talk about it any more." He sighed. "Something about the way you held yourself. Some guys seem ashamed that they're bears, or they're not proud of how they look. But you carried yourself like you knew who you were and what you wanted." He lay back down. "There's a spark sometimes in people. It's so rare, you only find it once in a while. And I guess I saw that spark." He cleared his throat. "Also, you had a cute butt."

"Thanks," Peter said after a moment.

"Don't mention it," Ben said, sounding embarrassed. He rolled over and his breathing slowed. Peter assumed he was falling asleep. But Ben didn't twitch, and finally Peter fell into a deep, dreamless sleep.

The morning of Valentine's Day, Peter woke up on the sofa bed with a cramp in his back and a dry mouth. He was completely lost for a moment, then remembered the accident and dinner.

"Ben?" Peter asked, rolling over. The other side of the sofa bed was empty except for a pile of rumpled blankets.

There was a note pinned to Peter's pillow. "I went to get help. Ben." Peter smiled, then got out of bed and stretched until all of his bones cracked back into place. Ben had left a box of matches in front of the cold fireplace.

He didn't know how long he'd been asleep, but the footprints in the snow leading away from the cabin were still fairly fresh, despite the snowfall. That meant that Peter had time.

He washed the pans in snow, then dried them off and set out to make breakfast. Soon, he had eggs, bacon, and hash browns cooking over the fire. The smell warmed him and made his stomach rumble. Peter checked his watch. He'd wait another ten minutes.

Peter waited a half hour, then an hour. Finally, when he heard a car pull into the driveway, he quickly pulled the pan out of the fireplace and served up the meal on two gleaming dishes, flanked by the best silverware he could find.

"Dan?" a voice called out as the door opened. "Are you all right?"

It was Will, followed by Jason, both looking worried. Peter wiped his greasy hands on his jeans.

"We got a call from Ben," Jason said. "He told us everything."

Will and Jason took in the scene, and Peter stood in front of the table nonchalantly. "Well, as long as you're here," he said, "you might as well sit down and have a big breakfast."

Like any bears, they quickly set to work eating the food, and neither of them asked Peter why he'd prepared a large meal for two. Even if he'd been asked, Peter wasn't sure he could have answered.

"So what happened to Ben?" Peter asked lightly once the two men were in full feed mode.

"He had to go to work. Valentine's Day is his busiest day of the year." Will shook his head. "If I knew what was going to happen to you guys, I swear . . ."

Peter took the pots and pans back into the kitchen and put them into the sink, biting his lip. He wandered over to the window overlooking the woods and blinked.

A burly snowman stood just outside the cabin, standing guard and waving at Peter jauntily with branches for arms. It was at least six feet tall and massively broad. Peter didn't have to ask who'd built it; a large carrot pointed out of its crotch area.

Despite himself, Peter grinned.

– 15 –

A few days later, when Peter went to a beer bust at the Eagle, he recognized everyone, but like some parallel-universe science fiction, the bears were all playing different roles. Aside from Will and Jason, who were talking intently by the pool table, almost everyone else seemed to have swapped partners, found a boyfriend, or left a boyfriend. Clearly, Valentine's Day had been eventful for people other than him and Ben.

"It's like a game of musical chairs," Mac commented to Peter as they stood by the jukebox, sipping microbrewery beers.

"Musical bears," Peter said, nodding. "Everyone except Will and Jason, and Sasha and his husbear, whoever he is. I think there must be some sort of biological imperative that kicks in on February fourteenth. Isn't that when salmon swim upstream to spawn?"

"I thought that was every seven years," Mac said idly. Peter watched his friend push the coaster around on the counter.

"Were you hoping to find someone special this year?" Peter asked.

"No!" Mac said. "Not now, at least. We're two weeks away from GBG. I want to leave myself wide open—if you pardon the expression—to enjoy it."

GBG. As soon as Mac said the word, Peter started hearing it everywhere in the room, just hovering above the low buzz of conversation. "Are you going to GBG, Chris?" "Did you get a room to yourself, or are you staying with Bruce again?" "Do you think they'll have the Solid Bear Dancers at GBG again this year?" "I read on the BLS that there are some super-cheap airfares . . . if you're willing to fly in from Texas."

"I guess that's where the bears go to spawn," Peter said to Mac, thinking. Global Bear Gathering happened to be scheduled on the same weekend as the Queermedia Annual General Meeting, so there was no possible way he could make it, but still . . .

"You should go," Mac said. "If anything defines and sums up the bear community, it's GBG. It's like one of those episodes of a TV show where they have clips of the last five years."

Peter waved to Frank as he saw him pass by in the distance. "I don't want to miss the Queermedia AGM," he said to Mac regretfully. "If I'm going to have a chance to do anything major to *Phag,* it's going to be there. I don't know what I'm going to do, but there has to be something. The current Queermedia board's going to be re-elected, and they're all in Chester's pocket."

Mac sighed. "You're just one man. And how are you going to get into the meeting? You have to let go of this thing, before it eats you up inside."

"I'm a shareholder," Peter said. "I own all of ten shares of Queermedia Group. They can't not let me in."

A bear with a camera came up and manually posed Mac and Peter together. "Now both of you smile and say woof!" he instructed, then snapped a shot. "It'll be in the club newsletter."

After the photographer went off in search of more victims, Peter asked Mac, "The club newsletter?"

Mac rolled his eyes. "If you did a search-and-replace of the word *woof* with *Christ,* it could double as the *Watchtower.*" He put a hand on Peter's shoulder. "You're changing the subject. Don't you think it's time to give up your vendetta?"

"No," Peter said definitely, shrugging off Mac's hand and looking at him uncomprehendingly. "I'm going to teach them a lesson and show them up for the idiots they are, not let them get away with it. What am I supposed to do—turn my back on that?"

Mac nodded. "Yeah, yeah, I think that would be a good idea. You've already turned your back on a lot of things, and I think you're a better person for it." He drank the last of his beer. "But hey, when you start talking about teaching them a lesson, that's when I start to get worried. Something tells me it's more about getting revenge on them than anything else."

Turned his back? Peter thought about Danny, about his job at *Phag,* about his life in the mainstream gay community. "I haven't turned my back on everything," he replied. "A lot of this is just a temporary phase while I write the book."

"I guess that's up to you," Mac said, lifting his empty beer bottle. "I'm going to get another drink—but think about this. You might not find it all that easy to go back."

Peter watched Mac make his way through the bears and to the bar. Give up fighting against *Phag*? he thought. Never. Mac was right—he'd given up a lot of things in the last few months, but he'd never give up that.

Peter headed off in the opposite direction, giving Frank a friendly pat on the shoulder as he passed him and his husbear, then stopping to watch Jason play pool against some hulking bear he didn't know.

"Everything okay?" Jason asked once he'd made his shot, standing up straight and giving Peter a bone-crushing hug. "Looked like you and Mac were doing some heavy talking over there."

Peter felt his bones slowly move back into position. "I was going to ask you the same thing. Everything okay with you and Will?"

Jason pursed his lips. "These two weeks between Valentine's Day and GBG are always a bit dicey."

Peter nodded but said nothing. He'd already heard from a few people that Will and Jason were having problems dealing with Jason's newfound wealth.

"So," Jason said, chalking the end of his cue, "speaking of which, are you coming to GBG, Dan?"

"Oh, I don't think I'm going to be able to make it," Peter said. "Work has me on a pretty tight leash."

Jason shook his head. "Not Will. He's easygoing."

"No . . . my other job."

Jason leaned over the pool table, and Peter couldn't help but admire his butt. "Seems to me like Will should become a bit more easygoing," Jason said, almost to himself. "No need for him to work ten-hour days at Bear Essentials."

Peter took his half-empty beer bottle and continued through the crowd. He said hello to Wolf, Ursus, and Grizzly, gave Polarbear a hug, and when he saw Sasha approaching, hid behind Moose's bulk.

With Moose's hand rubbing his head affectionately, Peter smiled. It was then that the realization struck him—he felt at home. Mac was partly right; he'd left the mainstream gay community behind, but he'd found another community. And this one, with all its quirks and rituals, was starting to feel more and more like home. Even the book, which he was still working on in his spare time, was less and less important to him; while he kept working at it, he was living it more than writing it.

Peter turned to get a refill on the beer (which was so good he could almost forget it *was* beer), and collided with Ben.

"Hi," Peter said.

"Hi," Ben replied. They stood in the middle of the bar looking at each other awkwardly.

"So you got home all right from the cabin," Peter said at last.

"Oh yeah." Ben scratched his head. "Guess I should've waited for you to wake up."

"No, I was pretty tired." Peter stared at the floor for a long second, then brought his eyes back up to Ben's. "Look, what happened at the cabin. . . . I mean, circumstances were kind of stacked against us."

Ben nodded. "We had a run of bad luck."

"Exactly." Peter gestured with the beer bottle. "It doesn't mean we have to treat each other like lepers every time we run into each other."

Ben smiled. "That sounds good." Another pause. "Actually, I wanted to ask you a favor."

"Sure," Peter said hastily. "I mean, if I can help."

"I'm working on rewriting my résumé, and I could use your help. Will says you're a pretty good writer. I have the main points down, but I need someone to . . . help me smooth them out."

Peter nodded. "Fine," he said. "I'd be glad to help you smooth anything out that needs smoothing out." He blushed.

Ben didn't seem to notice. He took a business card out of his pocket and handed it to Peter. Peter glanced at the bear paw print on the card and put it away in his jacket.

"Say tomorrow night at seven-thirty?" Ben asked.

"I'll see you there," Peter said.

Ben turned to go. "Are you going to go to GBG?" he asked suddenly.

Peter shook his head. "Probably not. I have . . . other commitments."

"Too bad," Ben said. "See you tomorrow."

The next day, Peter was rearranging the stock at Bear Essentials. First he had to clear out the Valentine's Day overstock into the clearance bin, which included the chocolate dildos and talking teddy bear. Then he had to put up the next holiday's decorations.

Will was idling by the video rack, and when Peter passed him with a handful of decorations, he couldn't resist saying something to the owner.

"Easter?" Peter asked. "In February?"

"Don't knock it," Will said absently. "Bears love chocolate. And we have an Easter bear instead of an Easter bunny."

Peter looked around. "I didn't see any Easter eggs in the stockroom yet."

"I'll let you in on a little secret. Any of the chocolate dildos we don't sell, we knock the testicles off and rewrap them as mini-Easter eggs."

Peter shook his head. "Promise me you won't tell me what we do for the Fourth of July."

He and Chloe started to put up the Easter decorations. "Will seems to be a bit distracted lately," Peter said, helping Chloe nail an Easter bunny to the front of the leather aisle.

"He's got something on his mind," Chloe explained. "Something big."

"I should go talk to him," Peter mused, looking at the door to Will's office. "By the way, are you going to GBG?"

Chloe laughed. "You think they'd let a woman go and cramp their style?" She shook her head and picked up an Easter garland. "They can't *not* let me in, but they definitely would make my life difficult if I went. Don't fool yourself—the bear community is only inclusive up to a point."

"Do you want to go?" Peter asked, thinking of his own deception and feeling intensely uncomfortable.

Chloe put her hands on her hips. "No," she admitted at last. "But that's because I know I'm not welcome." She shrugged. "It's what makes it so insidious. They don't have to actually restrict it to men—they just make you not *want* to go."

Peter found Will sitting in his office, going over some papers. "Seems like you have a lot on your mind," Peter said.

Will motioned Peter to sit down in the chair in front of his desk. "I do," he said heavily. "I have a big decision to make."

"About Jason?"

Will smiled faintly. "Not exactly. Somebody wants to buy the store."

Peter blinked. "Who?"

"It's a private offer. I can't tell you, but I can tell you that the amount of money they're willing to pay is really good." Will sighed and leaned back in his chair, putting his hands behind his head. "I have to admit, I'm tempted."

"I thought you loved running Bear Essentials," Peter protested.

"I'm tired," Will said. "It's such a grind. I mean, we're not a high-margin business; you know that. And even though we have good jobbers, I still have a lot of hassle with our suppliers. Because we're gay, we don't get good credit terms. Or maybe it's because we're bears."

"Is this private offer from a bear?" Peter asked. Will said nothing. "Oh, come on," Peter said. "You're not going to sell it to some . . . outsider, are you?"

Will picked up the pile of papers and turned them over so that Peter couldn't see what was printed on them. "I'm thinking of taking some time off."

"Jason wants you to take some time off," Peter said slowly.

Their eyes met. "You don't understand," Will said, almost helplessly. "All of a sudden, he's got all this money. New friends, new social connections. He can afford to go out every night if he wants to and take a vacation every month." Will rubbed the edge of his worn desk. "There's a part of me that just wants to fit in. Even if it means giving up something that's important to me. Jason's willing to pay my way, and I don't feel like he's going to be my sugar daddy bear or anything."

"You might not think so," Peter said, "but I do understand. Just do me a favor—don't sell the store right away. Think about it—Bear Essentials is at the heart of this town's bear community."

Will shook his head. "That's not what I hear. Every business owner in the ghetto gets told they're making money off of the gay or bear community, not contributing to it."

Peter thought about that on his way over to Ben's apartment that evening. Maybe Will was right, but Peter doubted it. Every community needed its hubs and meeting places, and a bar only went so far in terms of providing that. What was more interesting was the source of the private offer; Peter had his suspicions, but he couldn't confirm them.

Peter hadn't planned on staying long; he was expected at his janitorial job at 10 p.m., and a résumé didn't take all that long to edit. When he arrived at Ben's apartment, though, nobody answered the doorbell. Peter pushed it repeatedly, then, thinking it might be out of order, knocked on the door a few times.

Finally he tried the doorknob, and the door opened. Peter was suddenly hit with a burst of techno music. He covered his ears and followed the loud music down a narrow hallway. Then he turned the corner and saw something he wasn't expecting to see.

Ben was leaning back on a weight bench, covered in sweat, straining against a loaded barbell as he lifted it off of his bare chest. Not only was his chest covered with red fur, but so were his belly and his crotch—Ben wasn't wearing any clothes at all. Peter couldn't help but stare at Ben's heavy uncut cock, and he rubbed his own crotch as he watched Ben's large muscles strain and shift under his hairy skin.

Ben finally noticed him and dropped the barbell onto the weight bench with a clang. "Didn't hear you ring the doorbell," he said, covering himself with a towel and blushing a bit. "I'm in the middle of a workout. Want to give me a few minutes?"

Peter also blushed furiously and nodded, going back down the hall to the living room. He batted at his crotch, trying to get his erection to subside, but in the end had to make do with rearranging it so that it wasn't so noticeable. Peter tried to block the techno music out of his mind and started to scan the bookshelves. He saw *A Brief History of Time* by Stephen Hawking and shook his head. Must have been a gift. Then he saw *Zen and the Art of Motorcycle Maintenance, Cosmos* by Carl Sagan, and *The Greening of America.* Peter took the Hawking book down from the shelf and riffled through it; there were notes scrawled in Ben's handwriting and dog-eared corners on most pages—definitely not a book meant only for show.

Peter turned to the odd large table at one end of the living room. He didn't know what to make of it. It looked like a large sandbox at waist level, with inflated supports beneath. Stuck at various points in the sand were tiny mirrors and little soldiers. There was also a metal box labeled He-Ne that looked ominous.

Bored, Peter started moving the soldiers around on the sand. "Ooh, don't ask, don't tell," he said, moving two soldiers together. "What were you doing at the base gym with Lieutenant Studmuffin, soldier?" Then, moving them over an embankment, he put four of them together. "So . . . have you ever been with an enlisted man before?" "Gee, I'm really drunk tonight."

"What the hell are you doing?" Ben yelled. Peter dropped the remaining soldiers into the sand; one fell onto the floor and rolled under the couch.

"I was just playing," Peter said sheepishly. Ben had changed into a tank top and shorts, with red fur poking everywhere out of the tank top.

Ben shook his head and pushed Peter out of the way. "That's my holography setup. Do you know how long it took to get all those mirrors in position?" He glared at Peter, then surveyed the damage. "What the hell, it's ruined."

"I think this mirror went here," Peter said, reaching toward the table.

Ben grabbed his hand and moved it aside. Peter could see Ben was making a definite effort not to get angry.

"No," Ben said quietly, gritting his teeth. "Let me fix it later."

Peter could smell the sweat on Ben, and considered readjusting his jeans again. He tried not to stare at the other man's large biceps. "You sure have a lot of interesting books," Peter said at last.

Ben's eyes strayed to the bookshelf. "Yeah, I'm interested in science."

"I wouldn't have guessed . . ." Peter said, then fell silent.

"Because I'm a jobber?" Ben nodded. "No, I suppose you wouldn't have guessed a lot of things about me."

Peter bent over and picked up the stray soldier, still powerfully aware of Ben's presence only inches from him. "Can I get you a drink?" Ben asked awkwardly.

"No," Peter said, his mind made up. "I don't want any excuses for what I'm about to do next." He stepped forward and kissed Ben on the lips.

Ben looked at him, startled, then pressed his beard to Peter's goatee, his tongue exploring Peter's mouth. "God, I've been waiting for this for a long time," Ben growled through the two sets of facial fur, and wrapped his powerful arms around Peter. Peter felt Ben's hands roam up and down his back and then cup and grab his butt cheeks and squeeze them hard.

Surprised at Ben's ardor, Peter kissed him hard, and felt Ben gently push him backward until his back was pressing into the edge of the holography table. A lift and a push from Ben, and Peter was sitting, then lying back on the sandy table. Ben pressed himself forward and ground his crotch into Peter's. The table groaned, then slowly started to collapse as Ben and Peter wrapped their legs around each other, and each started biting and nibbling at the other man's beard.

As the balloons supporting the table deflated, the wind whistled past Peter's ears and he felt Ben's weight press him deeper into the sandy surface of the table. He sighed with contentment.

"Everything okay?" Ben asked through a mouthful of fur. Ben had already taken down Peter's jeans and was unbuttoning Peter's flannel shirt and tweaking his nipples through the T-shirt underneath.

Peter smiled. "I feel like I'm Deborah Kerr in *From Here to Eternity* . . . well, except without the crashing waves."

"I'll give you crashing waves," Ben growled, and put his mouth to Peter's left nipple.

Peter yelped. "Ow! It hurts! Get it out, get it out!"

Ben withdrew his head like he'd touched it to fire. "What, what? I'm biting you too hard?"

Peter shook his head. "My butt! I got one of your toy soldiers in my butt—the wrong side up."

Ben stood up, picked up Peter as if he weighed nothing at all, and put him gently over his shoulder. Peter felt Ben's beard nuzzle against his leg, then against his butt, and then Ben's tongue worked its way into Peter's ass and dislodged the toy soldier.

"Better," Peter murmured.

Ben spat the toy soldier out onto the floor and kissed Peter hard once again. "And now that I have you exactly where I want you . . ." he said, grinning. Ben sprinted faster than Peter could imagine a man of his size moving, dodging the coffee table, kitchen table, chairs, and racing into the bedroom, where he tossed Peter down onto the bed, which promptly sloshed up around Peter's half-clad body.

"A waterbed," Peter said, stripping off his T-shirt and shirt. "Kinky."

Ben looked down on him and stroked his crotch; Peter could see his cock hardening through the gym shorts. With two quick movements he was naked, his fur barely visible in the dim light. With a final growl, Ben leapt onto the bed and onto Peter.

"Ooh," Peter mumbled under the weight. "Crushing me . . . can't breathe." But at the same time he felt Ben's cock slide against his. They turned sideways so that Peter could catch his breath, and then Peter grabbed Ben's head and slid his goatee along Ben's beard.

Ben soon caught on and they were growling and groaning as they rubbed facial fur until Peter knew he was going to have a bad case of beard burn the next day. Then, just when he couldn't take it any longer, Peter felt Ben slide his bearded mouth downward, down Peter's hairy chest, and around his incredibly hard dick.

Peter scooted his body around and found Ben's own massive dick, then started slurping on the end, working his tongue under the foreskin. Huge, he thought. God, I hope he doesn't want to do anything else with this monster.

A few minutes later, Peter felt that he was close to coming, and pushed on Ben's shoulders to tell him to ease up. Ben kissed Peter, letting him taste his own juices, and muttered, "I want to fuck you."

Peter's eyes grew wide as he shot a look down at Ben's crotch. "It's pretty big . . ."

Ben nibbled his earlobe affectionately. "I'll be gentle, I promise." He leaned over to the night table and picked up a wrapped condom. "Want to help me on with this?"

Ben's large fingers skidded over the small plastic square in his impatience, and soon Peter was trying to help him open it. "There's supposed to be a tear mark," Peter said, as they both tugged at the wrapped condom. "Keep pulling."

The condom wrapper burst open, and they both fell backward onto the bed. Then Peter and Ben confronted each other with the two halves of the wrapper.

"Where did it go?" Ben demanded. "Did you see it?"

Peter hunted around on the floor, dick still hard. "Probably slipped under the bed. Can't you just get another one?"

Ben blushed. "It's the last one I had."

Peter collapsed onto his side on the bed, dick pointing straight up. "You don't *have* to fuck me."

Ben put his hairy chest to Peter's back and Peter felt Ben slowly rub his hard cock along Peter's ass. "But I *want* to fuck you."

"Oh, all right, if you ask me again like that . . ." Peter relaxed as Ben's meaty paw started jerking him off. Then he stiffened. "Hey, what the hell are you doing—get your cock out of my ass!"

Ben bit Peter's neck and growled. "That's my *thumb,* you idiot." He kept jacking Peter off while he worked his thumb in and out of Peter's butt. "Feel it? Like that?"

"Oh yeah," Peter said, getting more comfortable and letting Ben do all the work. "I feel it." Then, realizing how big Ben's thumb was, he added, "Geez, were you always this big?"

Ben wedged his thumb all the way up Peter's ass and massaged his prostate. "Nah, I just grew that way . . ."

Ben flipped him over and grabbed their cocks together in one big hand. Peter felt Ben slide his foreskin over both of their cockheads, while his other hand kept up his relentless in-and-out motion up Peter's ass. Ben's eyes stayed locked on Peter's, and Peter leaned forward and sucked Ben's tongue into his mouth just as he felt his cock spasm, spraying come all over both of them, and his ass clamped tight around Ben's thumb.

Ben grinned, then pushed Peter onto his back. He grabbed onto Peter's nipples with his hands and pushed Peter's hairy pecs together, slamming his large dick back and forth along the crevice between the pecs.

"Christ!" Ben yelled at last in a voice loud enough to wake the dead, and Peter got the load in his face.

Ben looked down and seemed embarrassed. "Sorry about that—let me get you a towel." He returned from the bathroom with two wet washcloths, and carefully and gently rubbed the come off Peter and himself. Then Ben gave Peter a tender kiss, snuggled up against him, and closed his eyes.

"Man, I loved that," Ben mumbled.

Soon he was snoring lightly, one arm over Peter's chest. Peter watched him sleep, and smiled. He had to go to work, but he really didn't want to disturb Ben . . .

"Mmf," Ben said, still asleep. "The box."

"The box?" Peter asked.

"The pancake mix," Ben mumbled. "Where is the pancake mix?"

"In the kitchen?"

Ben grabbed Peter. "Dan!" he said in his sleep. "I need you."

"What do you need me for?" Peter asked, bemused. "You want me to make some pancakes?"

"No," Ben said, his voice growing fainter. "I . . . need you." Then he started to snore again.

Peter froze. Dan, he thought. It wasn't him that Ben had just had sex with, but Dan. And what, he wondered, caressing the edge of Ben's cheek with his hand, would happen when Ben found out he wasn't really Dan after all?

— 16 —

The next evening, Peter snuck into the maintenance room in the building where the *Phag* offices were, trying to avoid the security guard. This was only his second absence on the job, but the guard had been explicit about absenteeism when Peter had signed up. "Two strikes and you're out."

"Two strikes? I thought it was three?"

"Like I know anything about baseball? Just don't miss more than two days without a doctor's note."

Peter had been unable to find a bear doctor to see him, and even if he had, he wouldn't have known what ailment to claim. Lovesickness? Achy breaky heart? Sexual overindulgence causing cardiac arrest?

With a quick glance around the room, Peter slipped into his overalls and grabbed the push broom. He dashed into the elevator and breathed a sigh of relief; the guard was probably watching *Springer.*

For the first time since he'd taken the job, Peter allowed himself a small smile as he walked through the glass doors into the *Phag* offices. Lovesickness? Was he really that serious? For that matter, was Ben?

He shook his head and starting moving the broom along the usual path. Ben knew all the right buttons to push . . . those eyes . . . those fingers . . . but there was more to an attraction than that. More to a relationship than that.

Peter stopped in front of one of his framed magazine cover articles: "The New Gay Man: Losing Your Identity." He looked at his faint reflection in the Lucite that covered the article. He hadn't lost his identity, after all. He'd found it, or rather, another facet. Slipping into Dan's shoes had been as easy as slipping on a plaid shirt jacket. And that was what being with Ben felt like. Frighteningly easy. Everything that easy had to have a price.

Unlike the price that Danny had exacted. For his ex-boyfriend, it had always been about money; money had been the true measure of Peter's love for Danny, and Danny's respect for him. The second of the three postdated checks had come due the other day, and Peter had barely managed to cover it with his bank account. But soon that part of his life would be over. No matter what Mac said, he felt he owed Danny that much. Or at least he felt that he had to assuage his guilt over leaving him in a cash-strapped situation. But Ben, on the other hand . . .

Peter held the push broom away from him and eyed it. "Now if I told you I was Peter and not Dan, what would you say?" He waved the broom back and forth. "You love me, and you want to dance?" Peter rolled his eyes. "Now if only it was that easy." The broom stood there reprovingly. "All right," Peter said.

He drew the broom close to him, imagining Ben's strong hands around his waist, dim candlelight lighting the corners of the room, and some soft rock playing in the background. No techno, Peter thought, swaying back and forth, eyes closed. All he had to do was open his eyes and say those three words that would mean so much. "I'm not Dan." As he swept the broom around the office, Peter found that he couldn't say it. The broom might forgive him, but Ben never would.

"I thought guys were supposed to lead," the security guard said, nearly scaring Peter out of his skin. He dropped the broom, which fell in a straight arc away from him, slapping Bette's desk as it hit. "When did you get here?"

Peter blushed. "I got in early. You know, about last night. I was meaning to call in . . ."

The security guard shook his head, and Peter wondered how he was able to shake it with no visible neck. "You're fired."

Peter felt his shoulders slump. "I can explain—"

"Don't bother. I already got someone else," the guard said. "You'd just be giving me more work to do."

"I'll complain to the government!"

Another shake of the guard's massive head. "I paid you under the table. What, you think they care about illegal labor?"

Peter gritted his teeth as he leaned against Bette's desk. He felt a magazine slide under his hands and looked down at it. What the hell? he thought, startled.

"Come on," the guard said, snapping his fingers. "It's my duty to escort you from the building. Hey," he grinned, showing uneven teeth, "it's my duty, and it's also fun. How about that?"

The guard waited as Peter slowly walked out to *Phag*'s reception area, then locked the door behind them. The guard looked at Peter strangely all of a sudden, and scratched his head.

"You know, there's something awfully familiar about this whole situation . . ."

Oh yes, Peter thought bitterly, except this time I don't even have a box of things to take with me. But that thought was soon replaced by curiosity at what he'd seen on Bette's desk. He couldn't stop thinking about it, even on the bus home.

What was Bette doing with a dog-eared, Post-it note-annotated copy of *BEAR Magazine?*

"Maybe she's going to become the first lesbian radical feminist bear," Mac said the next morning as they had breakfast. "Oh, wait, I think Janet Reno beat her to it."

"I bet *Phag*'s going to do something with the bear community," Peter said. "That's got to be it." He made notes on a small pad of paper as they ate, circular diagrams with *Phag* and Chester and Bette and bears.

"They're not going to bother with a niche market," Mac said, shoveling bacon onto a wedge of toast and using it as a scraper to pick up the last of the scrambled eggs before folding it in half and neatly putting it in his mouth. "Now, if you were talking leather, or S&M, I'd think you might have something."

Peter pressed down with the pencil as he circled Chester's name, and the pencil's point snapped. "I'm not through with them yet."

Mac picked the pencil lead out of the jam. "Let me recap for you," he said gently. "You lost your job with them twice. You nearly got caught, oh about four times, trying to spy on them. Don't you think it's time to give up?"

Peter shook his head violently. "You have to fight for the principles you believe in."

"Revenge? Spite?" Mac put down his cutlery, so Peter knew he was about to say something serious. "I think you've got some principles worth fighting for, and they don't involve *Phag*."

"What are you talking about?" Peter asked.

"Jason, Will, and I all think that Ben's probably the best thing that could happen to you in a long time." Mac shrugged. "Not every day that you find someone who could be *the one*."

Peter laughed. "Oh God, that statement is wrong on so many levels. First, even if he's interested—and I'm not saying he is—he's interested in Dan, not me."

"So tell him."

"Yes, and then we can join hands and skip merrily down Denial Avenue," Peter said. "Second, you're as bad as he is, jumping to conclusions. I met him a month ago, and already everyone knows he's the one?"

Mac couldn't help taking one last slice of toast. "Are you done?" he asked around a mouthful.

"The third point isn't about me, it's about you." Peter searched for the right words. "When did you—of all people—suddenly start preaching relationships? No offense, but you go through them faster than *International Male* catalogs."

"I'm not slutty; I'm just drawn that way." Then, more soberly, Mac added, "Sometimes you get a chance at something good. And sometimes, like me, you only get a lot of chances at something that's okay. It's not bad, and maybe you figure that's all you'll get. Sooner or later, you fall into this pattern . . ." He smiled wryly.

"I'm sorry," Peter said.

"Then go to GBG," Mac said, instantly cheerful. "And tell Ben."

"He won't understand."

"He will if he loves you," Mac said sagely.

Mac's words echoed in Peter's ears that afternoon as he and Ben set out cross-country skiing at the local ski hills. Peter watched Ben angle his way up a steep hill by wishboning his skis. But he doesn't love me, Peter thought, smile fading from his face. It was Dan, the cuddly cub with the job at Bear Essentials, the one with the potential to be a writer someday, who Ben loved.

"You look serious," Ben huffed as he approached Peter, sliding back and forth in the ski ruts. He breathed out clouds of white air that condensed on his red beard.

Peter smiled and wiped away the drops from Ben's beard with his hand. "I'm enjoying myself," he said.

Ben kissed Peter's fingers. "You want some cider?"

They found an overturned tree, and Ben wiped away the snow so they could sit down. He had brought a flask of hot cider, and it coursed through Peter's veins instants after he had a deep sip.

"That's good cider," Peter murmured, leaning against Ben.

"I could fall asleep here," Ben said, yawning and lighting a cigarette.

"Then they'd find us in the spring, frozen together. Big bear and little cub."

Ben nuzzled his beard against Peter's neck. "That wouldn't be so bad, would it?" His eyes sparkled. "We'd be comfortable."

Peter nodded. Comfortable. That was the word he'd been looking for. He felt as if they already were in a relationship, for all intents and purposes. The only thing missing was the words.

Ben looked out into the distance. "Do you want to see where this goes?"

Peter punched Ben playfully in the gut. "That goes right into a ditch. Can't you see the 'No Entrance' sign?"

"I meant *us*."

Ben reached over and tugged on Peter's goatee until their eyes were only inches apart. "Do you want to say it, or do I have to?"

Say it, Peter thought. "Say what?"

"Dan, I want you to . . ." Ben said. Peter stiffened at the sound of his alter ego's name, and Ben took his hand away, looking hurt.

"I'm sorry," Peter said, looking down at the snow, unable to bring his eyes to meet Ben's.

"No," Ben said slowly, "I don't think you are." He struggled to his feet. "Does everything have to be on your terms?"

Peter shivered against the chill that blew against him. "I let you make the first move," Ben said, tugging on his gloves angrily. "I let you make the second, third, and fourth moves. Give me some credit already, will you? Let me do something for a change."

"Ben, I'm . . ."

"A control freak?" Ben asked, cutting him off. "I didn't want to believe it, but I'm starting to. Look, I'm going to ask you one simple favor. This isn't a hard one. Cut me some slack, okay?"

"Okay," Peter said, looking up and meeting Ben's eyes.

"Come with me to GBG," Ben said simply. "Let's take some time to get away from this city and see what happens. God knows we could both use a break."

Peter thought fleetingly of *Phag*. The Annual General Meeting, he thought. Going to GBG would mean he'd miss it, and any last chance at getting back at Chester.... And financially, he didn't know how he'd swing it, not with Danny's check coming due.

"I'll go," Peter said, rubbing his hands against the cold. "I'll go."

As the last week of February approached, the bears who were heading to GBG started their ritual preparations. Some bears, like Mac, had their packing down to a science.

Mac usually started with one duffel bag, but this year he decided to go with two, just in case. With a packing list labeled "GBG Survival Kit" in one hand, he went through his closet and cabinet drawers, ticking off items. "Plaid shirts, check. Jeans, check. Ripped jeans, check. Totally ripped slutty jeans, check. Condoms, check. Baseball cap, check. *BEAR Magazine* baseball cap, check. Teddy bear . . . teddy bear?"

Mac looked around frantically, then got down on his hands and knees and peered under the bed. "Noel, you bad thing you. Who put you under there? And what's that you have in your hands?"

"Teddy bear, check. Cowboy boots, check. Condoms, check. Astroglide, check." Mac looked at the remaining empty space in the duffel bag and tossed in some more condoms, then an entire case. You could never be too prepared . . .

Some bears, like Jason and Will, took this time to get the psychodrama out of their relationship and prepare for a good weekend of nonmonogamous sucking and fucking away from their problems.

"You're not taking that ratty old thing, are you?" Jason asked as Will tried to push another pair of faded jeans into the end of his battered suitcase.

"It was my dad's," Will said. "Now if you want to help, you can sit on it while I zip it shut."

Jason obliged, and Will strained to tug the zipper around the edge of the old suitcase. "I could buy you a new one," Jason said lightly.

Will smiled. "You could buy me a lot of things. Hell, you already bought me the ticket to GBG and the hotel room."

"I just want to share what I have with you," Jason replied, hopping off the bulging suitcase and taking his own brand-new suitcase out of the closet. "Does it really bother you?"

Will hoisted his suitcase and placed it by the bedroom door. "You know what, it does. I didn't think it would, but it does." He went over and hugged Jason. "Maybe if you could hold off a bit, you know? Not start buying up everything at once. You don't have to buy *me*."

Jason kissed Will. "I know," he said. "The money's burning a hole in my pocket. Maybe we can buy a house together . . ." He caught sight of Will's eyes. "*After* I hold off a bit."

The phone rang. Jason went over and picked it up. "Hello?" Will watched as Jason listened, his expression turning into a frown. "You're kidding. How did this happen?"

Jason listened for a few more minutes, then said goodbye and hung up. "So, dish already!" Will said, fairly hopping back and forth with anticipation.

"Oh, you're going to like this one," Jason said, shaking his head in puzzlement. "I think there's something that we may both be able to agree on . . ."

Some bears, like Peter, went to GBG for reasons other than wanting ursine camaraderie or just plain sex; usually, the sign was that they had packed too lightly (and had to borrow condoms from the more well-stocked bears).

Peter held the letter between the tips of his fingers, thinking furiously. He'd already put *Phag* out of his mind; the upcoming weekend was about GBG and Ben, mainly Ben. There was to be no more fighting either *Phag* or Ben. But now this . . .

"Queermedia Group is pleased to inform its shareholders that its upcoming Annual General Meeting will be held in San Francisco. Long known as Silicon Valley, this area of California is the perfect setting for Queermedia Group subsidiary Phag Corporation's announcement regarding its new Internet direction. Please see the attached flyer for a revised agenda . . ."

Throw it out, Peter thought. His fingers tightened on the letter, threatening to tear it apart. Who was he kidding? he said to himself, going over to the night table where the GBG brochure was. His destiny was bound up with *Phag*'s as much as it was with Ben, and he *would* see this through to the end.

Sitting down on the end of the bed, Peter started comparing the GBG schedule with the *Phag* agenda. There was time, he thought. Just enough time.

And some bears, like Sasha and his husbear, weren't packing at all.

"Come over here and take a look at this, dear," Sasha instructed his husbear, who was busy reading *Wired* magazine on the couch.

"You have that evil look in your eyes," his husbear said, coming over to where Sasha was sitting behind his reproduction Italian desk. "Did you put Richard Simmons's head on Carl Hardwick's body again?"

"Oh, hush," Sasha said, waving his hand. "I've cracked what has to be *the* mystery of the bear community this year." He started up an image-editing program and loaded a picture. "This is Dan Karn, in a photograph taken at the last beer bust."

"And a cute little cub, too."

"Shut up!" Sasha said, then calmed down. "Now, *this* is a photograph of one Peter Mallory from *Phag Magazine,* circa last October. I found it when I was browsing archives of their site while I was looking for a job." He manipulated the mouse, and slowly the two photographs superimposed themselves into one eerie image. The goatee and extra flesh on Dan couldn't mask the resemblance to Peter. "They're the same person. Peter Mallory is Dan Karn."

"You saw that on *Wonder Woman,* didn't you?" Sasha's husbear asked.

"Be quiet. You truly try my patience." Sasha smiled as he separated the photographs and placed them side by side, so that they looked like a before and after set. "This is simply delicious."

Richard Wentworth, Sasha's husbear, shook his head. "Hon, you're a bitch. What are you going to do?"

Sasha looked over at the GBG brochure on the desk and just smiled. "It's true, you know," he sighed. "I really am a bitch."

PART III
———

Once the bear's hug has got you, it is apt to be for keeps.

Harold Macmillan
Prime Minister of Great Britain

– 17 –

"Please fasten your seat belts in preparation for this aircraft's final approach to San Francisco." A chime sounded, and the seat belt sign came on, joining the "No Smoking" sign, which had been illuminated for the entire flight. Peter felt Ben fidget in the seat next to him, where he was already wedged in between the sharp armrests. And, of course, there was Peter's fellow passenger, who wasn't oversized at all, except perhaps in his own mind.

Peter watched Ted Dennison carefully fold his laptop and stow it away underneath the seat in front of him. When they'd first boarded, Peter had had the window seat, and Ben the horribly cramped middle seat. But Ted had graciously offered his aisle seat, which Ben had accepted with relief. "It's very nice of you," Peter had said, although he'd ended up squashed in the middle between a man who didn't recognize him for the journalist he was, and a bear who didn't recognize him for the man he was.

"Thanks," Ted said, settling into the aisle seat. "You going to the Global Bear Gathering?"

Peter simply looked at Ted. The entire plane was full of hairy, hefty bearded men, and both Peter and Ben were wearing plaid flannel shirts. "Sure," Peter said. "And what are you doing in SF?"

"Oh, I'm going to the GBG too," Ted said. He went on to explain that he was a journalist covering the event for a "national gay magazine." Peter participated in as much small talk as he could stand, then retreated into the in-flight magazine, pausing every now and then to sneak a look at Ted's laptop screen. Not only was Ted nice, he was a good writer too, Peter had to admit. "It's *woof,* not *arf,*" Peter had said at one point when the in-flight magazine's coverage of "Great Tropical Getaways" became too much.

"Woof, you say?"

"Woof, I say. Woof." Peter stole another look at the laptop. "Interesting that a mainstream magazine like *Phag* would want to cover a niche event like this."

Ted eyed Peter speculatively. "I never said I worked for *Phag Magazine.*"

Oh God, Peter thought. This wasn't how he wanted to be unmasked, caught between a jock and a soft place. He grinned. "Saw the magazine in your briefcase."

"Oh. Yes, that would explain it." Ted took another look at Peter and furrowed his brow. "You should be a writer. Good eye for detail."

"That's what I keep telling him," Ben rumbled, busy constructing a miniature model village out of the remains of the lunch tray.

"Maybe one day," Peter said, squeezing Ben's thigh affectionately. "So," he added, returning his attention to Ted, "you think your magazine might be having a change of direction any time soon?"

Ted smiled. "Don't ask me, I just work there. So, are you two an item? I was hoping to interview a real live bear couple, and you could save me some time."

Peter and Ben looked at each other. "We're friends," Ben said.

"Good friends," Peter added. "Intimate friends."

Ted nodded. "Well, woof to both of you. I'm going to get back to my article." And that was the last that Peter had heard from him until the plane started its descent.

The plane landed with a bump, and Ben was out of his seat even before they had taxied to a stop. "God, that chafes," he said, rubbing his sides. "You'd think they'd design some seats for normal-sized people."

Peter saw Ted open his mouth to say something, then apparently reconsider and close it again. He was so *nice,* Peter thought. Then again, Ben was twice his size.

Ben had his backpack out of the overhead storage and was nearly hopping with anticipation. "Will they let us out already?" he griped.

He wasn't alone; there was a palpable buzz of excitement among the other bears on the plane. At last the seat belt sign blinked off.

"Welcome to San Francisco," the pilot announced. "And for those of you attending Global Bear Gathering, have a woofy gathering."

Ben barreled down the aisle and dashed out of the plane. Peter rushed after him, barely keeping up as Ben raced out of the airport, surprisingly agile for such a large man.

"Yes!" Ben shouted, throwing his hands up into the warm, open air. Then he dropped to one knee and leaned down.

"What, are you going to kiss the ground?" Peter asked, incredulous.

Ben got up again and blushed. "Dropped my matches," he explained, then lit up a cigarette. Peter winced. Charming.

"I'm going back in for my luggage," he said, waiting for Ben to respond. "Do you want me to pick yours up, too?" Ben tossed his claim tags to Peter. "Fine, see you on the shuttle bus," Peter said, going back into the airport.

The automatic doors slid shut behind him, and he was back in the recycled cool air of the terminal, but Peter suddenly *knew* that he was in San Francisco. There was some irrational process going on in his mind, just below the conscious level. Maybe it was the sight of so many bears chatting and hugging by the baggage claim, maybe it was the subliminal scent of the sea air in his nostrils, or maybe it was the sight of palm trees in the parking lot, but he knew that this was, somehow, where he belonged. Like salmon returning to their birth stream to spawn (and what an apt simile that was), Peter and the bears had come home.

Then he saw Sasha at the baggage conveyor belt. Well, Peter reflected, every Eden had to have its snake. Before Sasha could spot him in the crush of people, Peter edged around another baggage claim area and walked over to the other side of the conveyor, where Sasha couldn't see him. Instead, he found himself face to face with Mac and Ted Dennison.

Mac observed Peter critically. "You feel it, don't you?"

"What's that?" Ted asked, taking notes.

"San Francisco Fever," Mac said grandly. "The Bear Flu. The I've Come Home to Tara Syndrome." He winked at Peter. "Odd that it doesn't seem to be a genetic trait, after all . . ."

Ted didn't seem to notice. "Now, you were talking about the whole purpose behind the bear community," he said as they watched endless sets of backpacks and duffel bags circle the baggage conveyor. Peter heard the quotation marks around Ted's last two words, and wondered when he'd stopped using them himself.

"Bears are all about individuality," Mac said, lunging forward to get his duffel bag from among three identical ones. "Expressing yourself without having to give in to the whole mainstream gay thing. Free from the constraints of any kind of peer pressure."

"Oh, get *her*," one bear whispered to another, pointing out a third one in the distance. "That torn claw T-shirt is so last year."

Peter soon had his own duffel bag, and they both helped Ted get his suitcase off the belt. "Just wait and see," Mac promised as they walked to the GBG shuttle bus. "It'll all become crystal clear."

They were among the last to board the bus, and Mac gave Ted a shove to make sure he fit in the last free space on the crowded vehicle. The three of them had to stand, and Peter surveyed the rows of bearded and buzz cut heads until he spotted Ben. He waved, and Ben grinned and waved back, his other paw around a new friend.

Peter saw Ted looking at him. "How did you spot him?" Ted asked, bewildered. "Don't they all look the same?"

"That's not what I'd call good j—" He caught himself. "Good ethics," Peter said. "I used to feel the same way as you did, but there's more to bears than that."

The bus went over a bump, and Peter and Ted jostled against several bears. "How did you come to change your point of view?" Ted asked.

Peter felt Ben's gaze on him. "Had a change of heart, I guess," he said, a bead of sweat trickling down the small of his back.

Peter barely got a look out of the bus window at the winding, hilly streets and old buildings before Mac got the other bears launched into a spirited rendition of "99 Bottles of Poppers on the Wall." Fortunately, they had only reached the number 86 when the bus pulled up in front of the Restwell Inn. "We're here!" somebody yelled, and everyone cheered.

Peter and Ted were pushed bodily out of the shuttle bus and onto the sidewalk in the human wave of excited bears. They joined Mac and Ben and collected their luggage.

"What's that pit in front of the hotel?" Ted asked.

"Mud pit," Mac said matter-of-factly. "Some bears get into mud. They like to roll around and play in it."

"And those guys taking pictures?" Ted asked. "Voyeurs?"

Peter, recognizing some of the men, shook his head. "Photographers," he said, barely concealing his disgust. "From the mainstream gay magazines. Give a straight magazine a gay parade, and they focus on the drag queens. Give a gay magazine a bear meet . . ."

Ted eyed him. "I should go over and talk to them," he said, then said his goodbyes to Mac and Ben and wandered over to the edge of the mud pit. Three bears, coated from head to toe in mud, were frolicking with each other in the pit, oblivious to the photographers.

"You better watch that bile," Mac said, shaking his head. "Not good for the complexion."

Peter shrugged and slipped off his flannel shirt, then tied it around his waist, already sweating into his T-shirt from the heat. "It burns me up to see someone like that who just doesn't get it," he said, starting toward the hotel entrance.

"Yeah," Mac said behind him. "That's got to be it."

But once they were standing in the hotel lobby, even Mac was speechless. Bears of all sizes and shapes milled about, going from the registration tables to the vendor booths, and then to the hotel check-in and the elevators beyond. Instead of an alphabetical distribution, the registration tables were separated out by "Bear," "Cub," "Otter," and "Wolf."

"Seems like they should be playing the theme music to *Airport*," Ben commented.

"More like the theme music to *Airplane!*" Peter replied.

Peter and Ben stood in the Bear line while Mac went to stand in the Cub line. "There is no public sex in the lobby zone," a voice boomed out, and Peter recoiled. He located the speaker, a short, bald heavyset man with a thick goatee and a megaphone, standing at the center of the activities like an MC.

"No public sex in the lobby zone. Public sex only in the steam room. See your concierge for instructions."

"That's Canis Major!" Peter said, recognizing the man's face from the video box covers. "He directed *Bear Tearoom Party!*"

"Must've missed that one," Ben said, ruffling Peter's buzz cut.

"Will anybear who drives a four-by-four pickup please go to the parking lot," Canis Major barked into the megaphone. "Your lights are on." Twenty bears started toward the parking lot. "License plate M-U—"—the number of bears going in that direction diminished—"5835." At the recitation of the last digit, only one bear was left in front of Canis Major, and he hurried out in the direction of the parking lot.

Peter started filling out his registration form. Name, he understood. But totem? Bear code?

"Do T-shirt sizes really go up to 7XL?" he asked.

"Don't demean your bear brothers!" piped a voice behind him.

"All GBG Bear Contest contestants, please meet at the pool in thirty minutes for an undress rehearsal," Canis Major bellowed. "Vaseline will be provided for your teeth or . . . any other areas." The crowd roared its approval.

Peter and Ben stopped at the tattoo booth, where a sweet-looking young cub had his shirt off. "Now, I want a bear on my shoulder," the cub explained to the tattoo artist's assistant, a bear nearly entirely covered with ink. "With his claws grabbing over the edge of the shoulder, so it looks like it's climbing me." He smiled shyly. "Oh, and a pink triangle on his chest, and a speech bubble that says woof."

The assistant pursed his lips and pondered for a moment. Then he grabbed the tattoo book and flipped rapidly through it. "We need a number 138!" he yelled to the tattoo artist over the hubbub.

"Did you ever consider getting a tattoo?" Peter asked Ben as they pushed their way through the bearish crowd toward the hotel check-in counter.

"I have a tattoo! Didn't you notice it?" Ben said.

Peter looked at him. "You're kidding. Where is it?"

Ben grinned. "On my chest."

"Oh, that explains it," Peter said, rolling his eyes. "Let's get up to the hotel room so I can change. I'm dying in this heat."

Peter offered to take care of the check-in, and Ben didn't seem to notice that Peter was using cash to pay for the hotel room. Dan didn't have a credit card, after all.

"Auditions are being held this evening for *Bear Tearoom Party 2!*" Canis Major boomed as Peter and Ben wedged themselves into the packed elevator. "Come to the ballroom at 7:30 p.m. tonight, and be ready for your close-up!" The doors closed, shutting off most of the roar from the lobby.

"Someone press three," a bear said. "Someone press four!" another bear called out.

"I'll press *all* the buttons," Peter said, running his palm over the button panel. "Someone's probably getting off at every floor."

"No, don't do that!" the first bear said as the elevator groaned and squeaked. "I don't want to die before I get laid at GBG!"

A screech of metal, and the elevator slowly started to rise. "I hear a group of bears broke the roller coaster at Six Flags one year," another bear said as Peter tried to make some room between his face and the elevator wall.

"What happened?" Ben asked.

"They all crowded on, and it was too much for the roller coaster. It wouldn't even start. Good thing too—they could've been killed!"

"Urban legend," Peter managed to get out. "There was probably a killer in the last car, too." The elevator jerked and dipped suddenly, and Peter found himself holding on to Ben for dear life. He chuckled nervously, and felt relieved when the doors released them onto the third floor.

The room was not only warm, but stuffy. Peter cracked a window open while Ben started to unpack. The room was small and mostly taken up by a bed, which was only appropriate. Peter looked out the window and down at the pool, where the GBG Bear contestants were gathering.

"Is that Will?" he asked, peering down at the mass of fur and flesh. "It looks like him . . ."

Ben joined him at the narrow window. "Yeah, that's him. He's competing in the contest. Didn't you read the registration package?"

Peter shrugged while Ben went back to unpacking. "Those things are popularity contests. And they try to pretend it's about personality, or conviviality . . . but it's about looks."

Ben put down the duffel bag he was holding. "You sound like you got up on the wrong side of the bed this morning."

"That journalist," Peter said evasively. "I guess he put me on edge."

"You could be a journalist too," Ben protested. "If you wanted. You could change your life . . . make something of yourself."

Peter turned back to the window. "One day, maybe." He spotted Will among the crowd of bears. Directed by Canis Major, they had assembled themselves into a bottom-heavy human pyramid, with Will swaying back and forth just underneath the topmost bear.

"Dan!" Will suddenly called up to him, catching his eye.

Peter waved. "Will!" he shouted. "You competing in the bear contest?"

"Yeah, with the rest of these woofy guys," Will called back, and waving his arm to demonstrate. The pyramid started to lose internal cohesion, tilting crazily to one side, and assorted woofs and groans rose up as the contestant bears collapsed in a heap, with Will at their focal point. Will's anguished cry could be heard as far as Peter's hotel room as a dozen bears fell on top of him: "Ooh, my nose!"

"Oh God," Peter said, turning to Ben. "He's been flattened!"

Ben was lying on the bed in his underwear, reading the GBG agenda. "What's that, Lassie? Trouble down at the old mill?"

Peter shook his head. "It's Will—he's hurt!"

Ben massaged his forehead. "Does trouble always follow you around, or do you just generate it somehow?" He looked up at Peter. "Oh, get going, already. We can have sex later."

Peter sprinted to the door, then stopped. "You ate the bed mint, didn't you?"

Ben looked guilty. "They only left us one!"

The elevator was nearly empty on the way down, but still creaked and jerked alarmingly. When it got to the lobby, a crowd of GBG contestant bears got on, carrying an injured Will.

"Are you all right?" Peter asked.

Will put a hand to his swollen nose. "Does it really look that bad?" he asked, sounding like he had a bad cold. The elevator jerked upward.

Peter winced. "Maybe if we cover it up a bit." He took a tissue out of his pocket and placed it over Will's nose like a pathologist covering up a corpse. Peter surveyed the results. "One more ought to do it," he said uncertainly, reaching into his pocket again.

Will waved his hand away and blew the tissue off of his face. "All my dreams, torn asunder," he said, sounding on the verge of tears. "Help me to my room."

"Don't worry," another one of the bears whispered to Peter as Peter helped Will off of the elevator on the sixth floor. "It's the endorphins. Give him a good dose of Dramaquine and he'll be fine."

Peter was about to ask if the bear had meant Dramamine, but the doors had closed. He guided Will down the hall, and unlocked Will's hotel room for him. Will took three steps into the room and collapsed face first on the bed, then let out a howl and turned over.

"I'll get some ice," Peter said. Will shook his head and beckoned Peter over with a finger. Peter leaned down next to Will and listened.

"You have to replace me in the contest," Will whispered.

"Why?" Peter asked. "Aren't there a bunch of runners-up already selected from the club? Why me?"

Will closed his eyes and smiled. "There's something special about you . . ." Then he coughed and sneezed, not a pretty sight. "Sasha's the only runner-up; he won't mind. He's been a runner-up for the last ten years. We call him the Susan Lucci of the GBG Bear Contest."

"I don't think that's a good idea," Jason said from the doorway.

"Come over and give me a hug," Will said. Jason went over to the bed and gingerly hugged his boyfriend, then glanced at Peter. "I don't think you should just come out of nowhere to compete in the contest. It wouldn't be fair to the others . . . like Sasha."

Will sneezed again. "Oh God, somebody get me some ice." He sniffed and looked at Peter. "Think it over."

Jason mouthed the words "drama queen" to Peter and took a condom out of the dresser drawer. "I'm going to get ice," he said, and went out into the hallway.

Peter sat down on the bed next to Will and spotted the telephone. If anyone would have an opinion on whether he should compete, it would be Ben. Ben had an opinion on everything. Peter reached for the receiver, then stopped.

In the late afternoon light, the pad of paper next to the telephone looked as if it had writing on it, but when Peter picked it up, it was blank. A trick of the light, he thought until he angled it sideways. Peter's eyes widened. It couldn't be.

He rummaged around in the night table drawer for a pencil and found one stuck into a Gideon Bible. Quickly rubbing the edge of the pencil over the notepad, Peter saw words appear in Jason's angular handwriting. Queermedia Group . . . then *Phag Magazine* . . . and Chester Valentine.

"How's our patient doing?" Jason said. Peter whirled around, dropping the pad and paper. Jason had filled the condom with ice, and he now placed it gently against Will's nose.

"Doing fine," Will snuffled. "And I'll be doing even better once Dan agrees to be in the contest."

Peter and Jason exchanged looks. Peter had thought he could read Jason, but he no longer knew what to believe. He guessed that if Jason didn't want him to participate, he probably had a sinister reason.

"All right," Peter said, patting Will on the shoulder. "I'll take your place in the contest."

−18−

When Peter woke up the next morning, his first thought was: Today's the Mr. GBG Bear Contest. His second thought was: I can't breathe. He was being smothered. He tried to cry out, but his mouth was pressed closed, as was his nose. He pushed against an incredible weight and finally managed to move it enough so that he could catch a few halting, ragged breaths.

Ben rolled over and looked at him sleepily. "Did my snoring keep you awake?"

Peter coughed and drew in great lungfuls of air. "You nearly suffocated me. Next time, sleep on your own side of the bed!"

Ben stretched out lazily, his torso and limbs covering more or less the entire bed, including Peter. "All right, all right," Peter said. "I get it. Next time we get a king-sized bed."

"I must've thought you were a little pillow while I was asleep," Ben said, grabbing at him and squeezing him between his hands. "Sort of like this."

"I'll remember to have them put that on the tombstone," Peter muttered, evading Ben's grasp and slipping out of bed. "Are you going to come down with me to breakfast?"

Ben yawned. "Last night tired me out. I was going to sleep in a bit."

Peter smiled and rubbed his butt fondly. Last night had tired him out, too. But he knew one thing that would get Ben out of bed. "You can smoke down there."

He'd never seen anyone move from zero to sixty that quickly. Ben leaped into the shower and started singing the theme music to *Freaky Friday*. Peter rolled his eyes. He contemplated joining Ben in the shower, then caught sight of himself in the mirrored closet doors. The contest!

When Ben came out of the shower, fur dripping and beard bristling with water droplets, Peter had been through both of their suitcases twice, and he still wasn't satisfied with what he was wearing.

"So?" he asked Ben. "What do you think?"

Peter sensed that Ben was trying to hide a smile. "You know how I feel about you," Ben said at last, "but it looks like you were caught in a Samsonite explosion."

Peter tugged at the leather straps angrily. "It's not my fault I don't look good in leather. What am I going to wear to the contest?"

Ben started to towel himself dry, which was quite an undertaking. "Dress like you always do. You're cute enough to win."

"I don't want to be cute," Peter said, stepping out of the leather gear. "I want to be *hot*."

Ben snapped the towel at Peter's butt, and Peter yelped. "Be yourself," Ben said. "Isn't that enough?"

Peter watched Ben go back into the bathroom to brush his teeth. "Ben," he said after a long pause, "I'm really . . ."

Ben poked his head out of the bathroom door. "What?"

"Really hungry for breakfast. Let's get a move on before all the food's gone."

He was a coward, that was all there was to it. On the rickety elevator down to the buffet, Peter leaned back against Ben, who held him in his arms.

"How long have you two been together?" asked a young bearpup who couldn't have been more than twenty-one.

"Uh, we're not together," Peter said, then turned to Ben. "Are we?"

The elevator shuddered, and Ben held Peter more tightly. "I guess we aren't. Are we?"

The bearpup turned to his boyfriend, who had a similar goatee, glasses, and nose ring. "It's so cute; it's like they've been together ten years." He grinned. "Sorry, you two seem so comfortable around each other."

"How long have you been together?" Peter managed as the elevator gave another jolt and came to rest on the ground floor, the overhead light flickering. Anything to change the subject, he thought.

"Three years now," the man said, and hugged his partner. "We met while a cop was giving me a ticket."

Peter, Ben, and the other bears poured out of the elevator. "You were speeding?" Peter asked.

The bearpup laughed. "No, I was DWB. Driving While Bear. You know, just like they stop black people in cars, they stop big, hairy, bearded men in denim. My husbear's a civil rights lawyer, and he saw what was happening."

He picked up his boyfriend and swung him around the lobby, with much hooting and hollering from the assembled bears. "It's nice . . ." Peter said to Ben. "And I don't think I ever felt so old."

"Time for breakfast," Ben said lightly, hands on Peter's shoulders.

They were serving eggs, bacon, pancakes, real maple syrup, waffles, and sausage links. Peter looked around vainly and finally spotted a fruit platter. What with the 1970s hotel decor and the retro breakfast menu, he was half-expecting Florence Henderson to come out of the kitchen when the swinging doors opened, but it was only a bear in a chef's hat carrying a tray of smoked salmon.

"Do you have anything a little less . . . fattening?" Peter asked the server as he laid the tray down next to three flavored syrups.

The man glared at him. "Honey, you came to the wrong event. Try one of those mints the housecleaning staff puts on your bed."

"My boyfriend ate them."

"Even better," the server said, and left with a flourish.

My boyfriend? Peter thought. He looked over at Ben, who'd piled his plate high and was talking to Mac, who seemed to have spent a fun night, judging by the two men on his arms. Well, they already were boyfriends in everything but name, weren't they? There was just that one pesky thing . . .

"Ben," Peter said, making up his mind and coming over to Mac and Ben and the others. "I need to talk to you for a second."

"We were trying to figure out where to go today," Ben said. "I want to go to the teddy bear factory."

"Ben figured you'd want to go to that boring new gay media museum that opened up," Mac said, miming a yawn.

Peter dragged Ben into a corner. "Listen, there's something I have to tell you."

Ben dabbed at a bit of scrambled eggs on his beard, and his eyes narrowed. "What is it, Dan?"

Peter cringed. If only he hadn't said *that* name. "I," he started, then just looked at Ben helplessly. "I . . ."

Ben brushed Peter's lips with his fingers. "If you can't say the words, you don't have to," Ben whispered. "I don't need to hear the words to know how you feel."

Peter's heart sank. All he had to say was one sentence, one sentence and it would be over. But looking into Ben's eyes, he couldn't. I'm damning myself, Peter thought. This is my last chance.

"I love you," Ben said quietly, then looked down at the ground shyly and broke into a smile. "I didn't think it would feel like this, when I finally could say it." He gave Peter a lingering kiss. "But I'm glad I did."

"Ben . . ." Peter could stutter.

"The words will come," Ben said, putting down his plate and holding Peter close. "Give it time, and you'll know exactly what to say." He grinned. "You're a writer, a natural-born one. The words will just flow."

Peter buried his head in Ben's neck so that Ben wouldn't see the expression on his face. "Do me a favor?" Peter asked at last.

"Anything."

His face composed, Peter met Ben's eyes. "Go to the teddy bear factory without me. I really want to see the gay media museum. And I'll see you this afternoon before the contest."

Ben nodded. "Not a problem."

They spent a few minutes looking for a free table, and finally a familiar bear waved them over. Will was in a wheelchair, sitting at a reasonably empty table.

"He looks like he was born into that thing," Ben whispered as they walked over, balancing their plates above the buzz cut heads of bears, otters, and cubs.

"It's the drama," Peter whispered back. "He loves it."

Even at this time of morning, the unusual heat was starting to penetrate the buffet room. Peter took off his plaid flannel jacket and put it with the others on a spare chair, while Will showed the wheelchair's features to Ben.

"It's only temporary, but I feel like that Man in Motion guy," Will said proudly. "Do you want to see me play basketball?"

"They didn't have grapefruits on the fruit platter," Peter said apologetically. Then he noticed an odd absence. "Where's Jason?"

A shadow crossed Will's expression so quickly that Peter might have thought he'd imagined it, if it weren't for Will's quick shrug.

"He had to go out and do something. He didn't tell me what." Will started cutting into his pancakes with quick strokes of the knife.

"Ben, did you try these pancakes?" Will said, not looking at Peter. "Have a bite."

You're lying to me, Peter thought in wonderment as he watched Will feed a wedge of pancakes to a bemused Ben. You and Jason are lying to me, and for the life of me, I don't know why.

"The following tour buses are leaving in ten minutes!" Canis Major's voice boomed out over the loudspeaker. "Tour bus One: Bathhouse tour of San Francisco. Please have your trick towels, lubricant, and condoms ready when you board. Tour bus Two: Teddy Bear Factory, bearaphernalia tour of Castro Street, and the Lone Star. Tour bus Three: Black bears, Asian bears, and longhaired bears tour of SF. Please proceed to the departure area."

"There are black and Asian bears?" Peter asked as Ben got to his feet.

"Even ones with long hair," Will said offhandedly. "I think it's a minibus."

Ben gave Peter a bone-crushing hug. "That's my cue. See you this afternoon?"

"You bet." Peter watched Ben's large body disappear into the crowd, then realized that Will was observing him. "What are you doing this morning?" Peter asked.

Will glanced over at where Ben had gone. "You shouldn't let him go," Will said suddenly. "Don't let it happen."

Peter was getting riled at the increasingly odd and inappropriate conversation. "Where did that come from?" he said, trying not to let his temper show.

Will looked more serious. "You guys had a hard time getting together, is all I'm saying. I don't want to see anything happen to you two."

Peter was taking his jacket off of the chair when the light dawned on him. "It was you—you were the one who set us up in the first place."

"Guilty as charged." Will beamed. "Now, are you mad at me?"

Peter held the jacket to his chest and thought of Ben. "No," he said. "No, I'm not." He ruffled Will's buzz cut. "Thanks."

In the lobby, Peter asked the harried concierge for a pad of paper and a pen. More than half of the notepaper was taken up with the Restwell logo and what looked suspiciously like a bear in the ivy scroll. Peter sat down in one of the overstuffed chairs and did his best to ignore the bear buzz around him as he took pen to paper.

"Dear Ben," he wrote.

> I think we only get one chance at happiness. Or maybe we were lucky—we seemed to get a few chances to make it work, and somehow we didn't screw up. Or at least you didn't.
> What do you see when you look at me? A bear, a cub, someone named Dan Karn? Now what do you see when I stand before you and slowly peel back that outer layer? Just a man underneath. A twink, even. Call me Peter Mallory.
> It was so easy to do it. That's how I thought at first. Gain a little weight, stop shaving, change your wardrobe, but stay the same person inside. Only I'm not, Ben. I'm not.
> Time for me to stop lying to you. I don't have to lie to myself anymore; somehow I managed to grow into the role I play. But I'm not "Dan." And I wonder, after you read this, what will you see when you look at me? A coward, a liar; that's how I feel. I can't even bring myself to tell you face to face. But if it's any consolation, Ben, it was me you spent those nights with, the man beneath that outer layer. Forgive me, Ben.

Peter chewed the end of the pen and blinked back tears. He had to do this *now*, while he still had the courage. He got up, struggled into his jacket, and took the stairs two at a time up to the third floor.

He placed the folded paper on Ben's night table, then ran a hand over one of Ben's large belts that was hanging over the headboard and smiled. "I love you," Peter said into the silence. Too late.

The Lesbigay Media Museum was located on the periphery of the Castro district, between the older buildings and the converted lofts of the high-tech district. The Queermedia Group was one of the major contributors to the LMM, and Peter wasn't surprised to see that most of the exhibits were flashy computer-based or videotaped demonstrations. At this time of day, the museum was nearly empty.

He paused before a video of the abortive "Q-Channel," then tried an interactive quiz ("Can you put this activist's head on the right body?") before he wandered over to the printed reference materials. Ah, this was what he'd come for.

Before he knew what he was doing, Peter had opened up the *P* filing cabinet. There they were—all of the years of *Phag Magazine*, neatly laid out in pristine condition. Why did I come here? he asked himself, pulling out an old copy and looking at a story he'd written. Was it to remember what he'd once been, or to say goodbye to it for good?

He flipped through the issues chronologically, going backward through circuit parties, lesbian chic, and ACT UP, until he came to Vol. 1, #2. But where was the first *Phag* magazine, the one that had started it all?

"Can I help you?" a perky young woman with a severe red haircut asked, materializing at his elbow.

"I was looking for the very first issue," Peter said.

She was probably a refugee from the high-tech downsizing, Peter thought as he watched her. He could almost hear a voice in her mind saying "processing." After a moment she stopped and nodded. "Somebody took it. It's still in the museum, though—we have a security system. Just take a look around the reading room and you'll find it." The woman disappeared as quietly as she'd appeared.

The reading room was deserted, except for high-backed leather chairs. A stack of magazines lay on a modern low oak table, and the second one in the pile was the first issue of *Phag* (the headline read: "A Cure For AIDS?"). Peter smiled and reached for it.

The leather chair nearest to him swiveled around. "I was reading those magazines," Chester Valentine said snappishly. Then his eyes focused on Peter's face, and Peter watched confusion, bewilderment, and finally recognition and understanding pass over Chester's face.

"Hello, Peter," Chester said, folding his arms elegantly. "What a long, strange journey it's been."

– 19 –

Peter recoiled as if he'd been bitten by a snake. "Oh, do sit down," Chester said, pointing to a seat across the table. "It's been far too long, and we do have a few things to discuss."

Peter considered his options. There were only hours before the Queermedia Annual General Meeting, and if he had anything to learn from Chester, now was the time. He sat down reluctantly, shrugging his arms in the uncomfortable plaid flannel jacket.

Chester noticed it too. "Oh dear, what on earth possessed you to wear that white-trash dinner jacket?" he asked. When Peter said nothing, Chester snapped his fingers. "Oh yes, the *bears* are in town. It's their Global Bear Rendezvous, isn't it?"

"Global Bear Gathering," Peter allowed.

Chester nodded. "Well, I have to hand it to you, dear boy. You always were one for spotting the trends. The bears are the next big thing . . . for now."

Peter heard the front door to the museum open in the distance. "Are they?" he asked lightly. "That would explain why you've been trying to buy up Bear Essentials from Will Goldman these past few months."

Chester registered surprise, but only for a moment before his smooth exterior slipped back into place. "Yes, we were interested at one point, but not anymore. You've been doing your homework . . . one way or another."

Peter wondered about Will and Jason for a brief moment, but his mind raced on to other subjects. Chester didn't know about Peter's undercover work at *Phag,* Peter thought, or else he'd simply have had him arrested.

"You're going to launch some kind of new bear-related Internet thing at tonight's meeting, aren't you?" he said triumphantly. "Well, I can tell you, co-opting the bear community won't work."

In the distance, Peter heard a man's voice, and then the perky woman's voice reply. Chester chuckled. "You were always one to follow the trends, but the wrong *kind* of trends. The day-to-day trends are one thing, but to run a magazine company, you need to focus on the larger picture. Bears are a micro-trend." Chester seemed on the verge of saying more, but fell silent, watching Peter through narrowed eyes.

It sounded as if the man and the perky woman were getting into an argument on the far side of the oak bookcases.

"I'm waiting," Peter said. "Isn't this where you reveal your evil mastermind plan for conquering the world?"

Chester spoke at last. "True visionaries are never appreciated in their time. And I suppose you would think I'm evil. The vast majority of writers have been trained to see things as diametric opposites; that's what sells!" He lowered his voice. "But not anymore. You see, Peter, you've lost."

Peter felt anger course through his body. He balled up his fists to avoid banging them on the table and thrust them into his jacket pockets. Then he realized something.

"They're not going to call you writers much longer," Chester went on in that silky voice Peter remembered too well. "With the Internet, what you produce is now being called content. That's how I like to think of it—a sort of pie filling, that gets squeezed as needed between the crusts of the magazines, or Web sites, or whatever *Phag* is going to produce. Do you know what the crusts are?"

"Advertising?" Peter said reluctantly.

"There! You're not so slow after all," Chester said. "I used to think it was all about providing compelling writing—compelling *content.* It turns out that we don't have to do that anymore." He flipped through the stack of magazines. "Let me show you something."

Chester tossed an exercise magazine with an oiled-up, straight-acting and -appearing buffed model on the cover: *Exercise for Men's Men*—a Queermedia Group publication. Peter groaned. "Not that old piece of trash," he said, not touching the magazine. "I didn't realize they still printed it."

"They don't," Chester said, pointing to various parts of the cover with the precision of a surgeon. "It's all online now. 'Eight Ways to Thinner Thighs' . . . 'Five Diet Tips for Spring' . . . 'Six Ab Exercises for the New You.'" Chester tossed the magazine back on the pile.

"There are only so many stories to cover. My mistake was in believing we had to be *out there,* controversial, innovative."

"People won't buy the same crap over and over," Peter replied angrily.

"Do you remember the two covers we had a few years back?" Chester asked, almost regretfully. "One was a photograph of Urvashi Vaid, the other was of Marky Mark. Do you want to guess which one sold three times the amount of magazines?"

"Readers will always go for quality." Despite himself, Peter started getting into the argument. "You can only pander to the lowest common denominator for so long."

The man and the perky woman were definitely fighting in hushed voices at this point. Chester shook his head. "Queermedia Group made their success by pandering to the lowest common denominator, didn't they?"

The light finally came on in Peter's mind. "Queermedia's going to turn *Phag Magazine* into a carbon copy of all their other crappy magazines!"

Chester rolled his eyes. "Oh, the extra fat must be slowing down your thought processes, my dear boy. Of course they are; it's been in the works for months. *Phag* and Queermedia are going to pander to every denominator, just in different ways. The lower-income gay men will buy the trashy, wretched Queermedia magazines—oh, let's not even call them magazines any more—the *content*—for the beefcake. The higher-income gay men will read articles under the prestigious *Phag* imprint—daring, modern articles, but not *too* daring. The type Ted Dennison writes. We don't want to offend their sensibilities or their bank account. Queermedia will give us enough latitude to prop up their poorly done rags. *Phag* will lend them the sophistication they so desperately need."

"And the activists? The rebels?" Peter tried to look between the bookcases to see what was going on, but Chester was blocking his view. Finally, the front door slammed, and the museum fell silent.

"They don't buy Ford Tauruses, now do they?" Chester checked his Rolex. "It's time for me to leave, Peter. I have an Annual General Meeting to attend." He got to his feet. "Don't bother trying to crash it, either. The security guards will be alerted."

Peter just shook his head and grinned. "It all makes such perfect sense when you explain it. Until you start thinking about ethics and morality."

"Goodbye, Peter." Chester looked at him almost fondly. "Give my regards to the bears." He turned on his feet and left.

When Chester had gone, Peter felt his grin continue to spread. That morning, at the buffet, he hadn't taken his jacket, he'd taken Will's. And what Chester didn't realize was what Will always carried with him.

Peter took the pencorder out of his jacket pocket and pressed "Rewind" for a few seconds, then "Play." "Trashy, wretched Queermedia magazines," Chester's voice said tinnily. Peter pressed the buttons again. "Queermedia will give us enough latitude to prop up their poorly done rags. *Phag* will lend them the sophistication they so desperately need—need—need." Chester sounded like Max Headroom.

Peter pointed the pencorder in the direction that Chester had taken. Gotcha!

Now all he had to do was ace the Mr. GBG bear contest, crash the Queermedia Annual General Meeting, and something else . . . something else. What was it?

In his mind's eye he saw San Francisco zoom past as if he was on a cable car on speed, whirling down streets until he came to the Restwell Hotel, then zipping up three flights of stairs and into the hotel room, where a neatly folded note lay on a bed.

Peter leaped to his feet. No, he couldn't let Ben discover that note. It was the coward's way out. If he was going to tell him, he'd tell him in person.

The hotel was in pandemonium; bears milled about giving odds on who Mr. GBG Bear was going to be, while others were buying programs and evaluating the bear contest merchandise (you could stand in front of a cardboard cutout of Carl Hardwick and have a photo taken for $10).

Peter was about to head for the elevator when another thought struck him. If he had Will's jacket. . . . He searched all of the pockets. No, of course Will had his hotel room pass.

Peter stepped up to the front desk and rang the bell repeatedly. "Service?" he yelled. "Little help?"

"Honey," a passing bear said, "they're all busy setting up for the contest. You probably should go slip into your posing jockstrap."

Peter turned around and saw Ben disappear into the elevator. Dammit! Peter raced through the crowd and sprinted up the three flights of stairs, barely making it to the door of their hotel room before the elevator door creakily opened and dislodged Ben.

Peter leaned against the door, wheezing and trying to act casual. He was trying to come up with a clever excuse when he knew that it had to end—the lying, the deception, all of it. He knew what he had to say.

"Ben," Peter said, drawing a deep breath. "There's something about me that you have to know."

Ben looked at him evenly for a long moment. "What is it . . . Peter?"

– 20 –

"When did you find out?" Peter asked Ben, who was fumbling with the door pass. "How long did you know?"

Ben opened the door and went into the room. He sat down on the bed and took out a pack of cigarettes. He wouldn't even look at Peter.

"Does it really matter?" he asked, tapping a cigarette out of the pack and stuffing it between his lips. "I should've figured it out a long, long time ago."

Peter saw that the note was still on Ben's nighttable, neatly folded. He coughed as the smoke from Ben's cigarette reached him.

"Would you at least not smoke in the room?" he asked, then immediately regretted having said it.

Ben got up and brushed past him, back out into the hallway. Peter gave the note one last glance, then followed Ben and closed the door behind him. In the warm hallway, Ben was pacing back and forth, stopping only occasionally to toss an ash out of the open window.

"The teddy bear factory tour got cut short," Ben said finally, continuing to pace and puff furiously. "Seems like one of the cubs didn't realize that not all the teddy bears get past the inspector, and he freaked out when he saw the rejection pile." More puffs. "Things didn't go so well after that."

Peter tried to stifle a smile, but Ben shot him a glance that easily stifled it for him. "So I came to see what you—what *Dan*—was up to at the media museum." Ben shook his head, and tossed the butt out the window. "I figured I'd surprise you, but what did I know."

Ben punched the "Down" button to summon the elevator, then punched it a few more times for good measure. There was another grinding noise from the elevator shaft, and the doors creaked open. Peter had no choice but to follow Ben into the empty elevator. Ben pressed the "L" button.

"So I went to the woman who was hosting the exhibit, and I asked her if she'd seen a bear matching your description," Ben said, staring at the wall. "She didn't exactly know where you were in the museum, but she showed me what you'd been looking at."

"That was you, arguing with her," Peter said, the realization dawning.

Ben shrugged. "I started flipping through the *Phag* magazines, and I saw a picture of you . . . of Peter Mallory. I thought it was some kind of trick, or practical joke."

The elevator jerked and shuddered. Peter felt himself flung against the wall, followed by Ben crushing against him. The light went out, replaced by weak emergency lighting.

"That's just great," Ben said.

Peter straightened up and pressed the "Emergency Call" button, which had no effect. "Do you want to hear my side of the story?" he asked quietly. "Or are you going to walk out of the hotel for good?"

"My luggage is still in the hotel room, you idiot." Ben folded his arms and leaned against the opposing wall of the elevator. "I don't want to hear any more from you at this point. Just shut up."

"I lost my job," Peter said. When Ben didn't reply, he gathered more courage and went on. "And then I decided to write a book, about bears and the bear community. Mac helped turn me into a bear so I could go undercover. And then I met you, but by that time it was too late." He looked at Ben helplessly. "Every time I meant to tell you, I couldn't. It never seemed like there was a right time. Kind of like coming out of the closet to someone after you've known them for years."

Ben said nothing, just bristled in the semidarkness. Come on, Peter thought. You're a writer—convince him. Tell him you were right, that it's not the worst thing in the world. That your relationship can survive this. Say something. Say anything.

Then Peter looked at the pain in Ben's eyes, and he knew there was nothing he could say. "You're right," Peter said simply.

"What?" Ben asked.

"You're right. What I did was inexcusable. I don't expect you to forgive me." Peter started pressing the "Emergency Call" button himself, then turned back to Ben. "I always thought that when this moment came, I'd know the right thing to say. That I could somehow make you forgive me." He sighed. "I'm sorry, Ben."

Ben was silent for a moment. "I'm glad you said it," Ben said at last. "But you can't base a relationship on a deception."

"No," Peter said. Then, grasping at straws, he added, "Listen. Will you at least wait for me until tonight?" Maybe, he thought, once he'd had a chance to intervene at Queermedia's Annual General Meeting, he could explain to Ben what he'd been fighting for.

"The bear contest," Ben said, shaking his head. "I should've known. It's not enough for you to infiltrate our community, is it?" He laughed. "Okay, go win the contest. I'm taking the 8:30 p.m. flight out of here, with or without you."

"That's not why—" The elevator suddenly lurched and creaked, and the light flickered back up to full strength. The doors slid partly open to reveal that they were between two floors: above them were hairy calves and hiking boots, and below them buzz cuts and flattops. The elevator doors closed and Peter and Ben felt the elevator drop a floor. The doors opened fully this time, and Ben walked out without a look back.

"Ben . . ." Peter said, but he was gone. Peter stood in the lobby watching the bears go by, feeling utterly alone. Too late, he thought. Too late.

"Where the hell have you been?" Mac said, yanking him to one side. "You should be getting ready for the bear contest!" Will was next to Mac in his wheelchair, nodding. "Did you forget you have a contest to participate in?"

Peter took a last glance into the crowd. "No, I hadn't forgotten." He checked his watch. It was already 5:45 p.m. The contest started at 6:00 p.m., and the Annual General Meeting had its public forum starting at 7:30 p.m. It was going to be close.

"How long do these bear contests run, anyway?" he asked as Mac and Will dragged him off toward the conference room. "They don't usually run late, do they?"

Will chuckled. "The sooner we can get you into a jockstrap, the sooner the contest can get started."

"Jockstrap?"

There were nine other contestants waiting backstage, primping in front of full-length mirrors and tugging at their costumes. "Oh God," one of the bears wailed, "I can't fit into my leather tuxedo, and we're going to go on in ten minutes!" His manager was trying to console him and was tugging on the recalcitrant pants at the same time.

"I am not wearing a leather jockstrap," Peter said when he saw what Mac had for him. He held it up and peered at it. "And where's the front?"

"It's a big stage," Mac explained patiently, unhooking Peter's 501s with practiced hands. "If you don't have something to differentiate you from the others, you won't get noticed. Do you have any Vaseline?"

Peter batted Mac's hands away and changed into the jockstrap himself. "I'm afraid to ask why I need Vaseline."

Will rolled over with a tub of the stuff and drew out a finger coated with it. "For your teeth. Makes them gleam in the stage lighting."

"Next you're going to tell me there's a talent show."

Mac and Will exchanged glances. "You did prepare something for the talent show, didn't you?" Will asked, aghast.

"That's it," Peter said, grabbing his jacket from the back of a chair. "You can find someone else to go on; I'm leaving."

Mac shook his head. "Your name's already in the program. You *can't* leave, or our bear club forfeits."

Peter dug his fingers into the tub of Vaseline and rubbed them over his teeth. It was 5:56 p.m. "All right, I'm ready for my close-up now. Let's get this show on the road."

A synthesizer drum roll started the proceedings at 6:10 p.m., and Peter watched through a cutout in the curtain as Canis Major, resplendent in a plaid tux, strode out onto the darkened stage and propped himself onto a stool with a drink to thunderous applause. "A funny trick happened to me on the way to the bear contest . . ." Canis started, and Peter groaned. That was all he needed—a long-winded announcer.

Canis proceeded through the long, dull joke, which was punctuated by whoops from the audience every time Canis said the word "bear." Peter gave up looking through the cutout and gave the view over to the bear beside him, the one who'd been unable to fit into his leather pants.

"Don't get so cozy up front here," the bear said offhandedly to Peter as he bent down to look through the hole. "I've got this contest sewn up. I'm going to be the one out there wearing the GBG sash."

"Sure," Peter muttered, going to get a Vaseline refresher. "If you can fit into the sash."

"I heard that!"

"And now," Canis said once the joke was over, "let's start the festivities with a visit from our very own . . . Solid Gold GBG Dancers!"

Peter groaned. He couldn't get a view of what was happening on the stage, but the arrhythmic stomping and woofing (with the occasional yelp) were evidence enough. Canis Major came backstage a moment later, wiping his brow with a bandanna. "Somebody get me an iced tea!" he bellowed. "Stat!"

Peter sidled up to Canis. "Hi there," he said. Canis just looked at him. "You don't know me, but I have a favor to ask you," Peter pressed on.

"Dear," Canis sighed, "it's far too late for that. You should've signed up on the blow job sheet last night." He eyed Peter. "Maybe you could be a fluffer on my new movie shoot. No, I think your mouth's a bit too small."

Peter gritted his teeth. "I was hoping you could hurry things up . . . you know, we're already about fifteen minutes behind schedule."

Canis raised both eyebrows. "Oh my. I didn't realize we were inconveniencing you. Well, let me remedy that *tout suite*."

He disappeared into the curtains. "Now you've done it," the leatherbear whispered, horrified. "Nobody offends Canis Major."

At this point, Peter didn't much care. He'd managed to offend Sasha, Chester, Ben, and various others in the past few months. What was another bearporn director?

The Solid Gold GBG dance music screeched to a halt, and Peter heard several thuds as random dancing bears crashed into each other.

"It seems," Canis said from the stage, "that some of our contestants want to get this contest over . . . that they have better things to do. Well, I'm all for it. Let's bring out contestant number one. Dan Karn!"

The leatherbear looked at the number on the adhesive label on his chest. "I'm number one!" he said, hopping up and down in anger. "Not you! I'm number one!"

Peter reached over and ripped the number off of the leatherbear's hairy chest with one long r-i-i-i-i-p, then replaced it with his own.

"Bye!" Peter waved, then parted the curtains and stepped out onto the stage, to scattered applause.

"Dan here wanted me to hurry up with the show," Canis explained to the crowd. "Now, Dan, what could possibly prompt you to want to get away from the contest? Have some tricks lined up?"

"No, I was going to go to a comedy club. You know, where I could hear some funny jokes."

A few people in the audience chuckled, and Canis glared at Peter. "Well, then, what can you say is your most outstanding quality?" Canis looked at Peter appraisingly. "Not what's in your jockstrap, I'm sure."

"Getting paid thousands of dollars to point cameras at naked bears having sex, and getting paid thousands more for scripts that basically say Lather, Woof, Repeat?" Peter asked. "No, wait. That's you." More laughter from the crowd. Peter felt encouraged.

Canis was clearly not amused. "I come here to dispense the humor, not receive it," he said. "You're the half-naked contestant, not me."

"Thank God!" Peter said, clapping his hand to his head in mock alarm. "I don't think they have an iron backstage."

"I think it's time we turn to the talent part of the competition," Canis announced, changing the subject. "Now, of course you're not going to stand here and tell bad jokes, are you Dan?"

"No," Peter said, going over to the bear behind the synthesizer. "That's your job, Canis." Peter whispered in the keyboard player's ear, and the man nodded. "Can someone toss me a cane?"

Canis looked like he was about to toss his chair at Peter, but then a cane came flying out of the audience and clattered onto the stage. Peter recognized Will's smiling, encouraging face and smiled himself. He picked up the cane and nodded at the keyboard player. "Maestro . . . ?"

It had been the only song he could think of, and he would have to alter the lyrics off the top of his head, but things couldn't go much more wrong . . . Peter cleared his throat as the opening lilting chords played. Then, with a Maurice Chevalier accent, Peter began to sing:

> Each time I see a little cub
> Of twenty-five, twenty-six, or twenty-seven
> I can't resist a joyous urge
> To smile and say . . .

Thank heaven for little cubs
For little cubs get more fur every day
Thank heaven for little cubs
They fill out in the most delightful way
Those little nips so tiny and appealing
One day will swell and send you crashing through the ceiling
Thank heaven for little cubs
Thank heaven for them all, no matter where, no matter who
Without them what would bigger bears do?

It's working, Peter thought! At first the audience was just dumbstruck, but soon they started to clap along. I might even win this thing, he thought.

Then the lights and sound system went out. At first Peter thought it was a power failure, but then a single spotlight illuminated him in the dark. Peter shielded his eyes against the brilliance with a hand, but then another, more diffuse light fell upon him.

Something made him turn around. Projected as a hundred-foot image on the backdrop behind him, Peter saw an image of him from *Phag Magazine* next to an image of him taken at the last beer bust. The resemblance was unmistakable. He tried to figure who had done this. Not Ben, he'd never. . . . Then he knew.

Sasha's voice boomed out of the sound system. "You might be interested to know that this man, this GBG Bear contestant, isn't Dan Karn. He's a fraud." The audience started to mutter. "A journalist, come to spy on us. And what's worse," Sasha said with sanctimonious pleasure, "he's a *twink!*"

Nearly everyone in the audience gasped. Peter looked around like a cornered animal and tried to cover his leather jockstrap with his hands. "Uhh," he said. "Anyone want to hear the rest of the song?"

– 21 –

"You know," Peter said, glancing back and forth nervously between the overhead projection and the increasingly surly crowd, "there's a perfectly logical explanation for all of this."

"Get off the stage, you asshole!" some wag in one of the back rows yelled. "Let's get the real bears out here!"

"Hey!" Peter said, offended. "I'm a real bear, just like you." Although the crowd was getting restless, he found it reassuring that nobody had been moved to violence yet. "Take a look at this chest hair. If you shave me, do I not shed?"

A veal cutlet came sailing through the air from out of the crowd and smacked against the backdrop between the projected Peter's eyes. "Real bears are polite," Peter said huffily, "and real bears don't throw their dinner—"

An entire centerpiece flew at him, and Peter ducked as it crashed into the stage. "That wasn't dinner!" someone else yelled. Other bears shouted their agreement.

A hand suddenly grabbed Peter from behind and yanked him through the curtains backstage. Mac dusted bits of veal off of Peter's shaking body.

"What, all of a sudden you're a martyr?" Mac said, rolling his eyes. "You'd better get out of here before they swarm the stage."

Peter took his plaid jacket off of a chair. "At least there weren't any photographers out there. Were there?" He shook Mac by the shoulders. "Tell me there weren't any bear magazine photographers."

Will rolled up and shook his head. "They're banned from GBG Bear contests. Something happened a few years ago with a blind contestant and a few dozen roses. . . . Now they have to wait outside the hotel until Canis Major starts singing 'There He Goes, Mr. GBG.'" He gathered his thoughts visibly. "Just get out of here. I think you're about to have a bear posse on your heels."

Peter looked at his watch and nodded. 7:10 p.m. He was going to be late for the Queermedia Annual General Meeting if he didn't hurry. He thrust his hands in the jacket pockets to make sure he still had the pencorder, then turned to go. Peter hesitated.

"The meeting . . ." Mac said with meaning in his voice.

Peter turned back. "Ben," he asked. "Did you see him?"

Will shook his head and handed him his hotel pass. Mac put a hand on Peter's shoulder. "It's time to *go*," Mac said.

Peter went. Remembering the way the elevator had stopped, he decided to take the stairs. The lobby was oddly silent, but the random thumping and cheers from the ballroom made Peter realize that the contest was probably still on. Thank God for small mercies, he thought—with a plaid jacket and a latex jockstrap, he wasn't exactly the most inconspicuous target.

He ran up the stairs as fast as he could, but still found himself out of breath by the time he reached the third floor. Panting and gasping, Peter leaned against the wall outside of his hotel room, fumbling for the door pass. Even with all of his focus concentrated on opening the door and what he had to do to get to the Queermedia AGM, Peter heard the elevator doors slide open.

"Room for one more!" Sasha said cheerily.

"Oh God," Peter groaned, fiddling with the door pass; it seemed to be warped. "Can't an anvil just fall on you or something?"

Sasha stood in the opening to the elevator, arms holding the doors open. "Dear, I had to come and gloat. There's no fun in putting a plan in place unless you get to witness the consequences firsthand."

Peter gave up trying to jam the pass into the door's sensor and started trying to unbend it. "Fine," he said, distracted. "You won, I lost. Seems to be happening a lot to me. Now can you leave me the hell alone?"

Sasha grinned. "I feel all fuzzy and cuddly all over. I don't usually get to feel so self-satisfied." He pushed at the doors as they started to close. "It's like being able to rub your own tummy for a change."

"You *can* rub your own tummy, any time you want," Peter said.

Sasha glared at him. "Don't contradict me!" Then, in the same silky tone as before, he went on. "You're never going to be allowed into another bear club or beer bust in the country, you know. The photographers will be waiting for Dan Karn outside, and your face will be plastered all over every bear magazine from here to Tacoma."

"And if I take the back exit?"

"That's why I took the elevator," Sasha said, grinning like a Cheshire cat. At that moment the elevator groaned, and Sasha pushed against the doors again to keep them from closing. The floor lights above the doors started to flash alarmingly.

"Sasha, the elevator . . ." Peter warned.

"I think the best part was when I sabotaged your computer article," Sasha mused, pushing harder on the doors.

"Sasha, you're going to fall . . ." Peter said.

"If anyone's going to fall, *Dan,* it's going to be you." The elevator creaked and groaned like a cheap motel bed under bear pressure.

"Oh God," Peter sighed, "do I have to do everything myself?" For one second he considered doing nothing; then he sprinted forward and yanked Sasha out of the elevator. The doors slammed shut behind them. With a final screech the elevator plunged downwards. Peter watched with hideous fascination as the lights flashed 2, 1, and then L before the air was split with a horrible crash, followed by the alarmed sounds of bears below.

"You idiot!" Sasha yelled, holding up the sleeve of his plaid jacket. "You ripped it!"

Peter looked at the man disbelievingly. "Excuse me?"

"It was cashmere—brand new! And you ruined it!"

Peter started to feel his brain turn to mush. "I just saved you from an elevator crash," he muttered.

"Oh please," Sasha said dismissively. "Nobody ever died from a three-story fall."

"That's it!" Peter said, stepping forward. "Go to hell!" Sasha slapped him, and almost in shock, Peter slapped Sasha back, harder. Sasha slapped him again, and soon they were hitting each other like seals at the circus. Peter felt rage envelop his mind. There was nothing more he could do; he lost control.

With all his strength, Peter shoved Sasha as hard as he could. Sasha gave him a surprised look and a little "O" of his mouth as he stumbled backward. Then he shrieked as he toppled out of the open window. A few seconds later there was an ominous plop.

Oh my God, Peter thought. I've committed bearicide. He raced over to the window. What seemed like a million flashbulbs went off at once, illuminating the front of the hotel. Sasha had landed in the middle of the mud pit, and now all of the bear magazine photographers finally had something to shoot. "My cashmere jacket!" Peter heard Sasha yell. "It's ruined! What a world, what a world . . ."

Peter stepped away from the window, shaking. He supposed he should feel mildly guilty, but then again . . . "Nobody ever died from a three-story fall," he said, and returned to his hotel room door. This time the pass worked. There was no time to waste; he was onto the next crisis.

He quickly changed into a shirt and jeans, and put Ben's baseball cap on his head. Then, slipping into his plaid jacket, Peter headed down the stairs in search of a cab.

While most bears were still at the contest, some were examining the smoking wreckage of the elevator car and talking amongst themselves in hushed tones. Peter was afraid of being discovered, but he soon realized that with the baseball cap and his bear apparel, he had nothing to worry about.

"Did you see what happened?" one of the bears asked him. It was the same one who had thrown the veal cutlet earlier.

"Yeah," Peter said in a gruff voice. "I heard Dan Karn was in that crash. He was all bloody and ripped up."

The bear looked at him with wide eyes and hurried off. Then Peter had another idea. He walked over to another knot of bears and looked over his shoulder at the elevator wreckage. "That guy who was in the bear contest?" he said without being prompted. "The twink? I think he was in that elevator. Wouldn't that be awful? I mean, even though he's a twink?"

A few more comments like this, and Peter was on his way out the service entrance to the hotel. As he left, he heard the name Dan Karn being whispered over and over like a mantra. With any luck, Peter thought, most bears would end up thinking it had happened. The first urbear legend.

By the time Peter found a cab, it was 7:35. By the time it approached the Moscone Center, it was 7:45. He fidgeted nervously in the backseat of the cab; public comments would only be allowed until 8:00 p.m., and Peter still didn't know how he was going to sneak in.

The front of the Center was lit up with roving purple searchlights, and the sign announced "QUEERMEDIA ANNUAL GENERAL MEETING; Phag Bash at 9:00 p.m." Peter got out of the cab, paid, and stared at the entrance. Two burly security guards were checking latecomers' identification against a list.

He took another look at the sign. "How utterly tacky," he couldn't resist from saying.

"Honey, you are so right," a somewhat masculine voice said beside him. "Now what are you doing so far from the Restwell Inn? You look a bit out of your element, in a woofy way."

The voice belonged to the young bearpup Peter had seen in the elevator with his partner the other day. He was grinning behind his goatee, and wearing a white suit with a black tie, with a name tag reading "Scott."

Peter beamed. "This is perfect!" he exclaimed. "Okay, tell me you're a waiter and you're working this event. Then tell me you can sneak me in somehow."

Scott looked at Peter. "Wrong, dear."

Peter's shoulders slumped. "Okay, then at least tell me why you're wearing that name tag."

Scott puffed out his chest proudly. "I'm a *server.* Now, do you think you can fit under a serving cart?"

It was a tight fit, but after sleeping in the same bed as Ben, Peter was used to making the most of small spaces. He was lying on his back in the bottom of the serving cart, with his knees hunched up against his chest, his head bent forward, and his arms crossed around his legs. Scott draped the cart with a linen, then poked his head in. "One last look—you sure you want to do this?"

"Yes," Peter managed, looking at his watch. 7:52 p.m.

"Just don't have any of the dessert. This is the chocolate tray." Peter felt the cart begin to move.

"Can you pass me a truffle?" Peter asked, and reached his hand out of the linen.

He felt Scott slap his hand. "Wait for the next cart!"

From his weird vantage point, Peter heard the doors to the conference room open and a wave of sound wash over him. "As General Manager of the *Phag Magazine* subsidiary, I want to assure the shareholder who asked the question that *Phag* is committed to social equity," Chester was saying on a loudspeaker. "As a matter of fact, part of the proceeds of every copy of *Phag Magazine* go to a gay-owned and operated charity."

"Valentine's Kids," Peter muttered darkly from inside the serving cart.

"Did you say something?" a woman said next to the cart.

"No," Scott said grimly, and Peter got a sudden not-too-gentle kick. "Honestly," Scott hissed as they continued moving through the conference hall, "this is the last time I help a total stranger break the law."

"Which brings us to our last question," Chester said over the loudspeaker. "We still have the reelection"—he chuckled—"make that *election* of the Queermedia board to contend with, and of course you're all invited to the Phag Bash after the meeting concludes." Chester paused. "Any questions? Anyone?"

Peter burst out of the serving cart, sending chocolate showering over the shareholders at a nearby table. "Sorry," he said, then ran over to one of the empty standing microphones. "I have a question," he said into the microphone, his voice booming through the hall.

"Security, please remove this man," Chester said tiredly.

"I'm a shareholder," Peter said. "I have a right to be here, and I want to ask my question."

"Oh, let him ask the question already," Scott said. "The coffee service is delayed."

Peter took a deep breath and grasped the pencorder in his jacket pocket. Everything these past few months, everything in his life had led up to this moment. He knew exactly what he had to do. Peter whipped the pencorder out of his pocket and held it up to the microphone, pressing the button on the side.

Then he realized that he hadn't taken the pencorder. Instead of Will's jacket, he'd somehow managed to take Mac's. And Mac didn't own a pencorder.

"Woof! Woof! Woof!" the talking black leather dildo in his hand said into the microphone, to the dozens of shareholders. "Woof! Woof! Woof!"

– 22 –

There was a very long moment of silence as the woofs echoed away into nothingness. Peter leaned over to an elderly gentleman at the table next to him. "Do you ever have one of those days," Peter asked, "where nothing goes your way?"

The elderly man nodded vigorously. "I'm still waiting for my coffee!"

Chester's voice boomed out over the audience. "If our esteemed shareholder has finished with his comments, I think we can declare the question period closed."

Then Peter noticed a commotion at one end of the conference hall. An unlikely pair was making its way past the seated shareholders, only steps ahead of three security guards. Jason was pushing Will in the wheelchair, but when he spotted Peter, he tossed something at him and yelled "Peter, catch!"

The pencorder flew at Peter as if in slow motion, turning slowly end over end as it approached. Peter tried to duck, but it hit him square on the forehead and bounced off. He was about to give up when a long delicate hand reached out and held the pencorder up to him.

"They can butch you up," Caliph observed in a whisper, "but they can't make you a good catcher, can they?" Peter smiled and nodded in thanks. Caliph, who was wearing a stunning off-the-shoulder red dress, sat back down. Two security guards approached Peter, one from each side, but he held the pencorder up like a cross, warding them off.

"Chester's right," Peter said into the microphone. "I am a shareholder. And I still have five minutes left to say my piece."

He glanced around the conference room. "I've got a lot to say, but there's someone else who can say it for me even better." Peter pressed the button on the pencorder. "They're not going to call you writers much longer," Chester's voice said tinnily from the pencorder.

191

Peter watched Chester intently. When he first heard his own words repeated back to him, Chester blanched. Then he asked a few questions of the man sitting next to him (who Peter recognized as the CEO of Queermedia Group). Finally, as the recording came to a close, Chester sat stiffly in his chair, arms folded, looking at Peter and the pencorder. But was that the hint of a smile that was playing around the corners of his mouth?

"Goodbye, Peter," Chester's recorded voice said. "Give my regards to the bears." The pencorder shut off with a click. Peter surveyed the audience; most of them seemed to be still trying to take it all in.

"Are you quite finished?" Chester asked mildly.

Peter looked around again, expecting some kind of uproar. "Well, I guess I am," he said uncertainly. Then, to the audience: "Aren't any of you concerned about this?"

As he spoke his last few words, Peter heard his voice suddenly become much smaller; someone had turned his microphone off. "I'm going to comment on this very briefly," Chester said, "because I don't want this nonsense leaving a bad taste in our mouths as we press forward." He got to his feet and paced in front of the microphone before composing himself and starting to speak.

"Writing and media in the twentieth century," Chester began, "will be remembered much as cabinetry was in the nineteenth century. The vast majority of us don't have furniture made for us; we buy it mass-produced at stores. Mass production for mass consumption is a fact of life—and writing is going to be less and less a hand-tooled affair as we go on."

A young man dressed all in black stood up at a neighboring table. "But there are people who do buy quality handcrafted furniture," he said loudly. "And let's not forget all the people out there who would buy it if it was widely available at a reasonable price."

Aha, Peter thought—Chester was about to be hoisted by his own metaphorical petard.

"Are you suggesting that the *Phag* subsidiary should pander to the lowest common denominator?" asked a middle-aged woman in a sequined dress from the other side of the large room. "Surely there's enough of that out there already, even in the gay community. *Phag* used to be known as a high-quality media property."

"And if there's anything the high-tech industry's taught us," Jason piped up in his baritone, "is that you can't compete on price alone. You also have to give your customers quality." He winked at Peter.

"That's all very nice from an ivory tower perspective," Chester said slowly. Then, looking at the clock, he hurried up. "But the question period is over. I suggest we move on to new business."

Peter noticed that Will was rolling himself over to him, while the protests in the room started to bubble up from muted whispers to an angry buzz.

"Yes," Jason said, commandeering another microphone. "That's really a good idea. And that's why I'm here." He looked at Chester. "Are you familiar with Bylaw 47-B3?"

Chester looked blank, then bent down and whispered to his lawyer. A moment later he was at the microphone, shaking his head. "That doesn't apply anymore," he said confidently.

Jason shook his head. "No, actually it does. You just forgot to have it taken off the books when Queermedia acquired you. I checked the regulations—it carries forward and now it applies to Queermedia too." He looked around the audience. "What Bylaw 47-B3 means, folks, is that anyone can bring forward a proposal for a divestiture of any part of Queermedia Group at any Annual General Meeting . . . without prior notice. I'm proposing that Queermedia divest itself of *Phag Magazine*—and I'm willing to buy it at a significant premium."

Chester rolled his eyes. "We haven't used that bylaw in years. Back when we were a small company, maybe . . ." He suddenly looked stricken and exchanged words again with the Queermedia CEO. "Well," he said, much smoother, "we *could* go ahead with a vote, but do we really want to waste the time? The outcome is a given—the CEO of Queermedia and I control more than fifty percent of the shares in Queermedia Group."

Jason smiled. "Do you?" he asked. Then he raised his voice. "All right, folks, I propose a fifteen-minute recess to let you all read up on what's been going on at *Phag*. Fiscal mismanagement, poor management and human resource decisions, general incompetence. I've got photocopies right here, just come and take a look if you want." He pointed to Chester. "Of course, you can always vote for the status quo."

There was a moment of confusion. Then Peter yelled, "I second the motion!" and most of the audience got to its feet.

Will rolled up to Peter. "Bet you didn't expect us to show up here," he said, grinning. "I love secrets."

Peter was confused; it was all going too fast. "What's happening?" he asked. "Why you and Jason? Why *Phag*?"

"I don't understand all the details," Will said, "but Jason realized he had enough money from the inheritance to buy out *Phag* from Queermedia. All he has to do is win over some of the minor shareholders."

Peter shook his head. "Chester and Queermedia always held on to more than fifty percent of the total shares, though."

"No, they didn't," Will replied. "We took a look at the stock registration records. Did you ever get a really good bonus one year while you were working at *Phag*?"

Peter watched Chester moving through the crowd with purpose. He cast his mind back five years . . . the first Christmas party he'd attended at *Phag*. Chester had handed out envelopes to a few people, but not Peter. He'd always wondered . . .

"He couldn't be that dumb," Peter said.

"He never thought it'd come back to bite him in the butt," Will said. "And he probably didn't think *Phag* would be acquired back then. After *Phag* got acquired by Queermedia, there was some kind of complicated stock swap where Chester got tons of Queermedia stock in exchange for *Phag*'s brand equity—Queermedia really got taken for a ride. Jason told me that Queermedia and *Phag* together have about fifty percent ownership of Queermedia . . . but not everyone at *Phag* is sympathetic to Chester, right? Watch."

Chester walked over to Bette Chambers and placed a hand on her shoulder. She shrugged it off, and turned away.

"Bette owns two percent of Queermedia stock," Will said. Chester's face became an expressionless mask, and he started toward Peter and Will.

"Did they have a metal detector at the door?" Peter asked, alarmed.

"He's not coming to talk to us," Will said.

Peter looked on as Chester approached Caliph. Caliph flipped long brown curls in Chester's direction and studied the contents of a martini glass.

"Caliph also owns two percent of Queermedia," Will said. "Chester probably had them under his thumb for years."

Peter remembered Chester's reprimand for Bette's mistakes, and his offhanded callous comments to Caliph after the press conference. "Peons only put up with so much," Peter said.

He took hold of the handles on Will's wheelchair and pushed him over to the podium, where Jason was distributing photocopies and answering questions. Jason smiled and took a moment out of his work to go over and hug Peter.

"Looks like it's going to work," Jason said.

Peter looked at Will, then Jason. "Why?" he asked. "And when did you find out I wasn't Dan? What, did everyone in the club know?"

Jason shook his head. "Mac told us. He thought you were starting to obsess about the whole thing, and I had this money burning a hole in my pocket." He kissed Will on the forehead and grinned at Peter. "I didn't mind working at a magazine, but when I realized I had the opportunity to be managing editor . . . and own a magazine! We figured it was the best way we could help you out, and ourselves."

"So that explains—" Peter caught sight of Chester on the other side of the room and shook his head. "Just a second. There's something I have to do."

When he was sure Chester wasn't looking his way, Peter walked over to Chester's chair and took the black leather dildo out of his pocket. Then he wedged its base in the crease between the chair back and the seat, so that it was pointing upward at roughly a sixty-degree angle. He made his way back to Jason and Will, who were wrapping up their conversations with various shareholders.

"That explains why you wrote those notes about *Phag* and Queermedia," Peter mused. "But why the secrecy? Why not just tell me?"

Will and Jason exchanged glances. "Mac told us about your . . . uhh . . . undercover activities at *Phag*," Will said. "With the amount of money Jason was going to be working with on this, we didn't want to get you involved, in case we drew any interest from the government."

"We also figured Chester might recognize you from your janitorial job, and it could blow up in our faces," Jason said. "We had to do it without you."

Peter shook his head. "You just wanted to have a big secret, didn't you?" Jason nodded.

Will looked at the clock. "Time to vote," he said. Jason went to the podium and started calling the crowd to order.

"It all worked out," Will sighed contentedly, leaning back in the wheelchair. "Happy ending."

Peter felt all the blood drain out of him. The clock read 9:25 p.m. Ben, he thought. Oh my God, Ben!

"Can I borrow your cell phone?" Peter asked Will hurriedly. Will took it out of his pocket and handed it to Peter, concerned.

Peter dialed the hotel and waited impatiently until a clerk answered. "Restwell Inn," the clerk said above the bearish din in the background.

"This is . . . Dan Karn. Give me Room 306."

A pause. "Mr. Karn? There's nobody in Room 306."

"How the hell do you know that?" Peter nearly shouted into the phone.

"Sir, your roommate's checked out. A Ben Conaway? He left about twenty minutes ago."

Peter sat down heavily in a chair and ran a hand through his hair. "Did he say where he was going?"

"Well, he had his luggage with him, sir. And he asked me to confirm a flight leaving at 9:45 p.m. I'd say that was pretty conclusive."

Peter flipped the cell phone closed and handed it back to Will. "I really blew it," Peter said. "Didn't I?"

Will looked uncertain. "You'd better get to the airport."

Peter stood up, shaking his head. "I had to come here first. I just had to see this through, when I should've been . . . oh, what the hell. I put *Phag* in front of Ben. There's no other way to say it."

Shareholders were starting to file forward to register their votes on Jason's divestiture proposal.

"Peter," Will said gently, "I only have one piece of advice to give you."

"What's that?"

"Go to the airport. Now."

Chester Valentine was blocking Peter's way. You know, Peter was about to tell him, I've sent better men than you plunging out of third-story windows. Instead, Peter shook his head. "It's over. Isn't that what you told me?"

Chester didn't budge. "It's a silly trick," he said. "You won't get back into *Phag*, ever. We don't need you anymore."

Peter almost laughed. After all this time, Chester still thought Peter wanted his job back. "I'm leaving," he said, pushing Chester aside.

"I won't let you have the last word on this," Chester said warningly.

Peter grabbed Chester by the shoulders. "You're right—what was I thinking? Have a seat." He jammed Chester down into his chair, right on top of the dildo.

Chester yelped, and Peter raced out of the conference room, grinning. He might not get the last word, he thought, but the dildo certainly would. "Woof, woof, woof!" was the last thing he heard as he headed for the lobby to call a cab.

The airport was crowded with travelers and well-wishers, but no bears; they must all still be at GBG, Peter thought. At least it would make it easier to spot Ben.

Peter stopped at the counter of the airline they'd flown in on. "Is there a 9:45 flight out of here?" he asked, breathlessly.

"Oh yes," the Asian woman behind the counter said, nodding.

"And what's the flight number?" he prodded.

"Oh, that would be 416," she said.

"And where do I catch it?" Peter asked, ready to throttle her.

She swung around and pointed her finger. Peter watched it pass all the gates, then come to rest on a large plate glass window facing into the dark landing field. An airplane suddenly screamed by, then banked and started to dwindle into the distance.

"Oh, there it goes," the woman said.

Peter turned away from the airline counter. He found a bench in the middle of the airport and sat down, head in his hands. Travelers streamed past him on their way to gates, airplanes, and other destinations. That was what he needed to do. Peter thought. Go home.

It was over. Ben, the bears, everything. Chester had been right in one sense; he may have prevailed over *Phag,* but he'd lost everything else.

– 23 –

A broad shadow fell over Peter. "Have some complimentary nuts," Ben said, holding out a small bag of airline nuts.

Peter smiled wanly and took a handful out of the bag. Then, digging through the nuts with his fingers, he realized something. "You took all the cashews, didn't you?"

Ben sat down next to Peter and nodded. "You know me too well."

They sat there in silence for a moment. "I made it all the way to the airport and onto the plane," Ben said. "Then I knew there was something I had to do." His expression was utterly neutral; Peter wondered for one moment if he was in the classic B-movie dilemma—would Ben kiss him or kill him?

Ben took out a folded piece of paper from his plaid jacket pocket. Peter recognized it as the note he'd left on Ben's nighttable. "I found this while I was packing," Ben said. "First thing I did, of course, was throw it away and keep packing."

"Of course," Peter said, not daring to hope.

Ben shrugged. "Me and my temper. Anyway, as I was about to leave the room, I decided to give it another read. Figured it'd keep me mad at you while I was on the way to the airport."

Ben unfolded the note and looked at it. "You're a damn good writer, all right," he said. "It was enough to give me second thoughts. Not quite enough though, so I got on the plane." Ben looked sideways at Peter. "Then I started thinking about that night I saw you without your shirt on, working at Bear Essentials."

Peter nodded. "Man, was I ever turned on!" Ben said, chuckling. "Part of me thought it was love at first sight, but when we got together the first few times, it was more like hate at first sight." He smoothed out the notepaper. "I saw you as a bear first, and a person second. Maybe that's why it hurt me so much when I found out you weren't a bear; I don't know." Ben rubbed the bridge of his nose. "Maybe it was

199

just realizing I was attracted to your looks first. We bears are supposed to be able to see beyond all that."

"I lied to you," Peter said, feeling his hope rise. "There's no excuse for that."

Ben nodded. "No, there isn't. But the man I fell in love with eventually—Peter, Dan, *whatever* his name was—he wasn't a lie. You couldn't hide who you really were from me, even if the details were a bit off."

Their eyes met. "Does that mean . . . ?" Peter asked.

"Yes, you idiot," Ben said, rubbing Peter's beard fondly. "That's exactly what it means. I love you. Let me show you just how much."

He tore his shirt open to reveal several beige patches on his chest. "I even quit smoking for you," Ben said. "And you can imagine how much they're going to hurt when I have to rip them off."

Peter grabbed Ben and kissed him, hard, not caring what the other airport patrons might think.

"I love you," Peter said through both of their beards. "God help me, I love you. But it'll never work."

Ben drew back, looking at Peter quizzically. "You're not gonna throw up another barrier, are you?"

Peter sighed. "First off, I'm a twink and you're a bear. Mixed marriages never really work out, unless we celebrate all the holidays together. Christmas and Chanukah and Twink Day and Bear Day and God knows what else. Second, I'm ostracized from the bear community. And third, I don't have a real job, if Bear Essentials goes under."

Ben rubbed Peter's buzz cut. "The bear community will forget," he explained. "Give it a few months, and they'll be worrying about next year's Mr. GBG Contest, or who posted the latest stuff to the Bears ListServ. As for a job, Will will probably give you one, wherever he goes. He's pretty loyal to his employees." Peter nodded, thinking of *Phag.*

"Let's go home," Ben said, kissing Peter again lightly. "Enough drama for one lifetime."

Peter shook his head. "We can't."

"Oh God," Ben said, only half joking. "What now?"

"My luggage is still at the hotel."

They started toward one of the airport's exits and the taxi stand. "Do you think everything will go back to normal now?" Peter asked idly, feeling Ben's arm wrapped around his shoulder.

"With you," Ben replied, "nothing's ever normal. But it'll work out. We'll make it work."

Some Time Later

Peter sat at his desk, talking to Jason and trying to ignore the commotion going on behind him. "Do you have the editorial deadlines for the next issue yet?" he asked.

Jason pretended to ignore the commotion as well. "I'll send you an e-mail as soon as they're finalized. We've more or less booked most of the advertisers for the Media and Technology issue; all we have to do is handle the ones who want advertorial content."

Peter rolled his eyes. "Not again. After all this time, they still want us to write about them?" Ever since *Phag*'s new Statement of Editorial Integrity, they were still getting inquiries from advertisers who wanted product placement or the equivalent of a rewritten press release masquerading as content. Chester had trained them only too well.

Jason shrugged. "I'll get Bette on it." He looked down and typed a few lines. "You'd think it was the mainstream advertisers like the beer companies, but it's usually the smaller ones. They don't have the money to spend on big ads."

"Now I know how *Ms.* magazine felt," Peter said. Ever since they'd laterally promoted Bette Chambers to the Advertising Department, she'd blossomed. Nobody could sell advertising space or hunt down deadbeats who wouldn't pay their bills like Bette. He heard a crash in the background and ignored it. "While we're on the subject, have you heard anything from Global Viaticals?"

Global Viaticals was a viatical insurance company that was considering pulling its advertising coverage from *Phag* if Jason didn't halt Peter's upcoming article on Viaticals' reluctance to continue payments in the face of the new AIDS drugs.

Jason grinned. "If you're asking if I'm going to budge, I'm not. Is the article done yet?"

"I'll e-mail it to you as soon as I've finished the edit," Peter said, holding up a sheaf of paper. "I'm really glad you decided to run it," he added. "It's not quite in our business mandate, is it?"

"*Phag Magazine:* Technology and the Gay Community," Jason said, repeating the magazine's new slogan. "I'd say it's close enough." He pressed a key on his computer and *Phag*'s financials popped up in a window on Peter's monitor. "The shareholders aren't about to start complaining."

Another crash in the background. Jason's image on the videophone looked concerned. "Everything all right over there?"

Peter glanced over his shoulder. "One of the benefits of having a home office," he replied. A text message scrolled over Jason's videoconferencing window: INCOMING MESSAGE.

"I've got another call coming in; can I e-mail you this afternoon?"

"Sure," Jason said. "You guys going to join us for dinner?"

Peter nodded. "See you there." He closed the connection to Jason's office and was about to open the new call when MacGuyver burst into the office, holding something in his mouth and making a low, hissing growl. He leaped onto Peter's chair, then used Peter's body as a springboard and leaped away, racing into the next room.

Ben rushed into Peter's home office, looking flustered but delicious in his tank top and jeans. "He's got the piece I need for the latest hologram," Ben complained. "Can you get it back from him or something?"

"It's a toy mouse," Peter said, getting up and giving Ben a kiss. "You might as well douse the holography table in catnip. What do you expect?" Then, noticing Ben's sour expression, Peter added, "I'll do something about it in a minute."

Peter clicked a button, and Caliph's face appeared on-screen, subtitled Administrative Supervisor.

"Hi, Caliph," Peter said. "What can I do for you?"

Caliph was wearing a deep-blue jumpsuit with matching dangling earrings. "Dear, I wanted to get your list of office supplies that you need before I place this month's order. Can you press a button or click your mouse or do whatever you need to do to send me an e-mail?"

Peter smiled. Caliph always pretended not to know how to operate the new computer systems, but he had no doubt that Caliph knew them inside out.

"I don't really need anything. Maybe a cat muzzle."

"If Staples has one, I'll order it." Caliph looked ready to say something else, but remained silent.

"Okay, what is it?" Peter asked.

"Turn on Channel 12, dear. On the television. And hurry!" Caliph's image winked off, with the message TRANSMISSION COMPLETED.

Peter walked into the living room and rummaged around on the coffee table for the remote. He glanced fondly at the hardbound copy of *Bear Like Me* (by Peter Mallory, "with Dan Karn"); the book hadn't been a best-seller, but it had received enough positive reviews that the publishers had asked for a sequel about bear politics. He found the remote under a letter from a gallery about one of Ben's upcoming holography exhibits, then pointed it at the TV. Ben joined him a moment later.

"It slices, it dices, and it lets you tell the world you're out and you're proud!" Chester Valentine said from the television. He was wearing a white shirt, red suspenders, and a bow tie, and looked intensely uncomfortable. His cohost, a bubbly blonde woman, looked on in awe as Chester continued to demonstrate the Pride Food Chopper ("now with pink triangle attachment!"). "You won't want to miss this once-in-a-lifetime deal," Chester said, using the pink triangle attachment to extrude a carrot into a vaguely triangular shape. "Call now!"

Peter shook his head. "Oh, how the mighty have fallen," he murmured, then switched the TV off. "I wonder what happened to Sasha..."

"Well you know what they said at the bear club. Somebody heard he became a bear escort," Ben said.

"That's just an urbear legend," Peter protested. "They probably said that about us too, when we stopped going."

"We should go back one of these days," Ben said. "See how the old gang is doing."

Peter nodded. "See if Mac's continuing to abuse his authority. I still say a bear club president shouldn't insist on sleeping with every new member." He turned away from the TV and contemplated the mantel. "At least we'll always have something to remember Sasha by."

Ben and Peter looked at the two-by-three-foot photograph that hung over the fireplace; Sasha's mud pit picture had come out better than anyone had expected. Forever frozen in time, he was wallowing in the middle of the mud pit, just starting to get up and reaching his muddy fist into the air. Peter had heard that it was still one of the top downloads on the bear Web sites.

Ben put a paw on Peter's arm. "Speaking of old times, ever hear anything from Danny?"

Peter shrugged. "Just the usual. He's finished his psych degree, so he dumped Irving. Now he's looking for another man to help him finance his master's degree. No takers so far, though."

"I have to start developing the latest holograms," Ben said, then swatted Peter on the butt and headed back into the workroom. "Keep MacGuyver away if you see him."

Peter smiled and rubbed his chin, then rubbed it again. His beard was getting a little longer than he liked. He walked into the bathroom and looked at himself in the mirror.

He'd had a beard for how long now, he wondered? Nearly two years. Casting a look at the hallway to make sure Ben wasn't around, Peter dug into the drawer for a while, then finally pulled out an old Gillette razor. Maybe it was time to shave the beard, after all.

He contemplated the razor as it glinted in the light. Then Peter smiled. Not today, he thought, putting it back into the drawer and going to find Ben. Not today.

ABOUT THE AUTHOR

Jonathan Cohen was born to nonbear parents thirty-five years ago. After a brief dalliance at the altars of Gillette and Nair, he realized who and what he was—a bear. Terminally shy and terminally single, Jonathan lives in the urban wilds of Vancouver, Canada, with his feral cat, Shadow. This is his first novel.

SPECIAL 25%-OFF DISCOUNT!
Order a copy of this book with this form or online at:
http://www.haworthpressinc.com/store/product.asp?sku=4766

BEAR LIKE ME

_____ in hardbound at $22.46 (regularly $29.95) (ISBN: 1-56023-417-2)

_____ in softbound at $12.71 (regularly $16.95) (ISBN: 1-56023-418-0)

Or order online and use Code HEC25 in the shopping cart.

COST OF BOOKS_____

OUTSIDE USA/CANADA/
MEXICO: ADD 20%_____

POSTAGE & HANDLING_____
(US: $4.00 for first book & $1.50
for each additional book)
Outside US: $5.00 for first book
& $2.00 for each additional book)

SUBTOTAL_____

in Canada: add 7% GST_____

STATE TAX_____
(NY, OH & MIN residents, please
add appropriate local sales tax)

FINAL TOTAL_____
(If paying in Canadian funds,
convert using the current
exchange rate, UNESCO
coupons welcome.)

☐ **BILL ME LATER:** ($5 service charge will be added)
(Bill-me option is good on US/Canada/Mexico orders only;
not good to jobbers, wholesalers, or subscription agencies.)

☐ Check here if billing address is different from
shipping address and attach purchase order and
billing address information.

Signature_____

☐ **PAYMENT ENCLOSED: $**_____

☐ **PLEASE CHARGE TO MY CREDIT CARD.**

☐ Visa ☐ MasterCard ☐ AmEx ☐ Discover
☐ Diner's Club ☐ Eurocard ☐ JCB

Account # _____

Exp. Date _____

Signature _____

Prices in US dollars and subject to change without notice.

NAME_____
INSTITUTION_____
ADDRESS_____
CITY_____
STATE/ZIP_____
COUNTRY_____ COUNTY (NY residents only)_____
TEL_____ FAX_____
E-MAIL_____

May we use your e-mail address for confirmations and other types of information? ☐ Yes ☐ No
We appreciate receiving your e-mail address and fax number. Haworth would like to e-mail or fax special
discount offers to you, as a preferred customer. **We will never share, rent, or exchange your e-mail address
or fax number.** We regard such actions as an invasion of your privacy.

Order From Your Local Bookstore or Directly From
The Haworth Press, Inc.
10 Alice Street, Binghamton, New York 13904-1580 • USA
TELEPHONE: 1-800-HAWORTH (1-800-429-6784) / Outside US/Canada: (607) 722-5857
FAX: 1-800-895-0582 / Outside US/Canada: (607) 722-6362
E-mailto: getinfo@haworthpressinc.com
PLEASE PHOTOCOPY THIS FORM FOR YOUR PERSONAL USE.
http://www.HaworthPress.com   BOF02